Everything's
Not Fine

Turner Publishing Company
Nashville, Tennessee
www.turnerpublishing.com

Everything's Not Fine
Copyright © 2020 Sarah Carlson.
All rights reserved.

*This is a work of fiction. All the characters and events portrayed in this book
are either products of the author's imagination or are used fictitiously.*

Cover design: Rebecca Lown
Book design: Karen Sheets de Gracia

Library of Congress Cataloging-in-Publication Data
Names: Carlson, Sarah J., author.
Title: Everything is not fine / Sarah J Carlson.
Description: [Nashville : Turner Publishing Company, 2020] | Audience: Ages 4–18 |
    Audience: Grades 10–12 | Summary: Seventeen-year-old Rose Hemmersbach aspires to break
    out of small town Sparta, Wisconsin and achieve her artistic dreams, just like her aunt Colleen,
    but must face her mother's heroin addiction and its ramifications first.
Identifiers: LCCN 2019035589 (print) | LCCN 2019035590 (ebook) | ISBN 9781684424108
    (paperback) | ISBN 9781684424115 (hardcover) | ISBN 9781684424122 (ebook)
Subjects: CYAC: Drug abuse—Fiction. | Family problems—Fiction. | Dating (Social customs)—
    Fiction. | High schools—Fiction. | Schools—Fiction. | Artists—Fiction. | Wisconsin—Fiction.
Classification: LCC PZ7.1.C4115 Eve 2020 (print) | LCC PZ7.1.C4115 (ebook) | DDC [Fic]—dc23
LC record available at https://lccn.loc.gov/2019035589

Printed in the United States of America

20 21 22 23 24   10 9 8 7 6 5 4 3 2 1

JUL 3 0 2020

Everything's Not Fine

Sarah J. Carlson

TURNER
PUBLISHING COMPANY

Chapter 1

Hollis's chainsaw snore yanks me out of sleep. His lanky leg, half swathed in his Pikachu sheet, hangs off his bed.

I chuck my teal owl accent pillow at him.

"Huh? Don't!" he whines, then chucks it back at me.

I catch it and tuck it under my head. "Stop snoring then, Holly Dolly."

"Don't call me that, butthead," he mumbles into his Pokémon pillow.

God, I'm seventeen. I cannot believe I have to share a room with a nine-year-old who smells like sweaty pit. Especially when our room is currently like ninety degrees. I stretch my arm and turn the oscillating fan toward me, then snatch my phone from the bedside table. We ran out of minutes; thank God our neighbor Traci's Wi-Fi password is just her name.

I send Dad another link for those trundle bunk beds—because seriously, why can't Hollis, Vi, and Sage share a room?—then check Instagram. At the top of my feed is a selfie of Seraphina Abramsson. Behind her is an empty Broadway theater with golden

1

pillars and a crystal chandelier hanging from a ceiling covered with Renaissance-style frescoes. She's wearing her trademark red lipstick, offsetting her milky skin and long, silky white-blonde hair.

The caption:

Just finished my last show. Wicked, it's been an unbelievable year. While I've deeply loved playing Glinda, I'm ready for what lies ahead. For the next two weeks, I'll be traveling the world searching for the true meaning of love. I don't know what life will hold when I walk the streets of NYC again, but I'm okay with that. XO Sera.

I want her life. Not the acting part, but living far away and truly embracing your art. Traveling the world.

Her post has 1,352 likes. Still, I fight back the urge to heart it like always. It's dumb. She wouldn't even notice someone named "RoseMarie" liked her stuff. And even if she did, she wouldn't connect it to her niece in Sparta, Wisconsin.

My ears strain to hear the sound of the shower or a toilet flush, but the house is silent. Meaning the bathroom is mine. I scramble out of bed and yank a black Unrequited Death shirt from my top dresser drawer, then my black jean shorts from the bottom drawer.

Justin said these make my ass look hot. But last night it was Trina's ass he was grabbing behind a rack of animal print blouses in plain sight of my register. That dull ache throbs deep inside me.

I ram the shorts back in and grab some blue jean ones instead.

Those black shorts would be symbolically perfect for *Justin in My Mind* though. Shredded black to parallel Frida Kahlo's traditional Mexican attire in *Diego in My Thoughts*.

I should just shower, but I can't let inspiration slip through my fingers. If a bedroom door opens, I can beat any of the kiddos to the bathroom. I snatch my canvas and a graphite pencil from the mound of art stuff at the foot of my bed and then escape the land mines of Hollis's dirty socks and underwear to the living room. I set my canvas on Dad's *Field & Stream* magazines, circa 2014, layering our coffee table. I've already done the underpainting—pure cadmium red, because it'll be a good contrast to the brooding purples and darkness I've felt since Justin broke up with me.

My pencil scrapes across the layer of acrylic as I add those raggedy, cutoff black shorts to my self-portrait with Justin's face on my forehead, his strong Greek nose, cleft chin, and square jaw. To capture his piercing blue eyes, I'll use french ultramarine and white. The bust of Dad's twelve-point buck, the deer of legend from five years ago, watches with its dead eyes. That'd be an interesting element to add, especially since now I spend every night sitting on the couch watching *Cops* with Dad after the kiddos go to bed. A buck head mixed with a dash of Kahlo inspiration might really grab Belwyn's attention. The website said their viewbook with all the application requirements would be emailed out after Labor Day. So any day now.

I lightly sketch the buck head in a corner, its antlers twisting through the edge of the canvas.

"Shut up, stupid!" Sage's nails-on-chalkboard voice booms through their bedroom door adorned with princess coloring sheets and a Green Bay Packers poster.

The beasts are stirring. I grab my clothes and bolt for the bathroom.

I peel off my pj shorts and faded middle school band T-shirt. The plastic octopus shower curtain is grainy with soap scum, and all the caulking is black with mildew, but because I got here first, I get to savor a shower without fear of the hot water running out.

Today is the only day this week I'm free of cash registers and fingertips blackened by dollar bills and mountains of back-to-school clothes to de-hanger. I have the whole beautiful day with Mrs. Hoffman's oils in the art room to add the finishing touches to my summer masterpiece, *The Two Roses*.

I dry off and get dressed. My black eyeliner pencil scrapes across my eyelids as I draw thick black lines, making sure they match on both eyes. After mascara, I blow-dry my freshly dyed platinum blonde, bluntly cut chin-length hair, then spray my long bangs sweeping across my forehead.

A tiny fist pounds on the door. "Rosey, I gotta pee!" Vi squeaks.

"Use Mom and Dad's bathroom."

She pounds again. "Mommy's in there."

Probably shooting up, because that appears to be how she starts her day now.

"Ugh, fine." I pull the door open, and she pushes past me, a blur of blonde pigtails and pink Shimmer and Shine pajamas. She slams the door as soon as I slip out, muting the sound of her pee. Five-year-olds apparently have bladders the size of grapes that can hold a gallon of pee.

In the kitchen, the dishes are piled even higher than yesterday because Mom's not doing them anymore. C'mon, Captain Jobless, it's not like you're even watching the kids. Ever since summer school finished, they've just been running around Sparta.

Morning sunlight filters through the lace curtains covering the kitchen window, refracting through three empty Miller High Life bottles. Three, Dad, really?

At the kitchen table, Sage and Hollis shovel Lucky Charms into their mouths. Hollis sits up tall today, so you can really see the six inches he now has on Sage. Dad sets the milk and box of Lucky Charms in front of my bowl. Today, his tucked-in dusty-blue shirt accentuates his steel-blue eyes. His beer belly hangs over his John Deere belt buckle.

"Had a dream last night you were the champ of the whole dart league. Won it with a pink dart." Dad pops a mounding spoonful of cereal into his mouth. A dribble of milk runs into his blond five-o'clock shadow. He cuffs it away.

"Pink? Ugh. Bet Travis and them would flip their shit if I used a pink dart."

"Language, Rosey."

"Flip their crap just doesn't work, Dad." Lucky Charms clink as I shake some into my bowl. I get an unusually high ratio of pots of gold.

He messes up my hair.

"Stop." I bat his huge oil-stained hand away.

"Don't think I can mess that hair up." Dad shakes his hand out like something's stuck to it, wearing a million-dollar grin that allegedly melted all the girls' hearts senior year when he was voted "best smile." "I swear you use Gorilla Glue."

I roll my eyes with a smile I can't stop.

"Pink's the worst," Sage spouts from behind the Great Wall of Cereal Boxes she's constructed around herself in the epitome of eight-year-old orneriness.

Violet bounds out of the bathroom. "No, pink's the best!" she erupts with such conviction you'd think Sage said the sky was green. She jumps into her chair next to me. Judging by her pink nose, she'd been running around outside without sunblock again. Freckles speckle her cheeks.

Mom and Dad's bedroom door creaks open. Mom emerges, a shadow against the sun seeping through their curtains. She cuts through the muted light of the living room. A sheen of sweat glistens on her forehead, dotted with fresh red scars from picking.

"Mommy!" Vi launches at her and crushes her slight frame into a hug.

5

Even from across the kitchen, I can smell the stench of her dealer Jeremy's secondhand smoke.

"Hiya, Vi Pie." Her voice has a slight slur. Mom's fingers fumble into Vi's lopsided pigtails. Her blue-green eyes have an unfocused glaze to them, and her pupils are practically the size of periods. Yup, she's high.

"Happy birthday, Mommy!" Hollis strokes her arm. His hand freezes an inch above a dark patch on the back of her hand where she missed a vein. He pulls back.

"I want to make you a pink cake with pink frosting cuz pink's my favorite." Vi's high-pitched baby voice shreds my eardrums like a cheese grater.

Mom grips her upper arm, face half-hidden behind her dish-water blonde hair. "Daryl . . ." Her voice comes out soft and tiny, like a frightened kitten.

Sage lets out an exaggerated groan from behind her cereal box castle. We all know what's coming.

Dad's hands choke his favorite "World's Greatest Farter" mug. A Father's Day gift I bought on behalf of the kiddos last year.

"Yeah?" he asks.

"I got a couple job interviews coming up—Kwik Trip and Century Foods." She sniffles and rubs her nose with her arm. The skin around her nostrils is chapped.

My spoon freezes halfway to my mouth. That lie's more transparent than glass; even Vi knows that by now. Stifling an eye roll, I shove the spoon into my mouth and force down the pots of gold. Because that's what we do. Ignore the elephant in the room, because acknowledging it makes it real.

Dad slurps his coffee. "Good. We need the money."

Her fingers twitch against her jeans. "My . . . my interview clothes. They got all messed up when that red shirt got washed with the whites. I just need a few bucks is all. A couple twenties." Her eyes flit up to him, then fall. "Just this one time."

Her words flop out like limp fish; even she doesn't buy it. "Just this one time" happens pretty much on the daily now. It hurts my heart. Because that's not Mom.

Dad clears his throat as he checks something on his phone. "Now, Maureen, I ain't got that right now. We're outta minutes, and the truck needs a new fan belt."

"Please, Daryl, it's not much. Just a couple hundred. I know you hate what I gotta do otherwise." She paws at his arm.

Then I feel *it* watching me over the wood-panel half wall cordoning off the living room from the kitchen with a burning intensity far worse than the dead-eyed buck ever attempts. The painting Mom made her senior year, right before I was born. A pure-white dove in flight, struggling to escape a seething darkness.

Dad looks up from his phone. He's got too many wrinkles around his eyes to be only thirty-five. "We ain't got it."

Mom's eyes bulge like the pile of dead fish in Francisco Goya's *Still Life with Golden Bream*. Dad's a foot taller than her with shoulders twice as broad, but she's a giant looming over him. "It's my fucking birthday! It's the least you could do!"

I pound the table with my fist. The cereal boxes dance and collapse. "Maybe you could actually get a fricking job!"

I throw my chair back and head for the door.

Behind me, I hear a high, choked sound that comes from Mom only when she pretends to feel bad, and maybe sometimes does. Whatever.

"Where you going, Rosey?" Dad props his faded Packers hat on top of his messy blond mop.

I rip my black studded purse off the hook. "To paint."

"Let me drive you." Dad's keys rattle as he grabs them from

the heart-stamped red clay bowl I made in fifth grade. A Mother's Day present.

"I want to walk."

I slam the door behind me and tuck in my earbuds. "Mr. Self Destruct" by Nine Inch Nails fills my ears. The world outside is coated with fat drops of dew glistening in the soft light of the rising sun. The air's so muggy it's practically drinkable. As I cut across the yard, wet dandelion fluff clings to the black laces of my combat boots.

It's her birthday, a tiny voice in my head whispers. I haven't drawn her card yet this year. Whatever—I did dishes all last week so Dad wouldn't be pissed at her, even though *I'm* the one with the job.

I turn up the volume to max and let the throbbing industrial beats of Nine Inch Nails carry me away as I leave behind the faded plastic Little Tikes playset in our front yard and gardens now filled with weeds and the brown rotting carcasses of allium and tulips and daffodils.

As I walk down Black River Street, I imagine being at a concert. Feeling the beats reverberate in my chest. Screaming the lyrics along with all the other people who get it. You probably can't think at a concert.

One more year until I Seraphina. Then I'll be up in the Sierra Nevada Mountains learning from the best in-residence artists at Belwyn School for the Arts. Painting in state-of-the-art studios with other artists who let the world fall away as the creative flow consumes them.

I'll be free.

Chapter 2

The ripping guitars of Unrequited Death fill the space between my ears with raw energy that fuels my paintbrush. My brain bursts with images and colors. My brushstrokes bring them to life. I don't paint objects; I paint shapes and edges and spaces. I create an infinite range of colors from four little tubes.

I draw in a breath. The sharp metallic smell of oil paint fills my lungs—so different than the plastic scent of acrylic. My shoulders drop an inch. I dip my brush into the cup of Gamsol; pink swirls in the muddy brown. I wipe my brush clean on a paper towel and then paint the shades of pink into a fold of a dress on the canvas.

The oil paint is still wet, so even weeks later I can fix my mistakes. And I love the smooth feel of it spreading across the canvas, not instantly starting to dry like acrylic. Building my painting layer by layer from dark vague shapes and shadows to thick bright colors. You don't just paint with oils—you sculpt.

I still can't believe Mrs. Hoffman gave me private lessons and let me borrow her paints all summer. Ugh, and tomorrow it's back to cheap acrylics.

I dab my brush into light pink and barely touch it to the canvas to highlight the fold, then step back to take in my crowning summer achievement. Two pale-skinned girls hold hands, surrounded by boiling gray clouds. I could never create clouds with that depth of color and texture using acrylic. Pink Girl—with long, silky dishwater blonde hair and a pastry-colored dress—clenches a pair of bloody scissors, her chest ripped open and emptied. Dressed in all black, the other girl has an unevenly cut, chin-length platinum bob and bangs hiding one of her eyes. Her visible blue eye is lined with heavy black eyeliner. Her broken rib cage reveals her heart, connected to Pink Girl's empty cavity by an aorta. Getting their faces to look identical had taken almost two weeks.

The Two Roses. The top contender for my Belwyn portfolio.

I chew my lip; Pink Girl's blush is a little too bright. I add a tiny dot of phthalo blue to my semiwet layer of pink, blending it slightly, then gently touch the tip of my brush to her cheek.

Something pokes my arm. I jump. None other than Miss Class President Queen of the Cheerleaders stands next to me, her bright-yellow shirt almost blinding. I step in front of my painting and rip out my earbuds.

"Oh, man. What's that smell?" Kimmy waves her hand in front of her cute button nose.

Through my hairspray-stiffened bangs, I spot two boys behind her. Both have dark skin and jet-black hair. The boy wearing a T-shirt with a Flash lightning bolt ogles Kimmy's butt. The older-looking boy, dressed in skinny-fit khakis and a red polo shirt, studies the prints over the blank whiteboard—*Girl with a Pearl Earring, The Persistence of Memory,* and *The Kiss.* Then his gaze drops to me. His hair is shaped into a little fauxhawk. He's cute.

"Sober Sadness" leaks out of my earbuds, filling the silence between us. Fumbling, I pause my music.

"Whew, Rose, I hoped I'd find you here, you know, since you're always here." Kimmy looks past me. Her perpetually perfect smile falters. "Oh, that's, um, really . . . different. Cute you're working on something pink."

I cross my arms. "Can I help you?"

Kimmy's grin reforms even brighter than before. "This is Rafa. He's a senior too. Oh, and his brother, Omar. Hey, do you know about the art club?"

"Yeah, it meets on—"

"Oh, yeah, we've got so many clubs here! FBLA, FFA, DECA, Mock Trial," Kimmy says as she ticks each off on her fingers. "Spanish Club. Bet you'd like that!"

Khaki Boy visibly cringes before offering a hand to me. "Hey. I'm Rafa."

"Rose." I reach for his hand, then realize my fingertips are smudged with paint and it's oil, so definitely still wet. "Oh, sorry, I was—"

He takes my hand and shakes it. "It's okay. I paint too."

Now his burnt-sienna skin is smudged with somber purple-gray and pink like mine.

"Oil paint, huh?" He studies my plastic palette. "This school must be rich."

"Yeah, no. It's just a summer thing."

"Disappointing." Rafa peers around me. "Your painting looks just like *The Two Fridas*."

"I was inspired by it."

"Frida's awesome, but Diego Rivera is my hero." He glances back at the print of *Liberation of the Peon* over the door.

Slimy Diego who cheated on Frida. Okay, maybe Justin didn't outright cheat on me, but he stored those *Playboys* under his bed and went to strip clubs "because all guys do it" and waited barely

11

even five seconds before making out with Trina.

"Figures, you're a dude," I mutter.

"Hey"—Rafa tosses his hands up—"just cuz Rivera was some chauvinistic macho man doesn't mean we all are. Besides, Frida cheated on him with Trotsky."

"Touché." I raise an eyebrow. "You know your art history."

His black-and-red Air Jordans scrub at a splotch of muddied pink on the tile. "Why wouldn't I know that? It's a no-brainer."

"Well, I guess now there will be exactly two people at this school who know the no-brainer."

A smile pulls at the corner of Rafa's lips.

"Oh my God, Rafa!" his brother groans from behind him. "I got football practice in twenty minutes. And Kimmy's got cheerleading practice." He winks at her, triggering one of her flirty giggles even though she has a boyfriend.

"Shut up, *manito*," he shoots over his shoulder. "Guess I gotta go finish this riveting tour."

I smirk at his sarcasm. "All five hallways."

"I'm guessing I'll see you in art," Rafa says before his brother almost literally pulls him out the door.

In spite of the gaping hole left in Justin's wake, Rafa's mildly intriguing.

As Kimmy's white cheerleader shoes squeak on the freshly waxed floors, she mutters a little too loud for her own good, "Well, that's the most I've heard Rose say in like a year. Guess you're special, Rafa."

Their voices fade.

A message vibrates my phone, thanks to school Wi-Fi. My heart swoops into my throat like every time I've gotten a text the past two weeks. Maybe, just maybe, it'll be Justin apologizing.

I pull it out of my pocket.

Gretchen: I'm outside, here to rescue you from wallowing in self-pity.

Justin's a dick, but my heart still sinks. At least Gretchen's return from family vacation in Florida will liberate me from another night of *Cops* with Dad. I grab my palette and brushes and head for the back sink.

But shit, Monday's always Dad's dart night, meaning I'm on kiddo duty. And it's Mom's birthday. Ugh. Guess I'm trapped at home making pink cake with pink frosting.

Warm water flows over my hands as colors wash down the drain.

Screw it.

It's the last night of my last summer before I graduate. I'm not spending it listening to the brats argue over what to watch. And, whatever, their *mother* is home with them.

I shut off the faucet, dry my hands, and message Gretchen that I'm leaving the building.

As I throw open the glass doors to the parking lot, heat instantly prickles my bare legs and arms. The air smells like baking pavement. Cicadas buzz over the crack of colliding football pads from up on the practice field.

"Chica, where have you been all my life!" Gretchen calls as she hangs out the driver's window of her blue Prius. A skull-print bandanna holds back her Bettie Page–inspired bangs from her sun-streaked bob. She has a golden tan I can never achieve.

"Ringing up school supplies." I climb in.

The familiar scent of her tropical sunset car air freshener wraps around me. I brace myself for her victory dance celebrating the demise of Justin and me, but instead her car fills with 95.7 the Rock, my station.

"How was Florida?" I ask.

Gretchen shines me a wide grin as we pull out of the parking lot. "Let's just say . . . they don't make boys like that in Wisconsin."

"Why not tell me about, oh, I don't know, the ocean?"

"Meh. It's ocean-y. Lots of jellyfish."

Someday I want to stand on a beach and paint the sea.

We drive past the decaying tennis courts. Across the street, cornstalks sway in the breeze, a red barn and low rolling ridges as a backdrop. If I were painting the stalks, I'd use sap green, then mix it with aureolin yellow to get the color just right. Green is so hard to mix exactly the way I like it.

"So there's a new kid this year," I say.

"Senior year?" Gretchen pushes up her purple cat eye glasses. "Go on . . ."

"His name's Rafa, and he might actually appreciate art."

"He cute?"

"I mean, I don't know if he's *Florida* cute, but yeah."

"We could use some fresh meat. And by we, I mean you." She pokes my upper arm.

"Sure . . . " I roll down my window. The wind whips through my hair as Gretchen's car strains to climb Putnam Ridge. Trees hug the shoulders of the winding road.

Justin creeps back into my mind. His cocky smile while he pretends to zone Housewares just so he can see me at the registers. Catching me while I red line to whisper a few song lyrics in my ear, challenging me to guess the band. Sharing bags of Funyuns and Cool Ranch Doritos from the vending machines on break, sipping from the same can of Sun Drop. Now Trina's the one running her hands over his tribal chest tattoos. It all leaves me aching and empty.

A new Shinedown song fills the break in conversation as Gretchen whips around the sharp turns with the confidence of someone who drives this road daily. When Mom used to take me to Gretchen's house, she'd always remind me about the kids in her class who died when they hit black ice and lost control. There's still plastic crosses with faded artificial flowers at the bend in the road. Dad, on the other hand, always bragged about driving Travis's car so fast it went airborne at that very spot.

At the bottom of the ridge, the trees open up to cornfields and soybean fields and the smell of green things mixed with a burst of manure. The sky is huge and brilliant blue dry brushed with wispy clouds. Wires droop between telephone poles shrinking to their vanishing point along the long, straight road. Purple chicory and yellow tufts of goldenrod bob along the side of the road.

Gretchen pulls into the driveway of her white farmhouse complete with wraparound porch and gingerbread trim. It's so disgustingly charming, it should be a bed-and-breakfast. The music dies as she turns off her car.

I peel the backs of my bare legs from the hot leather seat. As we cut through their sunny kitchen with lemon wallpaper trim, Mrs. Osmundson calls, "Hi, Rosey! How are you? How's your mom?"

"Fine," I mutter.

Mrs. Osmundson's mouth presses into a tight-lipped smile. She worked with Mom at Piggly Wiggly before it became Hansen's IGA. She knows about Mom's extracurriculars.

"It's pool time, baby!" Gretchen tugs me toward the sliding glass door.

Outside, I pull off my combat boots and socks and leave them in a pile by the door. The planks of the deck surrounding their aboveground pool bake the soles of my feet. I stick them into the water and relish the coolness. A few helicopter seeds litter the surface like tiny boats. The sun bakes my shoulders.

Gretchen plops down next to me. Her vintage polka-dot skirt fluffs over my thigh.

"Hey, girls. I'm going to get the beer boiling for my famous brats. Know they're your favorite, Rosey," Mr. Osmundson calls through the screen door. He's brought a piece of Florida to Wisconsin, judging by his Hawaiian shirt.

"Thanks," I say.

"So, senior year," Gretchen says as she stares out past the rolling cornfields to the tree-covered ridges beyond. "Can you believe we're almost done?"

"Counting down the seconds." I lean back on my elbows. The edges of the boards dig into my skin.

Gretchen leans back too.

The sticky summer breeze rattles the cornstalks, carrying with it the smell of freshly cut grass and corn tassels mixed with chlorine. *But maybe this year will be better*, a voice whispers from the emptiness Justin left in his wake.

"Seraphina's going on a world tour." I dig out my phone and show her the post.

"That'll be you someday."

I tap my heel on the wall of the pool, feel the water flutter across my foot. "I mean, I won't get coaching to ditch my Wisconsin accent like Aunt Colleen during her metamorphosis into Seraphina, but . . . I'm not getting trapped anywhere *near* Sparta. I want to see real mountains and be whoever I want to be because no one knows the Hemmersbach brood."

"I'm totally hitchhiking and crashing in your dorm." Gretchen pushes my foot with hers. "Belwyn's museum has an Egyptian collection compete with three-thousand-year-old cat still in its sarcophagus."

"If you don't get murdered by a serial killer."

"Always the pessimist." She gives me a playful shove.

"Expect the worst and you'll never be disappointed." I shove her back.

"Well, cats were sacred in Egypt. So maybe their spirits will protect me on my pilgrimage."

I sneak a glance at my Instagram feed. Seraphina's post now has almost two thousand likes and over three hundred comments. My thumb hovers over the heart button. I press it.

She'll never even notice me.

Chapter 3

As Gretchen drives me home, she blasts Z93's pop music per our tradition; I pick on the drive out of town, she picks on the drive in. It's surprisingly cool tonight, probably fifty—a sign that fall is on the verge of kicking summer out.

The sky is a canvas painted burnt umber and ultramarine blue, a tiny hint of white, mix in some alizarin crimson to give it a purple hue. The stars are speckles of white with hints of red or blue or yellow scattered across the darkness. Up at Grammy's in Cataract—back when we still went there—I used to sit on her front steps and look up at the faint, patchy brightness of the Milky Way. Tonight, even though we're not too far from Sparta's light pollution, the sky's so clear I swear I can see a hint of it.

As Gretchen slows at the intersection, the blue light from the cross on top of the abandoned country church's steeple spills eeriness into the night. When we were in elementary school, Mr. Osmundson used to sneak us in to play school.

As the car accelerates, I dangle my hand out the window and let the air rush around it. The night is rich with the sweet smell of clove and violet. Dame's rocket, the purple flowers growing in the ditches, releases its smell in the evening. Mom had told me that on a late-night attempt to soothe screaming baby Violet with a drive. Mom learned everything she knew about flowers from Oma. That's how we got our names too, in honor of Oma's love of all things green.

It's past nine; the kids will be in bed, and I didn't help them cobble together a birthday celebration for Mom. My gut pinches. Whatever, that should be Dad's job.

I could still draw her the card though. She keeps them all in her top dresser drawer, all the way back to the first one I made when I was three. If I finished before midnight, it wouldn't even be belated. Maybe this year I could draw a blue aster, because they bloom so late in the year and they're one of the only blue flowers. Homage to Oma's favorite color.

We drive past Walmart. Its blazing parking lot lights are a beacon in the night. Justin's red Grand Am sits in the back of the lot next to Trina's Chevy Cavalier. Since he doesn't have to tow an obviously under-twenty-one-year-old around anymore, Justin will probably take Trina to the bars after work with the stockmen. I'll never get to run my fingers across his fresh crew cut again. Breathe in his Nautica cologne. Every day without his touch has scooped chunks of happiness from me.

Gretchen pulls up in front of our dark-blue ranch. Light spills through the windows, creating patches of brightness on the grass. Dad's truck isn't parked in the driveway; guess he decided not to celebrate her birthday today either.

I wave as Gretchen pulls away. Her taillights fade along with her thumping music. And, for the first time since Justin broke up with me, I feel a spark inside as I cut across the lawn. Blades of grass stick to my black combat boots. Our landlord, Randy, must have mowed today.

"Rosey!" Hollis bursts out from our little doorless entry shelter. His face is washed in shadow, but the streetlight filtering through our oak tree reflects off his tears.

Chills prickle up my neck. "Why are you guys outside?"

Hollis crashes into me. His arms are cold and clammy. "She's not answering the door."

"Where's Daddy?" wails Vi, curled up on the stoop.

"I told you, stupid, dart night!" shrieks Sage. Her teeth are chattering.

Something's not right.

With a shaking hand, I pull my keys from my purse. They slip through my fingers and clatter onto the sidewalk. I grab them, then manage to unlock the door.

Our creamy-yellow peel-and-stick vinyl flooring is splattered in bright red. My heart batters against my ribcage as buzzing adrenaline surges through my veins. "Mom!"

I push the door open all the way.

Mom lies facedown, needle sticking out of the crook of her elbow, that Western-embellished pleather belt laced tight around her arm. The burnt spoon lies inches from her open hand. Her fingernails are blue. Stringy dishwater-blonde hair covers her face.

Hollis screams next to me. He is titanium white. His eyes consume his face.

"Stay outside!" I shove him out, then slam the door.

I kneel in Mom's cold, sticky blood. I roll her frail body over. Her eyes are closed. Her nose is swollen and misshapen. Her face is caked with red, so is the pink Wisconsin Dells T-shirt from the last time we went to Noah's Ark five years ago. Where's the blood from?

Oh my God. Is this it? Is this an overdose?

"Mom? Mom!" I grab her shoulder and shake her. Her eyelids don't even twitch. The thick stink of her dealer Jeremy's cigarettes clings to her.

Dad says we aren't supposed to call 911 because Sparta cops are dicks, but her lips are blue.

She could die.

I fumble my phone out of my pocket. Drop it. Grab it. Then remember we're out of minutes. It takes me a second to figure out how to place an emergency call, then three tries to hit the right buttons.

"Nine-one-one, what is your emergency?"

"My . . . my mom." My words come out strangled. "I think she OD'd."

"Okay, hang with me, sweetheart. What's your address?"

The air throbs around me. I've never had to tell it to anyone. I can't remember it. Mom could be dead. I don't even know if she's breathing. And I can't remember my fricking address.

"Are you still there?"

My brain finally works, and I stammer it out.

"Okay, sweetheart. What's your name?"

"Rose Hemmersbach."

"Okay, Rose, can you check her pulse?"

I'm scared to touch her, but I take her pencil arm, slick with blood oozing from the puncture site, and press my fingers into her wrist. Nothing.

Her skin is so cold.

Nothing.

And her body is limp like the deer Dad bagged last hunting season, lying dead in his truck bed.

Maybe she's already dead, and I never even told her happy birthday.

"Does she have a pulse?" the tinny voice asks through my phone.

The sound of the bowl of apples wall clock over the sink ticks away the seconds. Finally, a weak twitch under my fingertips. "Yes."

"Is she breathing?"

I lean my ear an inch from her mouth like in the movies. My hair drags in the blood. Nothing. "No. I . . . I don't know CPR."

Nothing.

Please. I want to tell you happy birthday.

"Calm down, sweetheart," the 911 operator's voice cuts through. "Help is on the way. Do you know what she might have taken?"

The word sticks in my throat, but I force it out. "Heroin."

In the distance, the quiet wail of sirens somehow breaks through to our kitchen. And a jagged breath tickles my cheek.

"Mom, wake up! Please, wake up!"

Her painting watches me. That stupid fricking dove. The inky darkness coiling around its feet. Dragging her into the abyss.

As the seconds of Mom's life tick away, the peeling howl slowly crescendos until it's deafening. But I still feel her heartbeat. She's not dead yet.

Faceless guys carrying bags burst into the kitchen wearing blue T-shirts with fire department logos. One drops to his knees across Mom's body from me. He presses a mask with a bag over her nose and mouth and starts squeezing.

Pump, hiss, pump, hiss, pump, hiss.

I crawl away from her body. Press my back against a chair leg. A drop of Pink Girl's dress dots the toe of my combat boot. The crusty, sticky blood. On my fingers. Frosting the tips of my hair. Alizarin crimson plus burnt sienna. The glowing patch from the light over the sink cutting through a patch of red on the floor—add a bit of yellow.

A heavy black boot sends the scorched spoon rattling across the floor toward my pinky. Indistinct faces with dissonant expressions surround us, turning to Mom like she's the black horned Satan at the center of Francisco Goya's *The Great He-Goat*.

A firefighter talks into the walkie attached to his shoulder, "Dispatch, rescue nine-one-one, 120 South Black River Street, overdose."

Another one with a full beard crouches in front of me, nose inches from mine. "Let's get you out of here." He takes my arm.

My whole body, every cell in me, trembles as he pulls me up. My combat boots slip on the blood as I stumble after him. I trip off our stoop. The firefighter catches my arm. "You okay?"

People wearing different uniforms swarm around us through our open door. The patches on their navy-blue sleeves say "Sparta Area Ambulance Service Sparta Wi."

Outside, the blue-and-red flashing lights of a fire truck and ambulance beat back the stars, casting strange shadows on the leaves of our oak tree. The front yard is empty.

"Where are the kids?" I cry. "Where are the kids?"

"In the cop car." He points to it halfway down the block in front of the fire truck.

And I can see their heads through the back window.

"What's your name?" the firefighter asks. He's much younger than Dad.

I feel each heartbeat in my temples as my nails cut into my palms. "Rose. Is she gonna be okay?"

"What's her name?"

"Maureen Hemmersbach. Is she going to be okay? It's her birthday."

"We're helping her, Rose. Where's your dad? You got a number?"

"We're out of minutes." I realize I'm crying. I scrub at my cheeks with the backs of my hands because my fingers are stained with her blood. "He . . . he's at dart night. Market."

"Okay, we'll get that figured out." The firefighter waves a police officer over. They step aside and talk.

I sprint to the cop car. Tap on the window. Sage, Hollis, and Vi are all sobbing in the back seat. I can hear it through the thick glass. I try to open the door, but it's locked. I pound on the window. Hollis pulls at the door handle, but nothing happens.

Blue and red. Blue and red.

Faces bathed in shadow, Mr. and Mrs. Studebaker watch from their perfectly manicured lawn, heads tilted toward one another as they talk.

"Rose." A female police officer approaches me. "We're getting your dad. I'm going to take you kids to the station. He'll meet us there."

The cop directs me to ride shotgun. I'm crammed in with a laptop attached to the center console. The kids are separated from me by a solid wall of plastic. I can't even hold Vi's hand.

"I got some cookies from Linda's Bakery with your names on it," the cop says as she climbs in. She told me her name, I'm pretty sure, but I can't remember it.

Hollis chokes on a sob. "Is she dead?"

The cop glances at him in the rearview mirror as she pulls out. "No, honey. They're taking her to Gundersen Lutheran to make sure she's okay."

All I can smell is tangy, metallic blood. And vinegar, even though I know no one's cooking heroin in the cop car. There's a drop of Mom's blood on my jean shorts. Bile chokes up my throat.

The cop pulls to a stop outside the station. I've never been in a police station before. As I climb out, I realize I forgot to buckle my seatbelt. She lets the kids out of the back seat. They all have stuffed bears. I try to get my arms around all three at once as we squeeze through the glass door.

"I'm gonna put you all somewhere comfortable while we get things figured out." The cop leads us past a reception desk. The receptionist is a frequent flier at Walmart; she must have an army of cats with how much kitty litter she buys. Her eyes widen in recognition. Shame burns my face. I shake my bangs over my eyes.

The cop opens a door to a tiny room with four plastic chairs and a table and some kind of recording device stuck in the wall. A camera watches from the corner.

"Are you gonna interrogate us?" Sage whimpers. Her bear dangles by its tiny hand.

"No, just want to give you a quiet place to wait. I'll go get some stuff for you to do. Hang tight."

Hollis's cornflower-blue eyes outsize his face, cheeks wet with tears, begging for me to say or do something. But I've got nothing.

Vi's sobbing so hard that coughs rack her body, her face alizarin crimson. I pull Vi into my lap, then try to scoot closer to Hollis, but apparently the table and chairs are all bolted to the floor. I grab his clammy hand. Some holes have been picked in the soundproofing, titanium white touched with a tiny hint of blue. Vi shivers in my lap.

Hollis lets out a high keen as he presses the bear to his face.

I should say something to the kids. Make them feel better. But I can't move, not even to open my mouth.

A different lady drops an armload of water bottles and coloring books onto the table, then sets a paper plate with four cookies next to it. She says her name too, but my brain can't hold that either cuz Mom's blood is still on my knees and the cop said she was going to be all right, but how could she even know that?

The lady tells me to go to the bathroom and clean up, but I can't move.

Dad bursts through the door. The kiddos all launch at him.

"I'm sorry, I'm sorry, I'm sorry." He scoops up all three and then kneels in front of me and pulls me into a crushing bear hug too. He's shaking. I can't smell beer on him. Then he grabs my hands. "Rosey, oh shit! Are you hurt? Are you okay?"

"Daryl, we're gonna need to Breathalyze you before we can figure out what happens next," a new cop says from the doorway as he hitches up his utility belt.

"Rosey, talk to me." His thick, oil-stained fingers get stuck in my hairspray-crusty hair now tipped with a little blood.

"Daryl, I'm talking to you," the cop barks behind him.

"I'm fine," I croak.

Dad hugs me again. "I've only had the one beer," he snaps over his shoulder.

"You got two DUIs, Daryl."

Dad stands up to his full six foot five, fists clenched at his side like a raging Viking warrior. "That was two years ago! And that ain't got nothing to do with my kids."

"Daddy!" Hollis shrieks as tears and snot pour down his face.

Dad's heavy brow crushes down on the rest of his face. His fists relax. "I'll be right back."

The door clicks closed behind them. Did they lock us in?

Hollis's staccato cries fill the tiny room.

Finally I can move. I get my arms around Hollis and pull him into my lap even though he's only a few inches shorter than me now. I haven't held him like this since Mom and Dad had the Big Fight years ago, when Dad found out she was shooting heroin. I

26

rest my cheek on top of his head. The sharp tang of prepubescent sweat is mixed with the kiddos' watermelon shampoo and body-wash combo.

What if Dad fails the sobriety test?

Sage and Vi are crying too, but I can't hold them all; my arms aren't long enough. An air-conditioning vent hums and rattles directly over us. That's all I can hear. Like this room has become the whole world as the cookies start getting stale as they sit in the middle of that tiny interrogation table by the mountain of generic coloring books that cost a dollar each at Walmart.

What happens to us if he's drunk? Where will we go?

And Mom, oh God. Mom. Is she okay?

Finally the door opens. Dad comes in, head hung so low it's practically dragging on the floor.

Vi jumps into his arms. He cradles her against him, hand tucked around the back of her little head. Her blonde pigtails poke through his fingers.

"I just got off the phone with the hospital." The fine lines around his eyes cut deeper through his cheeks than they did this morning. "They say Mom's fine. She's going to be fine."

Hollis may be only sixty pounds of skinny legs and arms, but my thighs burn under his weight as his warm tears soak through my T-shirt.

Then in walks Grammy.

Grammy?

She looks the same as the last time we saw her two and a half years ago—short permed blonde hair with brown and gray roots growing out, tanned leathery skin, and deep wrinkles around her eyes and mouth from her liberal smiles.

Shit, maybe Dad is drunk and we have to go with her.

Grammy rams her finger right in Dad's face. "Damn it, Daryl!

This is why I told you to leave that woman ages ago!"

Dad sets Vi down. She crumbles onto the floor like a used tissue. He throws his hands up. "Mom, please. Not in front of the kids."

"There ain't nothing I can say or do that could possibly be worse than what they just went through. And you. You were out drinking at the bars. That ain't how your dad and I raised you."

Dad's chin sinks to his chest.

The adrenaline wears off, and I can't stop shaking. My tongue is sandpaper.

Grammy shakes her head at him one more time and then scoops Vi from the floor. "Look at you, such a big girl!" Her voice, raspy and deep from decades of smoking, is a ghost resurrected from the dead.

Vi clings to Grammy, even though she probably doesn't remember her. Her sobs slow.

"And Hollis . . . you're practically a grown man." She reaches for him.

Hollis shifts in my lap, his bony butt digging into my thighs. I hold him tighter.

Dad squeezes Sage's shoulders. "We're staying at Grammy's tonight."

"Do we get to skip the first day of school?" Sage asks.

Dad tugs off his Packers hat, revealing his major hat head. "I'll drive you back."

"But what about our clothes?" I ask.

Dad rubs the red imprint on his forehead. "Can't go home yet."

"I'll wash them tonight." Grammy kisses the top of Vi's head. "Good news is, since tomorrow's the first day, no one'll know you wore them today."

But can you wash out the spot of blood on my shorts?

Dad scoops Hollis off my lap, and I'm instantly shivering without his body heat. He pries Vi from Grammy. Sage trails behind them as we leave the room.

Grammy walks next to me. Her scuffed-up white gym shoes squeak on the floor. As she looks to me, her pale-blue eyes rimmed with navy blue tighten. "Oh, Rosey. You're almost a grown woman. And short hair looks good on you." She touches my hair. The smell of her Newport Menthol Blues brings this primal wave of comfort.

The last time she saw me was before Rose split in two and I chopped off what Mom called my "Rapunzel" hair.

"Well, we've been in the same house all this time. You knew where to find me."

Grammy's eyes widen like I slapped her. "Rosey . . ."

I throw open the police station door and walk into the slightly cooler night. I climb into Dad's rusted-out brown Chevy extended cab, a Calvin pissing on Ford window decal on the back window next to the NRA one. Then we're driving up Highway 27 all the way up to Cataract. The kids are all sleeping. It's 1:07 a.m.

Headlights slice into the darkness, barely illuminating the road ahead, the pine trees around us, the rear end of Grammy's rusty silver Lumina. The moon casts creamy light on the blacktop, highlighting the veins of tar patching up cracks in the road.

The truck cab is silent. No COW 97 Country even.

"What's gonna happen now?" I ask.

Dad's hands strangle the steering wheel. "Social worker's gonna come and talk to you guys at school tomorrow probably."

"Social worker?" I cough out. My arm hair stands on end. Her blood's still on me. Oh God. Her blood's still on me.

Dad flicks the heat on.

"This is bad. This is really bad, isn't it? Are we going to end up in foster care?"

Dad's shoulders wilt. He lets out a sigh heavier than a grain bin. "It's only Mom they're worried about right now."

The cab is lit only by the glow of the radio, but I can see millions of apologies brewing in Dad's exhausted eyes. "Everything's fine. It's going to be fine. I promise, Rosey. I promise."

I don't believe him, because the tightness in his voice proves he doesn't even believe himself.

Chapter 4

Something lands on my chest. I jump to a start and push it off.

A calico cat eyes me up from its landing spot a foot away.

I'm on a pile of quilts and pillows nestled between a cream-colored faux suede couch and a TV stand. My whole body aches. Sage lies next to me with pink cheeks and a tiny dribble of drool running from the corner of her mouth. Hollis isn't even snoring.

The cat forcefully rubs its head on my arm, its purr vibrating through my skin. It's Cleocatra.

"She remembers you, Rosey Rose," a raspy voice calls. Grammy. We're at Grammy's house. Crackling and the smell of frying bacon drifts from the kitchen.

The crumpled deer-hunting quilt Grammy made Grampy lies in a pile at the foot of the couch where Dad slept last night.

Grammy's living room. Where we had pancake breakfast every Saturday. Same brown plaid armchair. Same glass coffee table layered with tabloid magazines, now pushed against her curio cabinet filled with the same Precious Moments figurines to make room for our makeshift bed. My freshman picture from when I was still Pink Rapunzel Rose hangs over the TV by Mom and Dad's wedding picture. According to the Sparta 2001 yearbook, Mom was the girl voted "best smile." She used to joke they should have been voted cutest couple, especially with me on the way. In the wedding picture, Mom's shining her best smile like a beauty queen in her poufy, sequined, strapless heartline wedding dress, and Dad, before the beer belly, looks kind of like Chris Hemsworth in his tux.

Everything from last night rushes over me and I'm shivering. I hug my arms to my chest over a huge pink kitten shirt of Grammy's. The only thing she couldn't wash was my underwear. My hair is still slightly damp from my 2:00 a.m. shower. I scrubbed myself five times, but I still feel the blood burning my skin.

"Rosey, why don't you come get some breakfast?" Dad calls from the kitchen table through the narrow cooking area.

I drag myself up, squeeze past Grammy flipping a pancake, and drop into one of her carved wood chairs inherited from her grandma. Cleocatra jumps into my lap, her paws digging into my bare thighs. I almost push her off, but her warmth makes me feel something.

"Here you go, Rosey Rose." Grammy sets a plate in front of me piled with pancakes and scrambled eggs and bacon, complemented with a glass of orange juice. "Fuel for the first day."

Grammy watches me with a wide, anticipatory smile as a pancake *thwacks* against the pan again. I stab some eggs and pop them into my mouth. The perfect amount of salt and cheese and hint of onion powder. Mom could never make them as good, even when she was sober. But my stomach is too knotted for food.

Dad shovels a huge bite of pancake into his mouth and then grabs some bacon. I swear there are a few more gray hairs in his five-o'clock shadow.

"What now?" I ask.

"Police are done at the house. I'll drive you kids to school, then clean so we can go home. Buy more minutes for our phones."

"Don't you need to work?"

"Took the day off." Dad slurps some coffee from the "I'd Rather Be Fishing" mug he always used for Saturday Pancake Breakfast.

The thought of seeing that crusty blood, now smeared by footprints makes my stomach lurch. But how could he do it all himself?

"I'll help," I say. Holy shit, why did I say that?

"You need to be in school, Rosey. You kiddos need some normalcy," Grammy says as she waggles her greasy spatula in my direction.

"I'm sorry, who are you? Cuz I don't think I've seen you in years," I say.

"Rosey!" Dad massages his forehead.

"And neither of you were actually there. You don't know how bad it is! It's more than just blood. Mom hasn't done the dishes all week and the trash is piled up and there's a mountain of laundry and the kids' toys are literally everywhere. Cuz now there's apparently social workers involved."

Dad sucks in a sharp breath.

"Rosey's just telling it like it is." Grammy fires off an approving nod in my direction. "You got that from me, you know that, right, Rosey? The Bergstrom side. My grandma, she was a real pistol."

My jaw opens and closes as I fail to come up with a retort.

"I'll come help for a bit, Daryl. I don't work till three today, and the kiddos need to sleep in their own beds tonight."

Dad's eyes are lost in his mug, the contents of which are no longer steaming.

"Daryl!" Grammy smacks him lightly with a dish towel.

"Huh?" He drags his head up.

"I'm coming to help."

He slurps his cold coffee with a grimace. "Thanks, Mom."

"And Rosey, your clothes are folded on the washing machine," Grammy says.

"Whatever." I squeeze between the wall and Dad's chair and head for her bathroom, since apparently I have to go to school.

I don't have any makeup to wear today.

———

I'm pushed down the hall with the rest of the student body one-up-ping about their vacations, just like every other first day of school. Usually I feel a pang of jealousy. Today I want to smash a window. I'm a shaken pop bottle ready to explode.

The white cinder block walls are lined with posters recruiting for Future Farmers of America, Future Business Leaders of America, and the Academic Decathlon along with handcrafted construction paper signs coated in glitter inviting "all" to cheer-leader tryouts.

Someone taps my shoulder.

"Good morrow, m'lady!" Anderson says in a British accent with a flourished bow. He's wearing a Fullmetal Alchemist T-shirt accentuated with a black bow tie.

I roll my eyes and keep walking. Today I can't play along. I just. Cannot.

"Rose, love"—he chases after me, pushing up his glasses— "hath thou seen my dearest Gretchen?"

I spit through my teeth, "Lay off the Dungeons and Dragons."

Anderson's face scrunches up.

I keep walking.

Eisenhardt, decked out in a Hawaiian shirt, pushes through the rest of the crowd. He's apparently frosted his hair like he's one of Gretchen's Florida surfer dudes even though we live in *Wisconsin*. He jumps up and slaps a red-and-yellow banner hanging from the ceiling advertising "The Spartan Way: Respectful, Responsible, Safe." The irony.

As he barges into Mrs. Ebert's classroom, he belts, "Know your role, shut your hole! Know your role, shut your hole! Seniors, seniors!"

As I droop into an empty desk, I catch a whiff of Grammy's Laundry Fresh dryer sheets mixed with a hint of menthol cigarettes. I hope no one else can smell that. My brain throbs against my skull with each heartbeat, and my arms are so heavy I can't unzip my backpack even for my sketchbook.

But then I remember I don't even have a backpack, because it's trapped in the crime scene Dad and Grammy are cleaning right now.

A cacophony of conversation hums around me, but my ears are filled with this buzzing sound like a horde of ravenous mosquitos.

But through all that, Kimmy's sunshine slices.

"*Hola*, Rafa!" Kimmy bounces up the aisle in my direction, wearing blinding yellow and her perfect smile.

I peek through my bangs. That Rafa guy sits across the aisle from me.

"Hi, Kimmy," he says.

"Hey, your notebook's *amarillo*! That's my favorite color."

"I never would have guessed," he says with a hint of sarcasm.

Kimmy moves on, but Rafa's eyes catch mine and he smiles.

Rafa saw me yesterday. So did Kimmy. Did they notice I'm

wearing the same clothes? Shame burns my face. I hide behind my limp hair.

Then I catch someone saying my name. My scratchy eyes focus on Eisenhardt and Mike whispering in front of me. Mike wears his red-and-yellow varsity letter jacket, even though it's going to be well above eighty and the school doesn't have air conditioning. The medals on the front clang as he glances back with a sneer. Eisenhardt's mom is a janitor at the police station; he probably heard.

"Hey, what are you two talking about?" Kimmy sashays over to Mr. Quarterback.

"Just debating *War and Peace*," Eisenhardt says, feigning innocence.

Mrs. Ebert rushes in, sparkly shirt catching the morning sun leaking through the blind slats as she smooths a few of her blonde curlicues back into her ponytail. "Good morning, class. Hope you all had a good summer. You must be Rafael. Why don't you come up front and introduce yourself? Tell us where you're from and your favorite hobby."

I drag my eyes up from the glossy desktop. Rafa is on display, hands shoved in his skinny-fit khaki pockets. He stands out; we have like seven kids who aren't white at this school, and he's probably the only new senior.

"Um, Rafa, Milwaukee, painting."

"What brings you all the way from the big city?" she asks, hands clenched to her chest.

Rafa scratches the back of his head. "Dad's job." As she opens her mouth to ask another question, he heads back to his desk.

"Oh, okay then." Mrs. Ebert pushes up her little round glasses. "Thank you, Rafa."

As Mrs. Ebert launches into a play-by-play of our syllabus, my eyes are glued to the classroom phone as I wait for the social workers to pounce like it's some twisted Christmas Eve where you know Krampus is coming instead of Santa but you have no idea when.

I hope the kiddos are okay.

"Rose. What book are we reading first?" Mrs. Ebert asks.

I sink in my desk. I feel every single set of eyes staring at me.

"*War and Peace*," I mutter.

Pink blooms across Mrs. Ebert's cheeks as she scoffs. Last year, when we discussed whether Brutus or Caesar was truly the tragic hero in *Julius Caesar*, I had all the answers.

This year, apparently I don't.

"Dude, you're Omar's brother, right?"

I forgot I'm in Psychology. I don't remember walking here. I peek through my bangs. Eisenhardt leans on Rafa's desk next to me.

"Yup." Rafa spins a pencil on his desk just an inch from Eisenhardt's ass. It's the same brand of graphite pencil I use.

"He's, like, the king of juking!" Eisenhardt tosses up a hand for a high five.

"Good for him." Rafa spins his pencil again.

Eisenhardt's hand drops as his nose crinkles. Rafa's the only person I've ever witnessed leave Eisenhardt hanging.

The bell rings.

Mr. Smith saunters into the classroom wearing a T-shirt with a black blob on it that says "Does this inkblot make me look fat?"

"Psych, psych, psych!" he chants as his fist pumps until the whole class but Rafa and me are chanting too. Eisenhardt starts galloping around until Mr. Smith nails him with a neon Nerf football.

"Per my grand annual tradition, let's kick the school year off with a joke." Mr. Smith's voice drips with his usual joviality. "A man's walking down the street one day when he gets beaten and robbed. As he lays there unconscious and injured, a psychologist walks by. What do you think he says?"

Eisenhardt belts out from his desk a few rows up, "Oedipus complex. You know, where you want to screw your mom."

Snickers ripple through the classroom.

"What?" Mr. Smith squints at him. "While I'm slightly impressed you even know a term associated with Freudian theory, that makes absolutely no—"

The phone rings. Mr. Smith grabs it. His eyes dart to me.

Krampus has arrived. Or what if . . . is she dead? Coldness creeps up my spine as my vision narrows. No, Dad said she'll be fine.

"Rose, your presence is requested at the guidance office." Mr. Smith sweeps his hand toward the door garnished with a photo of a pink Freud, a pun probably lost on most of these people.

I drag myself up from my desk. My legs wobble, almost give out, as I walk down the aisle. Everyone stares.

"Rose, can't let you go without telling you the answer. It's the core of psychology," Mr. Smith booms as I grip the cold metal door handle. "As the dude lays there bleeding, the psychologist says, 'My God! Whoever did this really needs help!'"

I let the door slam behind me just as Mr. Smith says, "Rafael, my man, c'mon up and introduce—"

The empty hallway is a blur of lockers too bright red to be blood.

When I walk into the office, Mrs. Arnold looks up from her computer and frowns at me. But it's not her Judgy-McJudgerton frown, like when I used to get called down here freshman year for skipping; today it's pity tugging the corners of her lips down.

And Mrs. O'Neil stands outside her own office fidgeting with her American School Counselor Association lanyard.

Adrenaline thrums in my veins. Makes my head spin. My feet move forward toward her door, adorned with a black-and-white zigzag patterned sign that says "Welcome to the Counselor's Office." I'm wading through a foot of mud.

"Rose, honey, some people are here to ask you a couple questions." Mrs. O'Neil's fingers graze my upper arm. "They're here to help."

"People?" Dad just said it would be a social worker.

"Just . . . They'll explain." Her voice drips with an apology. She pushes the door open.

A middle-aged lady with thick permed bangs like you see in those eighties movies sits at the round table. A badge hangs around her neck that says "Monroe County Human Services." Next to her is a beefy man with a crew cut wearing a white polo and a police badge around his neck.

This is bad. Really bad. My head is swirling, swirling, twirling like I'm trapped on the Tilt-A-Whirl at Butterfest with Anderson in eighth grade when he wouldn't stop making our car spin.

"Hi, Rose. Why don't you take a seat?" The lady gestures to the blue plastic chair across from her.

My body sits on its own. Over the usual smell of Mrs. O'Neil's eucalyptus essential oil cuts a strong aftershave. It's hard to breathe. The same clay bowl sits in the middle of O'Neil's table, but it's filled with brand-new fidgets: Koosh balls, stress balls, and one of those rubber duckies with eyes that pop out.

"I'm Kristy, a social worker for the county." She holds out her hand. I lift my hand from my lap and barely touch hers.

"And I'm Detective Diggs." He offers his hand with a deceptively warm smile. His hand crushes mine as he shakes.

The social worker digs out a yellow notepad and slaps it on the table. Then she takes out a manila folder. "My job is to help families get what they need and to keep kids safe. Do you know why we're here, hon?"

I nod.

"We already know a lot of it. We're just here to get some more specifics, okay?" the social worker says as she clicks her pen. Her voice sounds kind, but she's here to get my mom in trouble.

"Who lives in the house with you?" she asks.

The saliva evaporates from my mouth.

"Rose?" the detective says.

I hide behind my bangs. "Uh, Mom, Dad, me, Hollis, Sage, Vi."

I hear pens scratching on notepads.

"Where'd you stay last night?" Detective Diggs asks.

"Our grandma's."

"That's good," says the social worker.

Finally my body can move. I scrape at the black nail polish on my thumb even though chipped nails look just plain sloppy and cheap. Tiny black flakes fall onto my jean shorts like snow. Grammy was able to get the blood out.

"Can you tell me about what happened last night?" Detective Diggs asks.

Cold sweat prickles my brow. I pull my eyes up. Past the detective and social worker is a window with the same ivy plant sitting on the sill as last year. Through the glass I can see Lawrence Lawson, the kiddos' school, across the street. Are they being asked that same question right now by a scary police officer?

As the adrenaline fades, inky tendrils of haze lace through my brain and it feels like it's thirty below and I have no coat. I shiver. Mom . . . they're investigating Mom because of drugs.

Our kitchen floor splashed with alizarin crimson and burnt sienna. Blue lips. Cold skin. Weak pulse. It's all I can see, like it's happening again. *Pump, hiss, pump, hiss.* But it's Mom. *My* mom. Tears choke my throat.

A loud throat clearing. I'm back in Mrs. O'Neil's room. One of her trademark posters taunts me from by the window: "The same power you have to destroy yourself, you have to save yourself."

"Rose?" That detective's beady eyes bore into me. Can he arrest me if I lie?

"I . . . I dunno. I came home from a friend's house. My siblings were sitting outside. I found her. I called 911." The words rip through my throat like barbed wire.

Their pens scrawl on their notebooks.

"You know the rest." I scrape the remaining black off my thumb.

"So the kids were outside alone. Did they see anything?" asks the social worker.

The look of pure horror on Hollis's face as he saw the red. Like the wide-eyed, soundless scream of Caravaggio's decapitated *Medusa* painting. So wide I could see the whites of his eyes all around his irises.

"Just for a second."

"What time did you come home?" the detective asks.

"I . . . I dunno. Like nine?"

"How come they were outside?" The social worker taps her pen on the notepad.

"The door was locked. And . . ." The haze clears and everything snaps into focus like someone threw a bucket of ice water in my face. "Oh my God, Hollis lost his key last week. I knew it was dart night, but I thought Dad would be home because it was her birthday."

"How long were they locked outside?" asks the detective, his words like bullets from a firing squad.

Each question carves a tiny chunk out of my skin. "I . . . I dunno."

Through my bangs, I see the social worker's pen flying.

The chair creaks as Detective Dick leans on the table. "That the only time it happened? The kids being locked outside for long periods of time?"

That carves another chunk out of me. They're both watching me. Pens ready.

Because Mom probably shouldn't be watching them. Last week, Travis found Vi all the way down at Memorial Park. Mom hadn't even noticed she'd left. And that witch Traci from next door complained to Randy about Sage stealing stuff from her yard. And I know they've been locked out before; that's why Dad gave Hollis the key.

But we couldn't afford Boys & Girls Club this summer because Mom's not working.

"Rose?" the social worker asks.

Sweat pools on my lower back. I purse my lips.

The social worker sighs. "Look, we're not trying to take you away. We're just trying to get a sense of how to make your family safe."

Detective Dick crosses his thick arms. "How long's your phone been out of minutes?"

For a fleeting second, the social worker shoots Detective Dick a look.

"Like a day. And, yes, it's the first time it's ever happened." That's true. "And I was still able to call 911, obviously."

"So your parents can't afford childcare and can't pay their cell phone bills. Where's the money going?" Detective Dick asks.

His dickish tone finally ignites my rage. I am strong again.

"You know the answer to that. Can I go now? I've got stuff to be learning."

Detective Dick and the social worker exchange a look. "All right, Rose," she says.

I leave.

I betrayed my family. My own mother.

I'm shaking.

I can't stay here. I can't. Besides, now I don't even know what hour it is or what class I'm even supposed to be in. All the colorful posters coating the walls are a blur as I rush down the hallway.

I throw open the doors to the side parking lot. Hot, sticky air brushes my skin, but I can't even feel the warmth. From the practice field on the hill leaks an off-key marching band attempt at "Wrecking Ball."

Now I can't even remember what I told the social worker and Detective Dick. And if I didn't tell them what they wanted, will they torture the kiddos even more than me? Hollis will crumble. And Sage, I wouldn't put it past her to tell him to screw off. Violet would probably just tell them everything. Shit. Shit, why did I storm out?

God, and how long were they trapped outside? It could have been literally all day. Did they even get dinner? Lunch? While I was eating Mr. Osmundson's legendary brats with my feet in the pool. They must have been so scared.

I need to see them. I need to make sure they're okay. But I can't. I can't get into their school.

I can't think. I can't breathe. I can run. My combat boots pound the parking lot pavement as I'm full-out sprinting like before Rose broke in two and I was one of the fastest girls at the one-hundred-meter dash on the track team.

A police car drives by. Shit. What if I get a ticket for skipping school? CPS might find out, then Mom and Dad will look even worse.

West Side Park. I'll hide there.

A car horn blares as it whizzes by, and I realize I'm stuck a few feet into the crosswalk on Black River Street.

I make it to the narrow grass path everyone forgets about that runs between houses. It's a tunnel of chain link and trees leading to a huge field with a baseball diamond sans bases littered with grass patches, a crooked swing set, and a wooden play structure. The castle Daddy Knight always rescued Princess Rose from. The steps creak as I climb to the top. I lean against a cracked post where someone carved C.B.+T.R. before I was born, avoiding protruding nailheads.

And Detective Dick's sneer and blue fingernails and Hollis's face as decapitated Medusa tears through my brain. I need to draw. I need to paint. Something. Art's the only way I can shut off my brain. But my stuff's back home with the blood.

My phone vibrates. Guess Dad got us more minutes. Take that, Detective Dick.

Gretchen: Hey, where are you?

I can't.

I curl up in a ball in the tower. Hot late summer sun sizzles my bare legs and arms. I'm so tired, and the wood is warm on my skin.

———

I wake with a start.

A little boy stares down at me with a sucker hanging out of his mouth. "Why are you sleeping here?"

My neck yelps as I sit up.

Through the planks, his mom watches us with her arms crossed. She's a Walmart frequent flier, just like that receptionist last night.

"Working on my tan." I jump down. The shallow, faded mulch crunches under my boots. And apparently I was working on my tan, because the skin on my neck stings as my shirt collar grazes it.

I check my phone as I emerge from the tunnel of green onto the sidewalk. Back into the real world. It's almost three. I have a message from Dad asking why I'm not in school. Thanks, robocall. I ignore it and head for Lawrence Lawson. The kiddos. I need to make sure they're okay.

The breeze, thick with the stench of car exhaust, blows through my naked hair as I walk along Lawrence Lawson's playground. The chain link is warm under my fingertips. On the other side is the massive field where I used to play freeze tag but now Sage plays football. Most of the playground equipment's red plastic has faded to pink now, but the metal poles are still the same shade of bright blue. After last night, it should look different. Smaller.

Parents dot the pavement by the door to the school. A mom and dad hold a bouquet of carnations and a sign that says "Good job on your first day of kindergarten." I bite my tongue before I point out that their precious kindergartener can't read.

The bell rings, and a teacher I don't remember leads a long string of what must be fifth graders out. The teacher eyes me up like she somehow knows I skipped, even though the high school's been out for ten minutes. Or maybe she knows Mom OD'd.

Hollis emerges from the glass double doors. He's clutching that bear the firefighter gave him.

"Holly!" I call.

His head inches up. The sun highlights his oily dark-blond Mohawk, at least a month overdue for a trim. Did the social worker and Detective Dick notice he hadn't had a bath in a couple days?

Hollis's brows pinch, and he runs to me. I pull him into a hug. He's trembling.

"Someone come talk to you too?" I ask.

He bursts into tears.

Crap. Maybe I shouldn't have started with that.

Mrs. Kenyon sweeps up to us. She has the same brown bob as when she was my teacher. "Gosh, Ring-around-the-Rosey. Look at you. You're practically an adult. What are you now, a junior?"

God. That nickname.

"Senior." I tighten my arms around Hollis. His hot, choppy breath, mixed with snot, leaks through the fabric of my shirt. He's seeing it again. I know he is. It's flashing before his eyes. I failed to stop him from seeing it, and now I can't delete it from his brain.

"I still have that daffodil picture you made me hanging up." Mrs. Kenyon shines her wide grin at me. It falters when her eyes fall to Hollis. "Anyway, I'm sure Hollis will talk more tomorrow." She waves to another parent and practically runs away.

I pull in a breath to fight back the burning sensation rising in my chest.

"It's okay. They already knew everything anyway," I say.

Hollis's body relaxes against mine. Finally found a right thing to say.

"Rosey!" Vi's skinny little arms tackle me into a hug from behind. It looks like she has twin black eyes from exhaustion.

One of the kindergarten teachers, a new one, comes up to me. "Are you Violet's mom?"

"What? No. I'm her sister."

The teacher frowns. "I'm just a little worried because she slept most of the day. And when she wasn't sleeping, she was crying."

I don't know what to say.

Mrs. Krause drags Sage up to me by the arm. The most powerful stain remover on earth can't make a dent in the grass stains on her jeans.

"She swore at me," Mrs. Krause says as she waggles a wrinkly finger in my face. "On the first day!"

Clearly the Hemmersbach brood is winning at normalcy today. Thanks, Grammy.

Oh God. Oh God. They'll tell CPS. My heart pounds against my ribcage as I peel Vi and Holly off me. I haul Sage toward the gate in the fence.

"If you think this is how the rest of third grade goes, missy, you're in for a surprise," Mrs. Krause barks at our backs.

She always was a bitch. Even Dad remembered that back from when he had her.

"Rose, you're hurting me!" cries Sage as she tries to pull free. I let her go. A red handprint lingers on her wrist.

"Well, stop swearing at your teachers, then."

"You're not my mom!"

"Yeah, but Mom's in the fricking hospital!" I snap back. "Not that she did anything before anyway!"

Now Vi and Hollis are crying again. Damn it.

"Let's . . . let's just get home."

Dad and Grammy better have finished cleaning.

As we walk, my phone vibrates in my back pocket. Gretchen sent me a picture of a banana split ten ice cream scoops high with syrup drooling down the sides.

Gretchen: Just cuz you skipped school doesn't mean you get outta this ;-)

Crap, our traditional first-day-of-school banana split at Ginny's Cupboard. But I don't have the energy to respond.

When we get home, Dad's truck is in the driveway, but not Grammy's Lumina. I walk into the kitchen. All I see is red eating away the yellow vinyl flooring. The scorched spoon. The needle. My heart roars in my ears, even though the kitchen floor sparkles and the air is thick with the smell of Pine-Sol. I grind my fingers into my sweat-slick forehead.

Mom, oh God, Mom. I didn't make her a card for the first time in fourteen years. I didn't even say happy birthday. And today I betrayed her. I can't remember what I told them, but I'm sure I did.

"Rosey, why are you crying?" Hollis paws at my arms.

"I'm not." I scrub my tears.

"Hiya, kiddos." Dad walks into the kitchen and manages to get his arms around all three of them at once. He glances at me over Sage's shoulder. I cross my arms as I wait for him to yell at me for skipping, but instead his eyes fall.

"When can we see Mommy?" asks Vi.

Dad lets them go and stands up. "We gotta talk. Family meeting."

We go to the living room. Hollis and Vi bookend me in warmth on the couch. Sage assumes her throne on the orange armchair.

Mom's painting watches us from over Sage's throne. Small impressionist brushstrokes building the shifting glow on the dove's feathery wings. The dove fights to break free of the seething darkness coiling around its feet, pulling it toward a black cavernous maw mixed from burnt umber and ultramarine blue.

I want to snap the frame and throw it away. Because now she's been sucked into the cavernous maw. And she's not even here to clean up her own fricking blood.

"Couple things." Dad tugs off his Packers hat, revealing his thick mop of hat-head hair. "Mom's fine. She's had a couple surgeries."

"Surgeries?" I squint at him.

"Don't you worry about that," Dad says.

"Stop treating me like a baby. I'm the one who found her dying!" I say.

Dad's brows pinch like I slapped him.

Hollis folds over himself, face buried in Teddy.

I rub his back, feel each of his vertebrae and ribs under my palm. "She wasn't dead, okay, Holly? I found her heartbeat."

His whole body heaves with sobs. I'm just making it worse. Again.

"I want to know too!" barks Sage.

"I'm the parent, and I decide what you get to know!" Dad roars.

That sucks the air from the room. A single tear streaks down Sage's face. Sage. Her lips form a perfect *o*. Even I sink back into the couch, because Dad almost never yells at us.

Dad twists his hat in his hands. "She's fine."

"Can we see Mommy?" Vi whimpers as she tugs at the hem of her pink dress.

"Soon. But let's keep the place tidy from now on, okay? Pick up your toys. Put the dishes in the sink. Your dirty clothes in the hamper." His eyes wander to Hollis.

"Is this cuz of those people today? Are they gonna take us away?" Hollis cries through his bear.

Dad drops to his knees in front of him. "No, Holly." He pulls down the bear and cradles Hollis's face in his huge hands. "Okay. Dinner. We need some dinner."

I snatch the remote and stream one of the *Toy Story* movie

using Travis's Netflix account and Traci's internet.

Dad pulls open the fridge, now stocked with more food than I've ever seen in it: apples and grapes and two gallons of milk and cheese and packs of hamburger. Dad even bought carrot sticks for like the first time ever. All his High Lifes are gone.

Dad grabs a pack of hamburger, opens it, and dumps it into a pan. He pulls a box of generic Hamburger Helper from the overstuffed cabinet. Hemmersbach special, one of the three things Dad knows how to cook. Slightly better than him slapping together braunschweiger and mustard sandwiches, but I hate Hamburger Helper. So, so much.

I climb onto the counter. The heel of my combat boot taps on the cabinet door.

"Two things. CPS is going to stop out and do a home visit at some point in the next week or so."

"They're stalking us here too?"

"It's just Mom, not me. Mom had a lung infection. That's what the surgery was for." Dad's chin dimples under his blond five-o'clock shadow as he stabs at the sizzling meat with a spatula. "Could've killed her in a matter of days."

In that singular moment, my skin stings like I'm sinking into ice cold water. It wasn't just the overdose. Mom's worse than we ever knew. She's using so much heroin her bodily functions are failing. Heroin isn't helping her "get through." And she sure as shit can't "stop when she wants to."

My *mom*.

No breath. No pulse. Tears pool over my lower lids, spill down my cheeks.

Dad pulls me off the counter into a hug that almost envelops my whole body like he hasn't since Vi was born. He smells like sweat and Old Spice, but not the usual raw metal because he had to clean up Mom's blood instead of working on the factory floor at Northern Engraving.

Heroin's killing her. And there's no surgery to fix being an addict.

———

After Dad gets the kids showering, I peel back my comforter and sink into my bed. For a moment, my body feels almost weightless. The spackled paint makes the white ceiling look like an inverse night sky sprinkled with gray stars. My eyes linger on the smudge of pink scarring the white—a reminder that Mom painted the walls teal per my request after I grew out of pink.

"Damn it, Sage, brush your teeth! You don't need another cap!" Dad's holler seeps under the door. I roll over and face the wall.

I know we already got Calculus homework, even though I wasn't there, because Mr. Ziegler is pretty much evil. And I should be reading *The Great Gatsby*, but I'm pretty sure I left that book in Psychology.

So much for this year being better than the last ones.

The bedroom door opens, and Hollis comes in, damp hair hanging in his eyes. His Minecraft pj pants are already a few inches too short, even though Dad just bought them at the beginning of summer. He grabs Teddy from his pillow, then stares at me wide-eyed, framed by *LEGO Movie* posters.

"Yes?"

"Can I sleep by you?"

I stifle a sigh. "Fine. Just for tonight."

He crawls into my bed. I toss my comforter over us. Our double body heat instantly warms the cold sheets. Hollis presses back against me like I'm the big spoon for the first time ever. I tuck an arm around his shoulders. And I'm glad he's here.

"Can I sleep with you too?" Vi whimpers from the doorway, arms hugged around her *Frozen* jammies. A bead of water drips from her limp curls.

"There's no room at the inn," I say, because literally there isn't. It's a twin bed.

"I'm scared about bad dreams." Vi's lower lip juts out a mile as her eyes fill with tears.

"Fine," I groan. Hollis helps me pile our comforters between our beds. Vi drags her *My Little Pony* one from her bedroom.

I dig the pink quilt Grammy made me from Hollis's and my train wreck of a closet and spread it over us, even our heads. The stiff blanket traps the warmth around us and muffles the sound of the next *Toy Story* movie Netflix autoplayed. Vi curls her little body into mine. I suck in the fresh smell of watermelon shampoo, feel her breathing slow as her shoulders relax. Hollis lays with his back against mine, hugging Teddy for dear life. My heart lifts a millimeter off the floor.

Soft cries come from the open door. I throw off the quilt, instantly feeling cooler, and find Sage in the doorway.

I wave her over.

Chapter 5

Vi started screaming bloody murder in the middle of the night. When I tried to wake her, she screamed even louder. When Dad burst in, he told me she's having night terrors like she used to get, that it was best to just let her be until she stopped. After ten minutes, like someone flipped a switch, she went back to sleep like nothing happened.

And whenever I closed my eyes, all I could see was Francisco Goya's painting *Saturn Devouring His Son*. Surrounded by blackness, a huge naked man with bulging eyes feasts on a small bloody body. But, according to Mrs. Hoffman, the look of horror on his face suggests he's trying, but failing, to stop himself.

Because right now, it kind of feels like that's what's happening to us.

When my phone says it's six, I shower to try and wash off the exhaustion, but I don't have it in me to do my makeup.

When I emerge, Dad's setting a bowl of Lucky Charms inside Sage's cereal box castle. The bags under his eyes could sink an aircraft carrier. He grabs a bowl for me from the cupboard. I sit in my spot because that's what I do.

"Is Mommy coming home today?" Vi whimpers as she pushes around a heart marshmallow in her milk.

"I hope she never comes home," erupts Sage from behind her boxes.

Dad pushes out a sigh as he dribbles milk from his spoon into the bowl. "She won't be home for about a week probably."

Hollis peeks over his knobby knees. "A week?"

"But she's going to rehab or whatever it's called, right?" I ask.

Until now, I hadn't been able to think three seconds ahead, but seriously. After you almost kill yourself with drugs, that's what has to happen. Isn't it? At least that's what happens on TV.

Dad clears his throat as he drips another spoonful of milk over the bloated remnants of cereal. "They're working on it."

Vi slides out of her seat and paws at Dad's thigh. "Can we go visit her in the hospital? I want to see Mommy."

"She still needs lots of rest." He massages the back of her tiny head.

Then I see it staining the baseboard under the sink—a splotch of red. I can't breathe. I can't stay.

I get up. I'm shaking.

"Rosey, where ya going?" Dad asks.

"Not hungry." I grab my backpack from the hook by the door.

"Rosey!" Hollis's cry escapes the house before the door slams.

My knees lock. And I see his face that night, the whites of his eyes surrounding his irises.

Dad's eyes widen as I walk back in; I storm out all the time, but I never come back. At least not right away.

Hollis buries his face into my shoulder. I hug him tight. My first sibling. I wish I could hold his whole body in my arms like when he was a baby, but he's so big now.

After Hollis's body has relaxed, I brush and braid Vi's hair. I pry Teddy away from Hollis long enough to make him put on some of Dad's deodorant. He can't bring Teddy again. The kids will make fun of him even more than last year.

But right now I kind of wish I had a teddy.

On my way out, I say to Dad, "Make sure he leaves the bear at home."

As I walk, Kenzie's VW jets by me, blasting some bouncy hip-hop song. I don't have the energy to dig out my earbuds. A thick haze clogs my ears, clouds my eyes as I drag my body to school and four hundred twenty minutes of teachers droning because CPS might stalk me again.

I suppose Great Novels happens, but I sleep through it. Then Senior Art. My sanctuary. My haven. But today when I cross the threshold, I feel nothing.

"Okay, okay everyone!" Mrs. Hoffman claps her hands, and the buzz of conversation fades. She tucks a strand of purple-streaked hair behind her ear. "My lovely Senior Art students, here is your first project." She scrawls on the SMART Board "Something from your life you can't express in words."

My entire fricking life.

Most of the class groans, but even though there's a row of easels between us, I can see Rafa's brows arch.

"World, hope you're ready for *Meditations on Cat, Part Thirteen.*" Gretchen sashays up to me, her bright red polka-dot fifties-style dress flaunting her hourglass waist. She grabs her usual easel next to mine. "What's your next *pièce de résistance?*"

I shrug.

"Rose!" Mrs. Hoffman rushes up to me, grinning. "The painting you've been working on this summer is amazing! Your centerpiece for Belwyn."

"Uh, yeah."

Thankfully she moves to the next easel.

I stare at the white void of canvas, and all I can think about is Seraphina's escape the second she graduated from this very high school. So weird to think this Broadway celebrity whose agent is trying to break her into film walked these very halls. They'd added on the math wing, but other than that, the building had the same polished stone pattern flooring and heavy red velvet curtains framing the stage Aunt Colleen first performed on. Probably three quarters of the trophies in the display case lining the main hall had been there too. I found her picture in Dad's freshman yearbook. She'd been stunning, even with her zigzag part, pastel-pink spaghetti strap dress, and black rope choker.

But to Seraphina, I need to paint a few more samples for my portfolio because most of my paintings are inspired by Kahlo and Francisco Goya, with the exception of *Mother's Love*. I need to show my artistic range.

As I stare at the infinitely vast eight-by-ten canvas, for the first time ever, I have nothing. No colors. No shapes. Not even the hint of inspiration. My head is empty. It's like that part of my brain got sliced out. A cold sweat prickles my brow.

What's wrong with me?

Gretchen's frowning at me, her purple-laden brush frozen to her canvas, because I can always paint. Always. It's my lifeblood.

Yesterday, I had no answers in Great Novels. Today I can't even paint.

―――

The day is moved by set changers as I wait for the social worker to show up again or to get called down to Principal Jorgenson's office for skipping the first day of school. I physically walk to class, but I don't remember moving. As soon as the bell rings, I head straight for Lawrence Lawson. Already had my backpack packed.

Hollis emerges with a burst of other fourth graders. He's clutching Teddy.

Damn it, Dad. You had one job this morning.

"Big baby!" A chubby, pig-nosed boy decked out in hunting camo rips Teddy from Hollis's arms and throws it on the ground.

Hollis bursts into tears.

"You little shit!" I charge at that kid. His eyes widen and he runs.

Someone grabs my arm. Mrs. Kenyon. "Rose, stop!"

Hollis melts into my side.

"Well, maybe if you actually did something!" I yank my arm free.

Principal Isensee surveils me from his post by the entrance, arms folded. My face blazes.

"Don't tell Dad. Don't tell Dad," Hollis begs. Dad might put him in football again to toughen him up. Cuz that went so well last time when he cried every time he got tackled.

I snatch his bear out from under a crowd of fourth graders. They scramble like I'm Chucky. I brush Holly's hair from his eyes and tilt his chin up. "You okay?"

Without meeting my gaze, he pries Teddy from my hands.

Now Vi's teacher comes to me holding Vi's hand, followed by fricking Mrs. Krause. "Vi slept the whole morning. Missed all of literacy. And from what I can tell, she's going to need every second of it because she doesn't even know her alphabet."

"Kids said Sage was swearing on the playground. And she kept making faces at Madison when I wasn't looking."

"I'm. Not. The. Parent." I grab Sage and drag her toward the gate in the playground fence.

"Well, your mom and dad never answer their phones," calls that witch.

"Why are you crying now, Holly *Dolly*? You're such a pussy!" Sage makes a face at him.

I almost slap her. "Shut up! Just shut up!"

Hollis sobs into his bear. Then Vi's crying again too, and I just want to scream, because I don't know what the hell to do.

Kimmy's bright-yellow CRV, loaded down with cheerleaders, drives past with K-Pop blaring out the open windows.

I'm too tired for this.

When we get home, I put the kiddos in front of the TV. In case today's surprise home visit day courtesy of CPS, I fill the sink with hot, soapy water and scrub the breakfast dishes with the dish wand. The hollow scraping sound grates at my ears. I spray the table and counters with 409 and scrub them until they shine. Then it's time for the spot of blood; I drop to my knees clenching that bottle of 409 and a wad of paper towel. Really, it's no bigger than a pencil eraser, but I swear I can smell the rust and copper.

And then it's like I'm kneeling in her blood again. I feel the slipperiness drying to crusty flakiness under my knees. Her blood. That's her blood.

My whole body tingles, and everything goes fuzzy—the cabinets, the music from *PAW Patrol*, even the bottle of 409 in my hand. The only thing that stays in focus is that spot of Mom's blood, like I'm looking through a telescope.

"Rosey?" Dad's voice rings out from behind me. "Are you cleaning?"

"Daddy, daddy!" Vi tugs on his belt loop. "Can we see Mommy now?"

"Not yet, Vi Pie."

Vi's chin trembles. "I miss Mommy."

Dad scoops her up and kisses his forehead. "I know. She misses you too."

My fingers work again. I spray a quick squirt and scrub at it. A ring of red lingers. I squirt and scrub again. Now all that's left is white.

"Go watch TV so I can talk to Rose."

After the kids leave the kitchen, Dad says, "Rosey, CPS isn't going to take you guys away because the breakfast dishes ain't cleaned. As long as I follow the safety plan."

"Safety plan?"

"The stuff CPS says I've gotta do to keep you safe."

"Which is . . . ?"

Dad rubs his face. "I can't drink when I'm watching you guys, and you kids can't have any contact with Mom until the social worker approves."

"We can't talk to our own mom?"

Dad's eyes tighten, accentuating the crow's-feet that have grown since yesterday.

"So that's why they can't visit her. Because of CPS."

Dad pushes a slow breath through his nostrils. He nods.

But . . . it's Mom. The thought of seeing her in the hospital hooked up to machines pushes the gas pedal on my heart, but still. How could these people tell us we couldn't even talk to her?

"That's fucked up."

"Language, Rosey." Dad shoots me a disapproving look before his long legs carry him into the living room. "Tonight's a special night, kiddos. Grammy's taking us to the Foxhole."

"So now we're just cool?" I lean on the half wall between the living room and kitchen, elbow an inch from a clay cat sculpture Hollis made last year.

"Yay!" Vi claps. "I like Grammy."

"Kids need some fun stuff right now," Dad says as he grabs a Hello Kitty cup from the coffee table and takes it to the sink.

That I couldn't argue.

We load up in the truck.

Crap, aren't the kiddos supposed to have booster seats or something? I think at one point they did, but Mom probably pawned them for dope. What if the social worker finds out?

Instead of taking my usual seat in the middle, I sit on the passenger side—Mom's spot. Mom probably weighs less than me now, but I'm too small to fill her seat.

Dad cranks the key. It takes a few tries before the engine roars to life. The fan belt squeals as he backs down the driveway. "Friends in Low Places" plays on COW 97. Dad always used to belt that one out at max volume.

I roll down my window and let the warm, sticky breeze blow through my hair. The cloudless sky is blue tinged with a hint of yellow ocher, the color of dying summer in the moments before twilight. Dad drives past Jake's Northwoods—the prime dining locale for the denizens of Snob Knob—to Foxhole Pub just outside of town. We used to go there almost every week for Friday fish fry. Grampy always said Foxhole had the best one in Monroe County.

Grammy's Lumina is already parked right in front of the neon open sign. I climb out and head through the little foyer littered with thumbtacked flyers for Sparta Summer Concerts in the Park and self-storage. I don't think you've been able to smoke in there since before I was born, but the stench of decades' worth of cigarette smoke still clings to the wooden booths, mixed with stale beer and old popcorn. A few old people sag over their beers at the bar as some sports show flashes on the muted screen over the racks of liquor. Grammy waits for us on the family dining side, separated from the bar area by wood rail dividers. That same fox statue watches from its perch on top of the back of a booth.

"It's the Hemmersbach brood!" Her smile's so wide it creases her wrinkles into canyons as she slides out of the booth. Warmth bubbles in my chest, like when we snuggled on her bed while she read *Oh, the Places You'll Go* and I nibbled from her blue tin of Danish butter cookies.

"Grammy!" Hollis and Vi charge her. Even Sage gets wrangled into a hug.

Dad musters a half smile that doesn't quite reach his eyes. "All right, kiddos, why don't we head to the salad bar?"

The lettuce is a little brown, but I douse it in ranch and bacon bits so it won't matter. Vi piles her plate with ham cubes; Mom said I always used to do that too. Must be genetic. Last time we were here, Mom still went to work every day and put little "love you" drawings in our lunch boxes. Back then it was easy to ignore the elephant in the room.

"You okay, Rosey?" Dad leans down and peers into my eyes.

I head back to our booth. Four Shirley Temples with maraschino cherries floating on the bubbles sit at our spots, like old times. But no beer for Dad. Good. The wooden booth creaks as I settle in. On the fake brick wall next to me is a quote: "believe you can and you're halfway there."

Too bad Mom can't believe herself out of being a heroin addict.

I take a sip of my Shirley Temple. Bubbly citrus tickles my tongue. Then my phone vibrates on top of a paper place mat covered with ads for Sparta businesses.

Gretchen: Just wanted you to know. It's from the La Crosse Tribune today.

It's a link to a newspaper article.
I expand it.

Three children trapped outside for hours while mom overdosed in house, Sparta police say.

The air vibrates around me. A fizzling sound fills my ears, drowning out Sam Smith's "Stay With Me" playing softly on the radio.

Three children — ages five, eight, and nine — were reportedly locked outside of their home for hours while their mother overdosed on heroin in the kitchen. "An older sibling, seventeen, found her and called 911," said police spokesperson Officer Jim Davis.

The incident was reported at about 9:00 p.m. at a private residence on the one hundred block of South Black River Street. Officers and the Sparta Fire Department paramedics found the unconscious mother as well as drug paraphernalia. The woman was given naloxone and taken to the hospital. Charges are still pending. The children were picked up by their father from the Sparta Police Station.

I'm the seventeen-year-old. Coldness pumps from my heart through my veins to every part of my body. Absorbs into my skin. Leaks from my pores.

This isn't just *As the Hemmersbachs Turn* being spread through the rumor mill around Sparta. It's in the *La Crosse Tribune*.

I'm shaking, shaking, shaking. I want to scream, but I can't even breathe because the air has been sucked out of the room.

Dad's voice is muffled like I'm underwater. Like I'm drowning.

He's saying my name over and over. Touching my arm. My cheek.

Everyone knows. Everyone.

"C'mon, Rosey." Dad gently pulls me up. He cradles me against his side as he guides me past gawking Foxhole patrons and video gambling machines outside into the stifling humidity. And I'm crying in the parking lot right next to a window that says "Buffalo Wings" in flaming orange letters. He takes my phone from me and flicks through the article.

Dad's brow crushes down as he hands my phone back to me. Now it weighs a hundred pounds in my hand. He kneads his forehead.

"How could they put that in the paper?" I scream. "How could they?"

Dad pulls me against him. Old Spice deodorant brings a small wave of classically conditioned comfort.

Dad—*Dad*—is trembling. Not Dad; he's my rock.

But he's trembling because he's the father in the article. And he had to pick the kids up at the police station because he wasn't there and now the whole world knows.

He kisses the top of my head, his stubble catching my hair. "It's . . . it's gonna be fine, Rosey. Stuff like this is in the paper all the time. People'll forget about it tomorrow. Maybe by the end of the week."

But shit stays on the internet forever.

"And charges?"

"Drug charges. Maybe neglect too, depending on CPS."

"Like she could go to jail?" I choke out.

Dad retracts from me. He lets out a sigh deeper than the Grand Canyon and nods once.

———

Sleep evades me again that night as I lay sandwiched between the kiddos on the floor. My eyes drift across my gallery of paintings. A macabre landscape with a brooding purple-black sky. A black dew-covered rose I did for Hoffman's name theme last year. A portrait of Hollis with a red sucker, all smiles when he was about four, realism style.

Mother's Love. A woman with long dishwater-blonde hair wearing a crown of wildflowers because Mom always says ditch flowers are underappreciated. The mother hugs a baby to her chest, eyes closed as she kisses her cheek. The baby's tiny, pale hand clenches her shirt. Mrs. Hoffman helped me approximate the color gold for the shimmery background—lemon yellow, yellow ocher, burnt sienna, add ultramarine blue for shadows and contrast.

It's both Mom and Dad's favorite.

Painted first semester freshman year before I knew about the heroin.

After I found out, knowing she was choosing to break the law just by using was one of the hardest things for me. That she was sneaking off to that drug house by Quilt Corner to meet criminals and buy something illegal because it made her feel good.

And then in Health class, Mr. Follendorf threw up pictures of strung-out junkies and showed that video of what heroin does to your body, about how it can kill you, about how it's the most addictive drug.

And that's what Mom was doing to herself. Moms were supposed to tell kids *not* to do drugs, not do it themselves.

Then came the lying. Next the stealing. Now the overdose.

And now she might go to jail. Mom in one of the orange jumpsuits getting her mug shot taken. *Mom.*

Rage ignites in my gut and tears through my limbs; my body shakes against Hollis and Vi. It's too much to contain.

That painting is a fucking lie.

I push myself up and step over the sleeping bodies onto my bed. I rip *Mother's Love* off the wall. I want to snap the frame, take it to the backyard, and set it on fire.

The canvas shakes in my fists as I hold it over my knee.

But I can't do it, because it's inspired by *The Kiss* and art nouveau and I need to show my artistic-fricking-range to Belwyn.

So I ram it under my bed with the other paintings I can't show anyone at home, cuz elephants. *Holding the Hand that Holds Me Down*: Kahlo-inspired devils crawling out of a sickly woman's skin. *Tiny Squares*: the crinkly paper with black residue painted in intricate detail, so you can see every grain of black tar heroin. *The Two Roses* will probably go down there after it dries too.

I settle back between Sage and Hollis. The spot where *Mother's Love* used to hang is darker than the rest of the wall. I roll to face Hollis's *Lion King* poster instead.

Chapter 6

The next day, I skip school. Sit in my castle at West Side Park. I don't care if CPS finds out. I'm not setting foot in that fricking building after that article. It'll spread like wildfire, and everyone will read it and know everything that happened. That I found her. That Dad left the kiddos alone with a raging heroin addict who overdosed.

This time I have my backpack. I pull out my sketchbook and graphite pencil. Press the tip to the sea of white. But it won't move. Because I have nothing. I curl into a ball, head on my backpack.

I wonder how Seraphina survived her senior year. Oma died in winter, then she and Mom had to move back in with their mother and abusive stepfather. Colleen didn't disappear to New York until the day after graduation. Just hopped on a Greyhound. Didn't tell anyone. That was before Instagram and Snapchat and even Facebook, so no one even knew where she was for days.

I open Instagram for the first time since before everything shattered. It feels like years ago. I check Seraphina's latest post: her trademark red lipstick selfie in front of a gigantic rock in the desert glowing ruddy orange in the setting sun, the sky light pinks fading to purples.

The caption:

After a 20-hour flight to Sydney and a 3-hour flight to Ayers Rock Airport, I've finally made it to Uluru. My aboriginal guide says this place is sacred to the Anangu, and as I take this selfie, I can feel it. It's magical, this sandstone structure standing out from the nothingness around it. Rising above. XO Sera.

That's what I'm trying to do. Which means I probably shouldn't have skipped school today. Seraphina's picture already has almost two thousand likes and over three hundred comments.

I comment too.

RoseMarie: I'm going there someday.

My thumb hovers over the post button. And I'm not sure why I hesitate, besides the whole she's-chosen-not-to-talk-to-us-ever thing.

I post it.

At a quarter after three, I head to pick the kids up. Now literally all the teachers stare at me when I get to the blacktop, even the ones who've never taught a Hemmersbach. So does Principal Isensee. Today, instead of launching into a laundry list of things wrong with my siblings, their three teachers huddle, heads tipped together while they look at me. They've all seen the article.

Shame burns my face. I shake my bangs over my eyes.

Holly clutches Teddy to his chest as he skulks up to me. Sage drags her backpack behind her, the scraping noise cutting over the shouts and laughs of all the other kids.

"Where's Vi?" I ask.

"How should I know?" Sage kicks a rock across the playground with her dirt-caked black sneaker.

Fists clenched, I storm up to the teacher gossip party. "Where's Violet?"

Vi's teacher tucks a golden curl behind her ear. "Oh, uh, she must still be with the nurse."

"Must be? Meaning you don't even know where she is?"

She huffs like I slapped her.

I head through the hall, past my coat hooks from first and second grade and a bunch of "Welcome Back" bulletin boards filled with the faces of smiling children, to the nurse's office.

Vi is curled up sleeping on one of the cots. Nurse Judy looks up from her computer. Except for the gray hair, she's exactly the same thorny beast I remember, sending kids back to class with headaches and fevers that weren't quite 101. Which makes it even worse that she let Vi sleep the day away.

"She's been out cold for the past two hours," says Nurse Judy.

Night terrors again last night.

"Tried calling your parents. Again," Nurse Judy adds, upper lip curled. "Well, your dad anyway."

She's seen the article too.

I want to tell her to screw off, but Principal Isensee glowers through the open door. I sit next to Vi's folded legs and whisper in her tiny ear. "Vi?"

"Wake up!" screams red-faced Sage.

Vi wakes with a start and bursts into tears. "Mommy!"

I pull her tiny body against me. "Shut up, Sage! Or you're going to be in big trouble."

"You're not my mom!" she yells.

"You're right! So I don't care what happens to you!"

Sage's face goes titanium white. Tears brim over her gold-tipped lower lashes. She bolts through the door.

My blood turns to ice. I made Sage cry. Sage . . .

I cradle Vi on my hip and follow her.

Hollis laps at my heels.

The secretary watches us through the office door, brows raised. She's seen the article too.

Sage isn't in the hallway. My arm burns under Vi's weight.

"Vi, you're going to have to walk." I set her down.

She throws her head back and cries.

Crap. I grab her hand and drag her behind me.

Sage isn't in either of the girl's bathrooms, her empty class-room, or the playground. Would she walk home? I'm the only one who has a key. Maybe that should be a part of this mythical safety plan. Keys for all of us.

I head out the main entrance. As I weave between teachers' cars in the parking lot, I spot a black sneaker sticking out from under a bush along a fence. I kneel and peek under. Bits of gravel scattering the grass dig into my bare knees. Sage hugs her body into a ball as snot and tears pour down her face.

"Sage—"

"Go away!" Her shriek rattles my eardrums.

"Fine!" I push myself to standing and grab Vi's hand.

A strangled cry leaks through the bushes.

Shit. Sage is still a little kid whose mom almost died. I dig the heels of my palms into my temples and shove down my irritation.

A branch catches my shirt as I sit next to her foot. "I'm not going away."

"You don't care about me!" She yelps into her grass-stained knees.

"Crap, look, I shouldn't have said that."

Now Sage is sobbing so hard she's hyperventilating.

I need to make her stop crying. Distract her or something. "Uh, I challenge you to a Pokémon duel or whatever."

"You only have that one crappy card!" Sage whimpers.

"Wait, you gave me a crappy card for my birthday?"

"I can still beat anything you got with my Rayquaza." Hollis stands tall on the threshold where blacktop meets grass.

Sage peels her face from her knees. Her brows arch as she looks up to Hollis. He reaches his hand down. Sniffling, Sage takes it.

Holy. Shit. I should have recorded this, cuz Dad's never going to believe it.

"You can never beat my Shining Mew!" Sage says as he pulls her up. Bits of leaves cling to her butt.

"Yes I can," Hollis says. "Sixty cards. Play for keeps. Unless you're too scared."

"Fine." Sage scrubs the moisture from her flushed cheeks and marches toward home.

Hollis shoots me a grin. Wow. Hollis to the rescue. I pull him in and kiss the top of his head. He smells like maple syrup and grass mixed with unwashed hair. "Shower tonight, Holly. And deodorant."

"Fine," he groans.

On the walk home, I fall into step with Sage. Her face is sheathed in her chin-length bob. She's shorter than Hollis, but her arms and shoulders are thicker thanks to football and baseball.

I lightly elbow her arm. "Look, I do care. Okay?"

Sage peeks at me through her hair. Her greenish-blue eyes—Mom's eyes—are still red from tears. She nods once like an umpire just signaled she was safe.

I check both ways before we cross the street, then grab Vi's tiny hand. "Even though you gave me that crappy card."

Sage wipes snot with the back of her arm. "You weren't going to use it anyway. Don't get your undies in a bundle."

Sage already picked that one up from Grammy.

"What if I'm not wearing any?"

"Ew!" Sage jumps away from me.

Hollis laughs.

As soon as I unlock the front door, Sage and Hollis race to their rooms to get their cards.

"I want to play!" Vi laps at their heels.

The kids actually listened to Dad this morning, so at least the place isn't a total disaster if Krampus comes down the chimney for the home visit today. My keys jangle as I drop them in the Mother's Day bowl on the kitchen counter. I settle into the couch as Sage and Hollis start chucking cards on the floor in front of the TV. Vi watches with greedy eyes.

Justin in My Mind still sits on the coffee table, an artifact from before. The deer head now watches me from the wall and the sketch on the red painting. So does Justin's tiny face sketched on my self-portrait's forehead. And it's almost laughable now, that *that* had felt like the end of the world. I snatch it and shove it under my bed with the other artwork I don't want to see.

On my way back to the couch, I catch a glint from something under the armchair. Is it a needle?

Heart pounding, I drop to my knees and look under. It's half an empty pop can, Dr. Pepper, black-scorched bottom. The edge is serrated. She cooked heroin in this, then sucked it in her syringe. Guess the cops missed this evidence when they tore apart our house. I grab it. The maroon cold metal cylinder shakes in my hand.

"What's that?" Vi tilts her head.

"Nothing."

Pinching it between my fingers, I storm to the kitchen and pitch it in the garbage can.

My toe is inches from where I cleaned that last remaining speck of blood yesterday.

Pump, hiss, pump, hiss, pump, hiss.

If I'd have come home five minutes later, I'd have found her dead.

It starts as a tiny throb and expands into a hammer slamming into my brain.

I bury the can under some junk mail that was piled on the counter, then check for needles in all her usual spots. In the cabinet under the sink. Behind the toilet tank. On the top shelf of a kitchen cupboard. In the back of the freezer under some venison steaks from Dad's deer last year.

The front door pops open.

"Uff da," Dad grunts as he tugs off his work boots. His gross toes poke through holes in his socks. Then his piercing blue eyes narrow at me, and I know I'm in trouble. The freezer door falls closed.

But then he looks to Sage. "You swear at anyone today? I got that message yesterday."

"No," she huffs from behind her cards.

His eyes swivel to me again. I wring my hands, still cold from digging in the freezer, and brace myself for being grounded until I leave for college. From what, I don't know, seeing as now I don't even have Justin.

"Holly, you do your work today? Your reading?" Dad calls into the living room.

The Pokémon cards fall from Hollis's fingers. He scrambles for his backpack.

"Cuz, would ya know it, calls from school keep filling up my voice mail." Dad casts me a fiery gaze.

I roll my eyes and storm to my room.

"Rose Marie Hemmersbach, you stop right there!"

I shoot a withering look over my shoulder. "How can you expect me to go to school after that article?"

Hollis peeks over *The Sorcerer's Stone*. "What article?"

Shit. Right, they don't know.

"Nothing." I yank the door closed, but Dad catches it before it slams.

I fold my arms against my chest.

"I went to work, didn't I?" he spits through his teeth.

People at Northern live to gossip, just like the teachers.

My arms fall to my side.

Dad yanks off his Packers hat and curls the bill in his fists. "Just . . . you need to go to school tomorrow. Please."

That's it? Wow. Things are different now.

Chapter 7

All my teachers have read the article. Probably sent out in a mass email. I can tell by the way their eyes all tighten and drop when they look at me. I survive the day by hiding behind my bangs, then Dad drops me off at Walmart for my five to eleven.

Surviving this shift, however . . .

"Heya, Rosey," Assistant Manager Tim calls from his office as I head to grab my vest. I make the mistake of looking up and seeing his eyes tighten too. He knows. He's been Dad's friend since elementary school. I grab my vest, ram my backpack into a locker, and clock in.

And I don't even make it to the front end before fear starts nibbling at my gut. Today might be the day CPS waltzes in, and I forgot to check for needles under the TV stand.

"You're on register five, Rosey," Cindy calls from the customer service desk.

Has she seen the article? I glance at her. Her reading glasses slip down her aquiline nose as she adds up receipts on her huge calculator.

I drag myself over to five and pull the cord for my register light. As I log in, Bette Midler belts out "Wind Beneath My Wings" over Walmart Radio. My *favorite*. It's the first home football game, which means it'll be a slow night. Last year, before Walmart became a necessity, I would have been sitting in the bleachers with Gretchen and the band geeks making fun of the other team's cheerleaders.

Justin swaggers through the front doors. He's wearing baggy jeans and the black I Prevail T-shirt he bought from Spencer's one time we wandered around Valley View Mall because we had nothing better to do. He doesn't look at me.

But now I don't feel that sick dropping sensation like on the Zipper. Not even the hollow emptiness desperate to be filled by any sign of recognition.

I draw six circles in my memo notebook with UPCs for Garden Center crap, then quarter them to represent the fifteen-minute increments of my shift.

"Hey, Rose, did you know they found the Garden of Eden in Colorado?" Ashlee calls from behind the latest edition of *Weekly World News*. Apparently space aliens backed Trump for a second term. "Even found the apple. Thought Adam and Eve ate it."

"You know everything in that magazine is crap, right?" I say. My eyes wander to the clock. I can almost fill in one section already.

"Rose, can you train our new cashier?"

Next to Cindy stands Rafa, hands shoved in the pockets of the skinny-fit khakis hugging his slim form. A pristine blue Walmart vest, still creased from being in the wrapping, hangs loose on his frame.

That's unexpected. I flip my notebook closed and jam it into my vest pocket. "Hey."

"Hey," Rafa says.

As he steps into my register area, I catch a whiff of lavender and lime. He's short compared to most guys I know, maybe an inch taller than me, and I'm only five foot four. Rafa glances at me again. I want to say something, but my brain feels like scrambled eggs.

The minute hand of the yellowed clock over Sam Walton's portrait shudders and then inches past the twelve like always.

Ashlee skips up to my counter. Her mousse-crusty curls have mostly fallen flat. She sticks out her hand. "Hi, I'm Ashlee. We got gym together."

Rafa shakes it. "Oh. Um, yeah. I think I remember you."

"Yeah, I s'pose I don't stand out like you," Ashlee says.

And even *I* cringe. His jaw drops a centimeter as she bounces back to her register.

Rafa clears his throat. "So, sensei, what's next?"

It sounds like an attempt at friendly sarcasm.

"Processing checks, I guess," I mumble.

A sharp giggle rings out over clicking heels. A college-aged couple saunters up to my register. The guy's lilac dress shirt under his black suit coat perfectly matches the woman's Marilyn Monroe dress.

"I can't believe he said that." The woman pats at her complex updo.

"Hi, did you find everything okay?" I can't even dig up my imitation of Kimmy's grin as I log in to my register.

The guy drops a wedding card on my counter. His eyes skip over me to his girlfriend. "Why not? He's a complete douche."

My scanner beeps as I swipe the bar code.

"But talking about her ex-husband? At *her* rehearsal dinner?" The girl titters, her mauve lips twisting up. "God, thirty-six more hours in this Podunk town for that? I don't care how barn chic the venue is."

"Your total is four ninety-five." I shove the card into a card bag.

The man swipes his card through the credit card reader. "Hey, at least we can buy four beers for the price of one in Chicago."

"Ugh. Can't wait to get back to civilization." The girl prances off in her silver heels.

Ashlee smacks her gum. "Frigging Illinois bastards."

I crumble up the receipt as the automatic doors slide open for them like they're royalty. A gust of muggy air brushes my face.

Rafa scrubs at some ancient blackened gum on the cashier mat with his spotless Air Jordan. What a contrast to my scuffed-up combat boots.

"They have a point," he says.

It catches me off guard, this spontaneous big-city pompous ass-ness.

"We need to red line." I shoo him out.

"What does that mean?" He follows me to the magazine rack.

"It means we stand on this literal red line and wait for customers."

Glitter from that cheesy card clings to my fingertips. I rub them on my jean skirt.

Dad would say Aunt Colleen is no better than those FIBs, but it doesn't even compare. Aunt Colleen decided she wanted more out of life than Butterfest and Saturday nights at crappy bars downtown with her coworkers at the restaurant formerly known as Happy Chef. That's not a crime. That's reaching for the stars. That's Uluru.

The night somehow ticks by even slower than the school day as I show Rafa how to scan and total items, process different forms of payment, and change register tape.

Rafa and I are scheduled to take break together. Ellen, the

cheeriest grandma people greeter ever, knits a green-and-yellow washcloth in the back corner of the break room. Rafa's nose is buried in *The Great Gatsby*. He brushes a crumb off his polo shirt, then takes another bite of some kind of Mexican food. The smell of spicy cheesiness leaks over, making my stomach grumble. Crap, I forgot to make my peanut butter sandwich, and I don't have any cash.

I should remove Calculus from my backpack or at the very least try to read for Great Novels, since we're already supposed to be through chapter five. But my head's being crushed in a vise of exhaustion.

I pull out my phone and text Dad.

RoseMarie: Kiddos ok?

The ellipsis flutters for about two minutes. Then finally . . .

Dad: Working on getting them to bed.

RoseMarie: Did the social workers come?

Dad: Not yet.

I need to be doing my homework. Because it's taken two years to resurrect my GPA since Rose split in two.

Belwyn, Rose.

I dig out my Calc book. I flip to our assignment. Rates of change. God, we *just* talked about that today, but Mom ripped holes in my cerebrum. I can't remember.

Someone clears their throat. I catch Rafa staring at me over his book.

"What?" I slam my book closed.

"Is it time?" Rafa points to the clock over the sink.

God, how is it only eight thirty? "Yeah."

———

The exit doors slide open for me just like those stuck-up FIBs. I walk past the candy machines and video games and out into freedom.

A refreshing, crisp dampness hangs in the air, the promise of fall. Parking lot lights and a line of headlights force away the stars. Rafa gets into a rusting blue Chevy minivan. Trina in her classy camo T-shirt that says "Country Girls Do It Better" climbs into my old seat in Justin's Grand Am. The angry, ripping electric guitar of Unrequited Death's "Rotten Kisses" blares out of his speakers.

As Justin's car peels out of the parking lot, I don't feel the sharp pang I felt last week. I don't feel anything. There's no room.299

I cut across the parking lot and tuck in my earbuds and let the throbbing industrial beats of "Mr. Self Destruct" carry me away. The weight of my backpack pinches the muscles between my shoulder blades. Stabbing pain spreads to the small of my back. As I walk, the moon fights to break free of the clouds but fails. Even in the patches of clear sky, I can't see any stars. The streetlights cast speckled light through the trees onto the sidewalk.

By the time I get home, I'm shivering because I didn't think to bring a sweatshirt. Our front windows glow like jack-o'-lantern eyes.

As I walk into the kitchen, her lifeless body and blue nails and scorched spoons scour through my brain.

Then the upbeat theme song for PAW Patrol bounces from the living room. It's eleven thirty. Fists clenched, I march through the kitchen. Dinner dishes are piled in the sink.

Vi's sleeping on Hollis's lap. Dad's hunched over his phone

next to them. Sage blinks in slow motion on her usual throne. The only saving grace is that they're in their pj's.

"Why are they still up?"

Dad drags his eyes up from his phone. "They can sleep in tomorrow."

I cross my arms.

Dad sighs and rubs his forehead. "They wouldn't go to bed without you." He grabs the remote off a scattered pile of Pokémon cards and shuts off the TV just before Marshall rolls out of the Lookout.

"Hey, it's not done!" Sage erupts.

"You're going to bed," I say.

I brush my teeth quick and throw on a faded seventh-grade track T-shirt and pair of shorts. By the time I'm done, Sage and Hollis have already recreated the makeshift bed on the bedroom floor.

Vi and Hollis sandwich me in body heat. As Hollis's breathing slows, I snake my arm out from under Vi's shoulder and grab my phone. I check Instagram. The glow of my screen fights back the darkness. Gretchen had posted a bunch of duck face selfies with Anderson and some other band geeks, all decked out in their red marching uniforms. Sometimes I wish I made friends as easily as she does.

Then I notice I have a message. Which is totally weird cuz I'm such an Insta loser even bots and pedophiles don't message me. I press the little paper airplane icon.

It's from Seraphina Abramsson Official. Next to her name is her red lipstick selfie.

A shock of cold runs through my veins.

No.

No way.

The message: What's your last name?

Holy shit. My comment. Seraphina Abramsson of legend reaching across the Pacific Ocean.

She remembers me.

I type: Hemmersbach.

Chapter 8

On Monday morning, instead of spending my usual thirty minutes on hair and makeup, I wash the mountain of dishes, because Mom overdosed a week ago today and CPS still hasn't shown up. Maybe today is Krampus Day.

And I don't even know how there can be so many dirty plates and forks, because Grammy came over on Saturday and Sunday to make her pancakes and she's a Nazi about dishes. I worked the whole weekend but managed to catch an argument between Grammy and Dad. Dad apparently visited Mom twice and was gone a long time. And Mom's going to be released from the hospital sometime soon, and we still aren't allowed to see her.

This past week, it's been like a vacation, not having the elephant in the room. Not having to watch Mom sneak off to shoot up all the time, sometimes conjuring cheap excuses to leave, sometimes not even bothering. Not having to move around her all day after she's fallen asleep on the couch or wait for her to emerge from the room she's been holed up in forever. Not having to worry that I haven't witnessed her eat all day. Not having to listen to all the lies and excuses as she extorts money from Dad that should be paying the cell bill.

And she probably can't overdose again while she's in the hospital.

Even Violet's stopped asking when she'll be back.

By the time I drag my body into Great Novels, fatigue cuts me to the bone. The smell of lemon dish soap clings to my hands.

Kimmy leans on Mike's desk, her white-skirt-covered ass practically in my face. Isn't there some rule about wearing white after Labor Day? Mike's away jersey hangs loose on her tiny body instead of her usual Monday yellow. I hate to admit it, but that stupid jersey is ten times more romantic than anything Justin ever gave me. She's literally wearing a piece of him, and he cared enough to give it to her.

Or he's going all alpha male and showcasing his property.

"So how's our float coming along?" Kimmy asks as she adjusts her "Homecoming Royalty" sash. Mike and Eisenhardt wear them too.

"Our tech ed boys're getting it done," VP QB Mike says. "But one of the junior's dads works at FAST, and he's gonna borrow them a fiberglass horse."

"Crap. That should be against the rules." Kimmy frowns. "God, if we lose homecoming to the juniors, I'll die."

Literally?

"Don't worry, Prez. We still got the window painting." Mike cops a sneaky feel of her perfectly tanned thigh.

She giggles. "Who's gonna paint that anyway?"

Your mom.

Mrs. Ebert swoops in just as the bell rings and calls on Rafa to kick off another rousing session of round-robin reading. Rafa even reads with emotion and expression, but his voice sounds garbled like we're both underwater in the deep end of a pool.

And Mrs. Ebert must still have that news article on her mind, because for the second day in a row she doesn't make me read, even though I tanked the pop quiz on Friday.

I swing by my locker before Senior Art to grab my sketchbook. Kenzie leans on a locker five down from mine talking to Carolyn, my former best friend from before Rose split in two. Neither of them look at me as I twist the dial on my padlock.

"I didn't even know you could turn down an invite from Kimmy," Carolyn gasps.

"And did you see his brother doing shots of Jäger?" Kenzie smacks her gum. "He's cute too."

Carolyn titters as her freshly manicured fingers glide down her glittery homecoming sash. "I never could have done that when I was a sophomore."

Normally I don't give two shits about their parties, but today I'm mildly curious who this mystery person is, so I adjust the print of Kahlo's *Without Hope* taped to the inside of my locker to buy time.

"OMG. It just makes me want in Rafa's khakis even more." Kenzie lets out a kitty growl as she paws at Carolyn's pastel-pink romper. "But seriously, what could be better to do in this town than Kimmy's party?"

I slam my locker. "He was working at Walmart."

Both their heads swivel to me, eyes wide like I just threw a bloody cat at them. Kenzie's gaze lingers on my black Unrequited Death tank top—*Add Violence*. To think, in seventh grade we used to share Gatorades after finishing our eight-hundred-meter relays at track meets.

Kenzie turns to Carolyn. "I like a man with a job. He can buy me things."

I roll my eyes, then get to art seconds before the bell rings. The smell of earthy clay fills my lungs, and today Mrs. Hoffman's even blaring my favorite album by Nine Inch Nails—*The Downward Spiral*—like it's just for me, but it does nothing to lift my shoulders.

Gretchen lifts her kitten bowler purse off the easel she saved for me in the back corner.

"Kenzie and Carolyn have eyes locked on Rafa," I say.

She follows my gaze to Rafa, whose easel is right in front of the SMART Board. His canvas is covered with a bunch of little people and buildings. Rafa has earbuds in again. As Anderson and Josh talk around him, Rafa dabs his brush into a pocket of orange on his brightly colored palette, then delicately fills in a patterned shirt.

"Little birdies told me that Kimmy even invited Luis hoping Rafa would come too."

"Luis?" My nose crinkles. Last year, his MO was "crop-dusting" girls with his most rancid farts. He'd even gotten me and Gretchen once.

"They're cousins," Gretchen says.

"Really?" I raise an eyebrow. "That's desperation. From Kimmy, no less."

"Cuz we never get any new kids. And cuz he's hot? Not only that, there's strong evidence to suggest he's actually a nice guy." Gretchen taps the end of her fan brush on her chin. "I heard last week he spent like thirty minutes after school helping Mrs. Petrowski lug in a book delivery cuz the custodian was busy. He's a man of mystery."

"I'll be your man of mystery, sugar," Anderson says with an attempt at a Southern drawl as he saunters over, thumbs hooked through his belt loops. Today it's a Dr. Who shirt and a loose purple tie.

"The only thing mysterious about you is why your Southern twang is so crappy," I say. "Your dad's from the South."

"'The lady doth protest too much!'" Anderson clutches his chest.

"Tone down the *Hamlet*, dingleberry," I say.

"Wait, you read *Hamlet*?" He pushes up his thick black-frame glasses. "It's going to be our fall theater performance. You should try out."

"Yeah, no."

"But seriously, who is this man of mystery?" He busts out a twenties gangster accent and pretends to pump a tommy gun.

"No one you need to worry about, sugar lips." Gretchen touches her finger to his lips, then licks it.

Anderson's face goes bright red as he grins.

Mrs. Hoffman starts down our row of easels. Anderson scrambles, and Gretchen dives into painting her latest iteration of a cat wearing cat eye glasses. My canvas is blank. Mrs. Hoffman's going to be disappointed in me. Thankfully she pauses at Anderson's slowly forming musical notes.

Something you can't express in words. C'mon, Rose. It's literally your whole life.

I try to summon images. I try to mix in my mind. I grab for bits of lyrics, scanning through every Unrequited Death song.

Maybe an adaptation of Goya's *Saturn Devouring His Son* featuring mom. *Saturn Devouring Her Children*.

Nope.

Mom's blue lips.

Nope.

A hand with blue fingernails, scorched, bent spoon inches away.

Nope.

Even though everyone probably already knows, I don't want them to.

I can't paint. This has literally never happened to me. Ever. Sweat tingles on my palms. Maybe I am broken.

"Rose." A gentle touch on my arm.

I glance through my limp bangs. Mrs. Hoffman's lips purse as her eyes drip with pity. She's read the article. I feel like someone ripped off my clothes. I hug my arms to my chest.

Mrs. Hoffman is the only teacher who never asks if I'm okay because she knows how meaningless that question can be. If she asks now, it's proof that things really are different now.

Mrs. Hoffman sighs and squeezes my shoulders.

I dredge up a small smile for her, then escape to the back table littered with paint tubes.

I have to try. Make my brush move.

I squirt some burnt umber on a palette. Next to me, Rafa spreads a line of french ultramarine, then snatches the burnt umber as soon as I set it down. He squeezes it next to the blue in the middle of his neatly mixed brilliant rainbow colors. Barely audible music leaks from his earbuds as his filbert brush gently blends them together into a brown. He adds a little more ultramarine to darken it. So he mixes his own black too, unlike the rest of the lazy people in this class. I squirt some french ultramarine on my palette.

Rafa's dark eyes meet mine. He pinches the inline volume remote between his knuckles and pauses his music. "So, Frida, you judging me for wasting my time mixing black?" He gives me a half smile like maybe he's playing.

And I want to say something clever back, but today my head is packed with Bubble Wrap and I can't hold onto a thought for more than twenty seconds.

Black. I can mix black with the colors on my palette. And a thousand shades of gray. I just need something to paint. But my mind is empty, and I don't even have the energy to grab a brush to mix.

I squirt red on my palette, not even checking if it's cadmium red or alizarin crimson, and head back to my easel. I attack the canvas with red straight from the tube. Today color cutting into white does nothing for me. I have no shapes. So my brush keeps finding the red paint until it covers the whole canvas.

Blood.

My paintbrush slips through my fingers and clatters on the floor, leaving red splotches on the tile.

Mrs. Hoffman walks back over and leans in so close I can smell her coffee breath. "Mrs. O'Neil wants to see you."

And for the first time ever, I'm actually glad she's pulling me from art.

After I clean up my paints, I head for the door. And catch Mrs. Hoffman frowning at my painting.

I just can't.

"Hey, Rose . . ."

Shit, here it comes.

I grip my upper arm.

"Just come see me at lunch, okay?" Mrs. Hoffman says as her eyes linger on me a few seconds too long.

Crap. It's going to be about Belwyn. And I don't even know what the application requirements are beyond the portfolio.

As I drag my feet to the office, I tell myself it's just going to be O'Neil badgering me about college too, but what if it's that social worker and Detective Dick again?

Or what if something happened to Mom? Dad says she's almost better. But, who knows, maybe she stole some pain meds and overdosed again. Or busted out before they can send her to rehab so she could shoot up with Jeremy.

When I get to the guidance office, Mrs. O'Neil isn't standing outside, and Mrs. Arnold pecks away at her keyboard with two fingers. So it's not CPS.

I go in. Mrs. O'Neil's unflinching bright smile fills her office. Now all I can smell is the eucalyptus mist curling out of her aromatherapy diffuser. It's weird, but I half expected Detective Dick's nasty aftershave to linger.

I collapse into a chair and cross my arms. "What?"

Her smile caves. "First off, Rose, I'm sorry the CPS interview was our first interaction this year. I know you're probably feeling a little betrayed."

I snatch a Koosh ball from her bowl and snap the orange and yellow elastic strings. I hadn't even realized it, but she's right. She lured me into this room with her vague "people here to help you" comment and trapped me alone with them for interrogation.

Mrs. O'Neil plucks the squeezy duck from her bowl and scrapes at something on its plastic googly eye with a beige nail. "I hope someday I'll be able to earn back your trust."

I raise my eyebrows as I pull a yellow string off the Koosh ball and drop it on the floor. My eyes wander to Lawrence Lawson through her window. Please don't sleep all day again, Vi. Hollis, don't let those asshats who are smaller than you push you around. And Sage, just don't cuss out your teacher. Can we agree to that?

"Rose, your dad asked me to check in with you."

The Koosh ball slips through my fingers into my lap. "What? Why?"

"He's worried about you."

After three years of telling us to ignore/deny/lie about the elephant, now he wants me to talk about it?

My fingers choke the Koosh ball. "I'm fine. Everything's fine."

"Rose . . ." My name is weighed down with so much concern it could sink to the bottom of the ocean and drag me with it. "I read the article."

Humiliation flames across my whole body. I shake my bangs over my eyes. "Well, that pretty much summed it up. So can I go now?"

Mrs. O'Neil leans in, her lanyard sliding across the table. "You're not fine, sweetheart. You saw your mom almost die. That's an incredibly heavy burden to carry."

All I see is the whites of Hollis's eyes as his face contorts into terrified Medusa when he sees Mom's crumpled body on the yellow vinyl flooring. And if I'd come three minutes later, she could be dead. My shoulders sag under the weight of it.

What's heavier than heavy? That's what this is.

"He should be more fricking worried about Hollis, then!" Tears thicken my throat. Tears I don't want O'Neil to see because I'm fricking fine. I head for the door.

"Look, Rose, I know you're not one for talking," Mrs. O'Neil says, "and sometimes, when kids have things going on at home, school is their escape. But you can't escape this right now. I can tell by looking at you."

"Don't you have college advising to do?"

Finally, some irritation cracks her perfect face. "Rose, please, you need to let it out of you. You don't have to talk to me, but talk to someone. Don't go through this alone. It'll tear you up inside."

"Yeah. Okay." I leave.

I'm not alone. I have Sage and Hollis and Violet to protect.

I lock myself in a stall in the girl's bathroom that perpetually smells like pot mixed with Japanese Cherry Blossom body spray, because it's not skipping if you were pulled out of class by a teacher. And if anyone asks, I'll just say I was puking because apparently I'm not fine.

"Is she breathing?" that faceless lady's voice echoes through my ears.

I draw my feet up onto the toilet seat and hug my legs to my chest.

The bell rings for third hour. Screw Psychology, even though I know Dad's going to get another robocall, because, really, what's he going to do? Ground me? From what, working at Walmart? I cannot listen to Mr. Smith talk about random intermittent reinforcement and gambling addiction. Or addiction period. The bell rings again. I don't have the energy to move. And screw Calculus, because I cannot with Mr. Ziegler's scowl.

At lunchtime, I head for the art room per Hoffman's request but only, only because I know I'm her favorite student.

Mrs. Hoffman's door is still shut when I get there, so I survey the display case. Most of it's totally amateur: cars, cats, and portraits painted in the last week. Rafa's is already on display; the only one that isn't crap. *Boy and His Horse, Acrylic, Rafa Hernández Muñoz,* the card below it says. Like Diego Rivera's works, every inch of Rafa's is filled with a bustling town featuring unique, colorful buildings and probably twenty people with different faces and clothing, each one in motion—laughing, selling flowers, eating, playing. A road cuts through the flurry of life, empty except for a horse being ridden by a boy whose face is hidden by a sombrero, completely unnoticed by the townspeople.

For the first time in all my years at Sparta High, I have nothing to display.

The art door pops open. Mrs. Hoffman's eyes dart past me. "Rose, Rafa, you made it."

I glance back to find Rafa carrying a blue lunch tray. Guess this isn't about Belywn. I follow Mrs. Hoffman in. Rafa sits across the table from me.

Mrs. Hoffman pulls off her glasses and lets them dangle from her Metallica strap. "Homecoming."

"Barf." I scrape at a chip in my black nail polish.

"Barf indeed, but I'm a senior advisor, and I hate losing to whiny underclassmen."

And I know exactly where this is going. I fold my arms across my chest. "I'm not window painting."

"Rose, you're not doing it for *them*," Mrs. Hoffman says in her freshman-stop-paint-fighting tone. "I have a bet going with Mr. Amundson. He's the tech ed teacher, Rafa. Loser has to buy Friday happy hour drinks for the rest of the year."

"Get Gretchen to do it," I mutter.

"No, no, no! No cats, please."

Even Rafa chuckles at that one. I shoot him a glare through strands of my platinum bangs.

He muffles his laugh with a hand. Clearing his throat, he says, "Sorry."

"Ask Anderson or Josh," I say. "They'd actually like to do it."

Mrs. Hoffman presses her fingers into a pyramid as she leans forward. "I don't want bubble letters and bobblehead Sparky. I want unique. I need Sparta's two best painters to make a masterpiece never before attempted on glass."

Rafa shrugs. "Guess I don't have anything better to do."

"Rose," Mrs. Hoffman says in a singsongy voice, "what a unique entry for your Belwyn portfolio. Bet nobody else will use a window as a medium, and showing you can work collaboratively will grab their attention."

But my brain is broken. I pick at a splotch of dried purple on the table.

"Rose, just . . . see what you and Rafa can come up with together." Her hazel eyes search mine.

I feel how much she cares. About me. It lifts my shoulders a millimeter. And I want to paint. More than anything.

I flick the last bit of purple onto the floor. "Fine."

Grinning, Mrs. Hoffman claps. "Okay, so the theme your lovely student council picked is 'riding in for the win.' Rafa, Tomah's mascot is a timber wolf."

"I'm good at painting horses," Rafa says. "Maybe we could paint the Spartan mascot riding a Clydesdale."

"Blood dripping from its mouth." I chip the last of the black off my thumbnail.

"Yeah, maybe some flames coming from its nostrils. Riding through a forest of creepy dead trees like in that." He points at the print of *The Wounded Deer* by Kahlo over the chalkboard. "Slogan could be something like 'Apocalypse Now: Tomah's Day of Reckoning.'"

Finally a faint image flits through my mind. "And Sparky the Spartan is wearing full medieval knight armor. Greek helmet though."

"Sparky's holding the timber wolf's bleeding decapitated head," Rafa says.

I glance up at him. There's this smile on his face that I know—the spark of inspiration.

I ache for it, but all I feel is that dull haze coiling around my brain.

Mrs. Hoffman grabs a sketchbook from her teacher's table and drops it between us.

Rafa snatches it, and graphite cuts into the pure-white paper. His pencil strokes are darker and more purposeful than mine as he draws the trees. The rearing Clydesdale's taut muscles and flying mane make it look like he's dancing off the page. From the wolf's severed neck spews stringy sinews and ragged bits of torn muscle. Rafa slides the notebook to me.

I press the pencil tip to the paper as I grasp for an image of Sparky, but it's sand slipping through my fingers. I want to scream. Because a day I can't create is a day I can't breathe, so I haven't been able to breathe for a week. And they're both watching me. My heart pumps faster.

No, Rose, you know how to draw fricking Sparky.

But my mind can't remember.

Then I notice someone left their assignment notebook next to Rafa. Sparky's on the cover. I draw in a breath and force my pencil to move.

And it happens. My hand takes over and my mind shuts off and my lines become a cross between medieval knight and Greek Spartan. And it's actually not half bad. I write the slogan in Gothic letters.

I feel a little lighter.

Mrs. Hoffman squeezes my shoulder. "Love it."

I brush my bangs out of my eyes.

"That's so cool. Love the lettering choice," Rafa says.

I bite in a smile as I add a drop of blood hanging from the horse's bottom jaw.

Mrs. Hoffman reaches between us and grabs the sketchbook. "Perfect. Come mix paint today after school."

Crap, the kiddos. My cheeks warm as I hide behind my bangs. "Can't."

"I can mix," Rafa says.

"Cool," I mutter as the pencil slips through my fingers. I leave.

Mixing's my favorite part.

As Sage and Hollis squabble over who won some Pokémon battle, I'm scrubbing coffee rings from the counter and kitchen table. Like, come on, Dad, were you raised in a barn? Dad alleges that CPS won't care about stuff like that. Well, I care. Because they have the power to take us away. And Dad certainly doesn't know everything about everything.

"Rose Marie Hemmersbach!" Dad comes into the kitchen bellowing so loud the walls shake. Veins bulge from his forehead. "You skipped again!"

This level of rage hasn't been directed at me since my grades got sucked down that black hole freshman year.

Even though he's a foot taller than me, I get on my tiptoes and yell in his face, "Well, why did you tell the counselor to talk to me?"

The kiddos stare at us wide-eyed from the couch. Sage's hand hovers an inch above the card pile. The card pinched between her fingers quivers.

The blood drains from Dad's face. He motions for me to follow him outside. The screen door clacks closed behind us. Light seeps through the rotting cracks in the base of the pressed particle board.

Dad lets out a sigh the size of a Mack truck that almost busts the roof off the cobweb-infested doorless entry shelter. "I'm worried about you, Rosey."

I kick at the half-empty bag of sidewalk salt leaning in the corner. "I'm fine!"

"Rosey, don't get me wrong. I'm glad you're finally taking more of an interest in the kiddos and keeping the house tidy, but it's taking over your life."

"So you're making me talk to a counselor because I'm trying to help my siblings?" I let out a wry laugh.

"And all this skipping . . . You're going to be the first Hemmersbach or Leis to go to college, and that's final." Dad's jaw sets as he looks down on me. His voice is strong again.

"How can we even be talking about that right now?"

Dad puts up his hands like I'm a feral cat. "Rosey, that's not what's going on here. You're still a kid too. You gotta let people take care of you."

I roll my eyes. "Too bad there's all those younger ones who need to come first."

"Rosey . . ."

He wants me to be a kid? Fine. He can watch them.

I walk down our front sidewalk.

"Rosey, where are you going?" he calls after me.

"I'm being a kid!"

I hide in my wooden castle in West Side Park. Early evening sunlight spills through the shifting leaves drooping over my castle, casting gold and shadows on my arms and legs. A lawn mower buzzes in the distance, but other than that I'm wrapped in silence. Breathing in the smell of the wood planks under my back slows my heart.

I check Instagram. Then as it opens I remember I don't want to check it because if Seraphina didn't respond, I don't know what I'll do. But I don't know what I'll do if she did. Part of me wishes I could travel back in time and never comment on Uluru.

The app loads, and there it is—a message notification. My stomach somersaults. I press it.

And sure as shit, it's her.

Seraphina Abramsson Official: I can't believe it's you! Last I
remember, you had hair practically to your knees and no front
teeth! You're so grown up and utterly beautiful. You like to
paint?

I have to read it three times to confirm it's real.

What do I say back? I don't want to go all fangirl and tell her
she's, like, the most gorgeous person on earth.

RoseMarie: Thanks! I'm hoping to go to art school in California.

And then I notice Aunt Colleen followed me back. Me. I have
only five followers, and one is Mom. Seraphina follows only 104
people.

A text pops up on my screen.

Dad: I need to take care of you. That's why I want you to talk to
the counselor.

I press my phone to my forehead. Our world really has been
knocked off its axis. And now how many days until Mom gets sent
to rehab? Or maybe jail. And would CPS even let us see her first?

And, if today is the day CPS graces us with their presence, I
want to be there. Plus, there's at least a 95 percent chance Dad will
forget its bath night.

I drag myself up and head home. But Seraphina Abramsson
followed me back. That I hold on to.

Chapter 9

For the first night in a week, all the kids slept in their own beds, and Hollis's snoring woke me up. I never in a million years thought that sound would reassure me. But today it does.

After I shower, I take the time to put on my makeup and style my hair. I pull on a black Three Days Grace shirt with a fist clenching roses, then I almost feel like myself again.

Dad doesn't say anything when I wash the dishes. Now it's officially been a week. Today Krampus is coming to the house; I can feel it.

When I get to my locker, I do a double take. Nope, 902; it's mine. And it's adorned with a bright-yellow locker tag with a huge red bow and a paintbrush made of rolled-up brown construction paper with a feather tucked in. Written in red glitter paint, "Go Rose! Help paint the seniors to V-I-C-T-O-R-Y!"

Not once in my entire life has anyone made me a locker tag. Ever. It was Kimmy, of course. It's actually pretty cool, for a cheerleader thing. I catch myself smiling as I ram my Chemistry book into the pile of old homework crumped on the top shelf.

As I walk by her desk in Great Novels, I thank her.

Accented by her yellow babydoll T-shirt, Kimmy's grin glows even brighter. "Sure thing, Rose. You're such an awesome artist. We're lucky to have you on our team!"

God, I'm part of a team. I settle into my seat. She, Eisenhardt, and Mike launch into an intense strategic discussion around the skit.

"So they found your locker too."

I drag my gaze up to Rafa. "You got one too?"

He nods. "I didn't even know they did those for art."

"Me neither. Cheerleaders must get top secret access to locker assignments."

"Imagine if it got into the wrong hands." Rafa's gaze wanders to Eisenhardt and his tuxedo T-shirt as he gallops down the aisle.

A smile pulls at the corner of my lips. "Yep."

After another rousing round of read alouds, Rafa and I meet in the cafeteria to kick off our mural. Three windows already have primary-colored blobs and various stages of bubble letters on them.

Rafa pops open the stepladder in front of our window. He nods to the box by his feet. "I did my best mixing."

I spread the capped containers on the floor. Drab grays, browns, and ochers blended with red and blue. A rich, beautiful purple with a hint of some kind of turquoise. Adding some gray and white would make the perfect color for the clouds. A tiny spark glows in my chest.

Rafa scrapes at a chunk of mashed pancake with his Air Jordan. "We can always mix them again. I don't want to wreck your art school portfolio."

His burnt-umber eyes meet mine, and I realize he's not being sarcastic. "No, it's all good." I grab the containers of ocher, yellow, and red. "I'll start on the slogan."

"Cool. I'll do the horse."

I tuck in my earbuds and climb up a few rungs. Crap, I'm wearing a skirt.

I jab the pointy end of my mottler brush at him. "Don't try to get a free show."

Rafa tosses his hands up, eyes on the bottom rung. "Just cuz I *like* Rivera doesn't mean I *am* a Rivera."

I smirk, then hit play. The angry, ripping electric guitar of Unrequited Death's "Rotten Kisses" fills my ears, and for the first time since Justin broke up with me, that song doesn't suck the life out of me. I can listen to it.

I can start on the letters. Letters are easy.

I dip my brush into the muted red, then press it to the glass. I suck in a breath. The brush moves. I bite in a smile as a perfect Gothic "A" takes shape, even though glass has to be the worst surface to paint on because it's translucent and the paint dries in a second, making it impossible to blend. My shoulders relax.

And my hand keeps going. A tiny hint of that intoxicating rush of warmth flows from my mind to my fingers as I paint all the letters, then outline them with ocher-muddied yellow.

Something pointy pokes my calf. Rafa jabs me again with the end of his filbert brush as he stares out the window. I pull out my earbuds.

"Bell's gonna ring in five minutes."

I look at what I created. The shapes and colors of my Gothic letters are perfect. Maybe I'm not broken.

A smile grows on my face. I cap my paints, clamp the brush between my teeth, and climb down. Rafa had finished the outline of the horse and started on the muscles. Its mane flies wild and free. It looks just about as good as on paper.

Rafa collapses the ladder. "Can you grab the paints, please?"

"Sure." I hug the box as Rafa tucks his arm through the rungs and slings the ladder over his shoulder. We walk through the empty halls to the art room.

Rafa's fingers lightly trace the glass display case protecting dusty, ancient trophies. "So I'll probably work on it during lunch. Don't know if you're free."

"I guess I could." The alternative being another lunch in the band room surrounded by discussions about the timing of various halftime show elements.

"Cool . . ." Rafa maneuvers the ladder through the art room door. The box of paints rattles as I drop it on one of the tables. Some sophomore wearing a Polaris shirt chucks a ball of clay at another guy.

And now Rafa and I are just standing by the art room door as *Pretty Hate Machine* by Nine Inch Nails fills the awkward silence between us.

The bell rings.

Rafa clears his throat as he shoves his hands into his pockets. "See you at lunch."

"Well, I'll see you in five seconds, seeing as we have an identical class schedule."

"Yeah. Guess fate brought us together through the miracle of schedules." He starts walking, but his eyes linger on me.

I guess we're walking to Psychology together.

"Or the fact that there's like no options for classes at this school," I say over the roar of dozens of conversations.

Rafa leans in and says, "Fact. I mean, you guys don't even have Filmmaking here."

"Well, aren't you just so special over in Milwaukee."

"Joking." Rafa throws up his hands. "We didn't have that either."

My hands are smeared with red and yellow ocher; his are clean.

"Oh. You're really sarcastic," I say.

As the crowd bottlenecks into the hall, Rafa's knuckles brush mine. I catch a whiff of lavender and lime.

"You're kind of really blunt," he says, "when you actually talk."

I cross my arms. "You're not exactly Mr. Conversation. Besides, life's too short to sugarcoat what matters." That's what Grammy always says.

"Touché. Makes me a little scared of what you're thinking all the time."

The smile playing on his lips suggests he's being sarcastic. My arms relax to my side. "You should be."

Rafa's eyes widen.

"Thought you were the King of Sarcasm."

"Wow, I get to be king?" Rafa laughs.

"Well, as long as I get to be Queen of Bluntness."

Rafa holds out a hand. "Deal."

I shake it. His hand is warm and calloused, which suggests he does more than studying and cashiering.

"So the real question is, what do you have eighth period?" I ask as my fingertips drag along the lockers, catching another glitter-caked locker tag. This one for that Tech Ed guru Konner celebrating his "valiant" efforts on the senior float.

"Some waste-of-space Criminalistics class." Rafa shoves his hands in his pockets. "Because apparently 'History of Latin American Civilizations' didn't transfer, and I need eight social studies credits to graduate."

"Well, that's bullshit."

"Pretty much." Rafa's brows crease. "What's your mysterious eighth period?"

"German Five. Also a waste of space."

"Doesn't everyone speak English over in Europe?"

"Yeah, probably."

As we walk into Psychology together, Kenzie's eyes widen.

"So I'll see you at lunch?" I say loud enough for her to hear.

She pouts, then turns back to Josh sitting on her desk.

Rafa slides into his desk. "You got it, Queen of Bluntness."

And I'm actually kind of looking forward to it.

———

After school, I spot Rafa through the cafeteria window. It stings a little that I can't stay, but the kiddos need me and I need to get through at least a few Calculus problems before my shift. And Krampus the CPS social worker is going to finally makes her grand appearance. I know it.

Today I have the kiddos meet me by the "Welcome to Lawrence Lawson" banner on the playground fence. I successfully avoid the teachers. Then, miraculously, I get the kids—even Sage—to read by bribing them with cookies.

I need to get Belwyn figured out. Sandwiched between Vi and Hollis, I open my email and scroll through a bunch of ads for Victoria's Secret and Bath & Body Works until I find an email from Belwyn from a week ago. The viewbook. I open it.

The trademark gold Gothic "B" fills my phone screen. I scroll down to the application requirements: a portfolio of twelve examples of recent work showing my artistic range, ACT scores, writing sample, letters of recommendation, and 3.25 GPA. I'd been there at the end of junior year. It's only been a week; my grades haven't been sucked back into the black hole of oblivion quite yet.

"What're you looking at?" *The Sorcerer's Stone* droops into Hollis's lap as he peeks at my phone.

"My Belwyn stuff."

Holly's head sinks as he grabs Teddy from between us. A few patches of crust dot Teddy's faux fur now.

Vi's crazy-haired Rapunzel Barbie faceplants against her thigh. She looks up at me with gigantic blue bush baby eyes, cookie crumbs and a little chocolate smearing her face.

"It's like a year from now anyway." But still, my heart tightens. I crack open *The Great Gatsby* because that feels less like climbing Mount Kilimanjaro than Calculus.

"Heya, kiddos." The screen door slaps closed as Dad strides in. "Well, lookee here, the whole Hemmersbach brood doing homework. Better take a picture."

The doorbell rings.

Nobody ever rings our doorbell. Not Travis. None of Sage's friends. Not Grammy.

It's finally happening. Pokémon cards and a variety of pink stuffed toys have exploded all over the living room. And Dad didn't wash his own breakfast dishes.

"Put something on for the kids to watch, Rosey," Dad says.

I turn on PBS Kids. Hugging my arms to my chest, my feet move me to the kitchen. The sickly sweet stench of copper fills my nose. It's not there. I know that. But I can still see the blood eating away the yellow vinyl flooring. The scorched spoon.

"Hi, Daryl," comes the voice I remember from a day that feels like years ago. A cold sweat coats my forehead. "We're here for your initial assessment. Just gotta ask you a few questions."

"How's it going, Kristy? Come on in." Dad's voice tightens

with forced friendliness.

Kristy walks in with her yellow legal pad, followed by Detective Dick. My shoulders hitch up to my ears. I stand in front of the sink to hide the dishes.

Dad looks the cop over, jaw cinched, then his eyes fall.

Kristy's shorter than me even, but she towers over Dad. "So how we doing, Daryl?"

Detective Dick strolls across the kitchen right through the spot where I found Mom's unconscious body, his toxic cologne trailing behind him. He stops at the half wall, hand inches from a little porcelain unicorn Vi picked for Mom's birthday last year, and scans the living room. Hollis's gaze bolts up to him. The color drains from his face.

Dad wrings his hands. "Can I get you guys some coffee?"

"Sure," Detective Dick says as he opens the fridge. Still no beer in there, dick.

"I got it," I say. I need an excuse to stay, because I won't be relegated to the children's table. I tuck a filter into the funnel, dump some Folgers and water in, and start it brewing. The coffee maker bubbles and chugs as the kitchen fills with the familiar smell of coffee.

Dad sits at the table. He tugs off his Packers hat and runs a hand through sweat-matted hair.

Kristy sets that yellow notepad on the table. Dad eyes up the blank page.

"I'm just taking a few notes for the initial assessment report," Kristy says. Detective Dick saunters over and slaps his own notepad on the table, then sits in my chair.

"Why don't we start by talking a little bit about Maureen's use?" Kristy says.

Detective Dick presses the tip of his black pen to his notepad.

"Started three years ago. Maybe longer." Dad's voice comes out like a deflated balloon as he twists his scratched wedding ring around his finger. "First I think it was just to take the edge off, but it got bad real quick. Then six months ago she got fired from Hansen's IGA for shooting up in the bathroom."

"That's why she got fired?" I utter. The world rushes around me. The only thing that stays still is Dad's face.

Dad's eyes pull up to me. What can be described only as despair seeps from him. His head slumps again. "If she's not high, she's looking for her next fix. Says if she doesn't use every three hours, she can't stop puking and feels like she's dying."

The noise of two pens frantically scratching across paper fills the whole room.

Every three hours?

I sink against the counter. The edge digs into my back. I've been thrown out into subzero temperatures; it's so cold my skin doesn't even feel anything for the first second, but then it burns.

I knew Mom slept a lot. And when she puked and even shitted herself, she claimed she had the flu, which I had stopped buying, but I didn't know she needed to use *every three hours*.

The coffee maker beeps behind me.

I can move again like someone pressed play. The coffee pot shakes as I dump some in three mismatched mugs. A few drops splash on the counter. I snatch our flower hand towel from the hook by the sink and wipe it up before they see.

"How's she get the money?" Detective Dick asks.

Dad's face tightens like he's Brutus about to stab Caesar. He presses his fingers to his forehead.

I almost drop the mugs as I bring them over. Detective Dick might have said thank you, but now my ears are filled with a thrumming sound that drowns out everything but Dad's voice.

"She blew through her oma's inheritance," Dad says through his hands. "Pawned the PS4, my hunting guns, the Blu-Ray player, vacuum cleaners, Oma's jewelry, my grandpa's gun from World War II. Steals from me. Final straw for my mom was the sterling silver flatware my great-great-grandparents brought over from Germany. She made me choose between her and Maureen."

Grammy polished that silverware every month but only used it for Christmas, Thanksgiving, and very special guests, like when Aunt Colleen visited Sparta when I was five. I figured we hadn't seen Grammy in two years because she was ticked at Dad for those DUIs, and Grammy and Mom fought a lot.

"Now, well," Dad's meek voice cuts through the mist coiling through my mind, "she finds receipts in the Walmart parking lot, then steals stuff and returns it."

Now the mist clears, and I see Detective Dick flip to a new page and continue writing. About our family. Kristy chewing the inside of her lip as she taps the end of her pen on her page filled with frenzied cursive. No one's touched their coffee.

"Does she do it when I'm working?" I choke out. "Like when she asks for my discount card?"

Dad's fingers press into his forehead so hard the skin goes sheet white around the pressure points. "I'm sorry, Rosey."

"She does!" A burning itchiness like my allergic reaction to bee stings spreads across my skin.

A guttural choking sound comes through Dad's huge oil-stained hands. Something drips from his chin. And another and another.

Holy shit. He's crying. *Oh, no, Dad, don't cry. Don't cry. You're my rock. If you crumble, how can the world stay together?*

He didn't even shed a tear at Grandpa's funeral.

Everything inside me shivers like a Jell-O salad.

A hot tear spills down my cheek, trailing eye makeup. I scrub it away.

"If I don't give her money, she threatens to blow her brains out. Threatens to fuck Jeremy."

I can't breathe in that house because all I smell is vinegar—the stench of little brown rocks of heroin being melted on a spoon. Or the bottom of a pop can. I grab my backpack, and I'm running, running, running down Black River Street. To the place Mom's been stealing from while I'm working.

How *could* she?

Oh, and now Detective Dick can tack that on top of all the other charges against her.

My boot strikes black pavement. I'm in the Walmart parking lot. As I cut across the vast, half-empty lot, I dig out my phone and check my eye makeup. Wipe away some of the smudges with a shaking hand.

When I walk through Walmart's sliding glass doors, Cindy gives me her usual wide smile, but I'm hollow and cold and quaking. Did Cindy suspect? It's probably her that processed most of those returns. Oh, God.

It's a battle to raise my hand to clock in.

"Hey." Rafa swipes his badge too. "So I got most of the horse done and some of the foreground."

Right. Mural. I don't have room for that.

"Great." I head out of the back room.

Rafa catches me by the explosion of fake flowers. He holds up his phone to show me a picture. "Here. How does it look? Hope it's not too Diego *Mexicanidad* for you."

I glance at his Samsung. The way the sunlight hits it, it's hard to make out details, but I can tell he's trying to go more realism than muralism. "Please. That's totally Velázquez."

His smile deflates. "Poorly used sarcasm. Even the King of Sarcasm does that sometimes."

"Not in the mood." I keep walking.

"Clearly."

Shit. He's just trying to be nice. And before Krampus busted through the front door, I was excited about the mural. I mutter over *Mamma Mia!* blaring from Electronics, "Sorry, shitty day."

"Yeah . . ."

We end up on four and five. I autopilot through the first two and a half hours. All I want to do is run out the exit door. Hide in West Side Park. I don't have energy to deal with all these customers, because Mom blew up our lives but we're the ones left to pick up the pieces.

But then a pack of guys wearing red-and-yellow football jerseys bursts through the entrance doors hooting and hollering. Rafa's younger brother, Omar, vaults into the basket of a shopping cart. Kameron jumps into another, and then the pack of rabid hooligans are off to the shopping cart races. Omar hangs out the front, arms wide like he's that chick from *Titanic*. Mom's favorite movie. Mom and I always kicked off Deer Hunter Widow's Weekend by watching it after the kiddos went to bed. At least we used to.

Rafa glares at them as they disappear into the food aisles. Their laughter echoes through the store.

"You open?" A lady with overly done blonde streaks in her mom cut pushes her cart bulging with snacks and cleaning products up to Rafa.

Rafa lightly shakes his head, then plasters a Kimmy grin on his face that doesn't reach his eyes for the first time I've noticed.

I work on stocking packs of gum in the candy section of my lane as "Wind Beneath My Wings" grates my eardrums.

Some douchey sophomore boy with overly styled hair pushes

the cart containing Omar, Doritos, and a shit ton of toilet paper up to Rafa's register just as Mom Pants pushes her cart toward the exit. Douche Boy makes a squealing brake sound as the cart crashes into the register. The stench of their sweat mixed with Axe punches my nose.

Rafa's jaw clenches.

"Hey, can I borrow your discount card?" Breathless and laughing, Omar holds out his hand.

Rafa pulls his cord to shut off his register light and points to the ice freezers. "We need to talk."

"Just say it here!" Omar laughs as he and Kameron try to shove each other out of their respective carts.

Rafa grabs Omar by his scrawny arm and pulls him out of the cart. Omar almost face-plants.

"What's shoved up your butt, bro?"

Rafa drags him to the freezers, and they exchange some heated words in Spanish. Meanwhile, the carts get rerouted to Darlene's register. Her reading glasses slip down her nose as she scans the last item. "Fifty-five seventy four," she says, voice bursting with disapproval.

One of the hooligans, whose parents live up on Snob Knob, slides Mommy's credit card through the card reader.

"What? It's homecoming week!" Omar puts his hands up as he peacock struts up to his friends at Darlene's counter. "Jealous much?"

"Just get out of here," Rafa spits through his teeth.

The pack departs to an end credits soundtrack of more hooting and laughing. The sliding glass doors slice closed behind them, bringing silence back to the front end. Besides some eighties ballad playing on Walmart radio.

"They're gonna TP Tomah's goalposts," Ashlee proclaims.

"Kids these days. No respect." Darlene's jowls waggle as she shakes her head at the doors.

"We're not all like that." Rafa yanks the cord for his light so hard it snaps back up against the sign.

"And my dad did crap like that all the time, and he's pretty old." I swipe off some slimy detergent that leaked on my counter.

"Well, I didn't mean *you* kids." Darlene fluffs her bouffant, probably carefully styled to hide her gray roots. She then digs out the *US Weekly* she keeps stashed under her register. "You're all hard workers."

"Are you sure you two are related?" Ashlee asks Rafa as she slips another pile of bags through the racks of her metal shopping bag holder stand.

Rafa scratches at the tape sealing his new roll of receipt tape. "He didn't use to act like this."

"Looks like maybe I'm not the only one having a shitty day," I say.

Rafa's eyes meet mine. "Guess not."

On break, I dig out my Calculus homework. Austin and Bobby are talking about NASCAR. Megan from Softlines taps away on her laptop, doing some assignment for her class at UW-La Crosse. Trina glares at me over her *National Enquirer* as she eats her Cheetos.

I pull out my phone and text Dad about the kids.

Dad instantly sends me a photo of Hollis and Vi playing our ancient Chutes and Ladders that I forgot we even had.

Dad: She was crying for Mom. Hollis decided to teach her how to play.

That kid. Never count him out.

Dad: Remember when we used to have Chutes and Ladders
tournaments? There's a scrap of paper in the box with our
tallies. I was ahead by seven games.

In true Dad style, he ends with ten different emojis of trophies
and medals and a devil face. We used to play during Packers
games while Mom painted in her spare bedroom "studio" at our
old house. Whenever I won, I got to tickle him.

I shake the thought from my head.

RoseMarie: Make sure the kiddos take baths.

I shove my phone into my purse.

Rafa reads *The Great Gatsby*, nibbling on his usual delicious-
smelling dinner carefully prepared by his loving mother. While my
mother . . . Tree roots split through my abdomen like in Kahlo's
Roots; granted, hers was a metaphor for fertility, but that's what my
insides feel like. Somehow, in spite of that, I'm starving. With forty
cents to my name, I can't even buy a bag of chips.

Then my stomach growls loud enough to draw Rafa's gaze. I
hide behind my bangs and press my arm to my gut. I want to crawl
under the table.

Instead, I flip to page twenty-seven, our homework on instan-
taneous rates of change. My eyes try to focus on the example, but
the symbols and numbers go fuzzy.

How could she let it get this bad? The only one shooting that
shit into her body was her. And why the hell did Dad keep giving
her all that money?

Dad's afraid she'll choose drugs over us. So am I. My skin
prickles from the inside.

How did I not know it had gotten this bad?

Because I ignored the elephant in the room, that's how. Because all I cared about was myself and Belwyn and stupid teal owl throw pillows. Because between work and art and Justin, I'd barely been home. And when Dad was working, the kids were home alone with Mom while she shot up every three hours. It's been there all along, but I wouldn't see it. I wasn't there.

That burden Mrs. O'Neil talked about, now it's the size of Jupiter.

Tears brim over my lower lids. *Don't cry. Don't cry. Crying makes it real.* I dab them away to protect my eyeliner. But it is fucking real. And it can't be ignored anymore.

The floodgates unleash and there I am, sobbing on my Calculus homework in the middle of the Walmart break room.

"If you're stuck on a problem, I can help." A chair scrapes on the floor next to me. The smell of lavender and lime cuts through the snot clogging my nose.

I squeeze my eyes shut. Hot tears run down my bare arms. *Breathe, just breathe. Get. It. Together.*

"Want some?"

I peek over my arm.

The way Rafa's eyebrows pucker just stirs more tears. He holds out this round tortilla thing. "C'mon, you didn't eat lunch while we were painting. Just take it."

I scrub under my eyes. My fingertips are blackened by the remnants of grimy eyeliner. I want to crawl under the table, but the best I can do is shake my stiff bangs over my eyes. The tortilla inches closer to my nose. The yummy smell of melted cheese makes my stomach grumble again.

I'm so hungry and pathetic, I take it. I brace myself for a burst of tongue-scalding jalapeno as I nibble on it. But it's just cheese and chicken. I devour it.

The world feels a little better. "Um, thanks."

"Better than Taco Bell?" Rafa asks.

I chew the inside of my lip. I don't want to say anything racist.

"Relax, I'm joking. Taco Bell's fake Mexican. You just got the real deal."

I laugh-cough up some snot and scrub at my cheeks again. "I feel special."

He gets a little smile. "Guess you are. No sarcasm."

Then it strikes me deep in the chest. I'm crying in front of Rafa. Even Gretchen's only seen me cry a few times, and Justin only when we were breaking up. Rafa and I *just met*. Everything fizzes up inside me. I draw my legs up and bury my face in my knees.

"Hey, uh, did I say something wrong?" There's this sincerity there that I can actually feel in my chest. And it makes me . . . uncomfortable.

Sniffling, I shake my head. My forehead slides against the stubble on my bare knees. Right. I haven't shaved in like a week.

"*Chin*, break's over. Want me to ask Cindy if you can zone so you don't have to deal with customers?"

"Thanks," I say through my arms. Because if I have to look at him, I know I'm going to just cry more.

God, how many more minutes? Not that I really want to go home.

When I get home, at least the kiddos are in bed.

Dad's sitting on the couch staring at his hands, looking like he just found out Aaron Rodgers pulled a Brett Favre and joined the Vikings. Even the TV is off. A week ago, he'd have had a beer in his hand. Dad drags his eyes up, messy hair falling across his forehead. Yellowed light from the kitchen spills across his face, catching his red-rimmed steel-blue eyes.

I don't know what to say to him. Because now I know what she says to extort money out of him.

Because I saw him cry.

Dad stands with a grunt, hand on his lower back. "Let me warm you up a plate of Hamburger Helper."

"Um, that's okay." I wring my hands. A few threads of carpet hang long and loose by the foot of the couch.

Dad collapses back into the couch. "Kristy's gonna help me fill out this waiver so the kids can go to Boys & Girls Club again. Since Mom's cooperating with the investigation, Kristy's going to allow Mom to have supervised contact with you kiddos once she's out of the hospital."

"Supervised contact?"

"Means she can't ever be alone with you guys."

"What, like I have to babysit Mom?"

Dad's eyes wander to the spot on the kitchen floor where I found Mom. "You're one of the victims. You can't be alone with her either."

I sink against the couch. I'm a victim. And I can't be alone with my own mom.

"But she's going to treatment, right?"

Dad's eyes squeeze closed, cutting wrinkles deep into his cheeks. He tugs on his mess of hair. "She wants to. Hospital social worker's still working on it. But there's wait lists and insurance problems. It's complicated."

"But . . . where's she going to go? Jail?"

Dad blows out a sigh heavy enough to crumble mountains. "Maybe. But probably not. Not right away."

My heart speeds up as my skin tingles. "Where, then?"

Dad's eyes meet mine. "Grammy won't have her under her roof, and we ain't got no one else."

"So she just gets to waltz back in here like nothing happened?"

"Well, she ain't living on the street!"

"When?" I spit through my teeth. "When?"

"Two days."

Chapter 10

Mom's coming home in less than two days.

That thought clings to me like a thousand cockleburs as I drag myself down the long hallway to Great Novels. All the concealer in the world, the thickest black eyeliner, can't distract from the dark, puffy circles under my eyes.

But what if she doesn't come home? What if she goes straight to Jeremy?

Through the haze, I notice a locker covered with so many glittery locker tags you can't even see the red paint. "Omar: Keep Calm and Play Football!" and "#23 Varsity!" on a football helmet cutout. "Omar! Roll over the Raiders!" on a football with a red-and-white bow attached. Omar, King of Jäger Bombs, football hero of the day, and day ruiner for one Rafa Hernández Muñoz.

As I drop into my seat, my head is pounding with exhaustion. Carolyn squeals. "I finally found him. I'm pretty sure."

"So over it," Kenzie says in her ditzy eye-roll voice, but snatches the phone. "I dunno, it's kind of blurry."

"But the handle's Rafa HM. Doesn't he have like two last

names?"

"And there's a metric on Instagram that brings up people in your geographic vicinity," Anderson calls over his shoulder in his Boston accent.

"Follow request sent." Kenzie shines a diabolical grin.

"Bitch!" Carolyn snatches her phone. Her fingers dart across her screen. "Is there any way to unsend?"

"Whatever. He's probably only into his own kind." Kenzie tosses her auburn curls over her shoulder.

Bitter much? No one ever rejects her. Ever. Until now.

"But his brother's been sneaking kisses from a quarter of the sophomore class, from what I hear," I say.

Kenzie and Carolyn both gape at me.

Just then, the man of the hour walks into class gripping his backpack straps, head down. Kenzie claps her mouth closed. Carolyn's still frantically fidgeting on her phone as Rafa slides into his desk kitty-corner from me. I catch a whiff of lavender and lime.

He's seen me ugly cry.

"Hey, Queen of Bluntness."

I pull up my gaze. His smile is so radiant I have to feel it. I sit up a little straighter. "Hey. Long time no see."

"I know, right? We're practically living together." Then his eyes widen. He scratches the back of his neck. "Uh, yeah. Can I delete that?"

"Rose Hemmersbach!" Mrs. Ebert barks as she rushes in.

I sink in my seat.

"I finally finished grading essays, and yours is the only one missing!" Her voice gets higher with each word until it ends in a mouse squeak.

A chorus of *ooh*s breaks out across the classroom. I hide my burning face behind my bangs. Guess I shouldn't ask her for a letter of recommendation anymore.

She waggles a pastel-pink fingernail in my face. "First thing tomorrow or else!"

Apparently my mom-overdosing-get-out-of-jail-free card has expired. Everyone else is moving on, but we can't.

Mrs. Ebert retreats to her desk and launches into a class discussion around themes in *The Great Gatsby*.

But all I can think about is Mom. I'm not ready to see her. I don't have room in my head, my chest, to even look at her, let alone figure out what to say to her besides go to fricking treatment.

I can't see her, because all I'll see is her blue bottom lip. Because I couldn't find her pulse. Because based on my observations of how her pupils react to light, she's only ever stayed clean a day or two. And she was using every three hours. Heroin has consumed her.

God, and now whenever she comes into Walmart, I'll know what she's doing.

My stomach almost evicts the Lucky Charms I forced down.

I hear the discussion going on around us, but I can't lift my pencil to copy down the outline from the SMART Board. All I can do is stare out the window at the floats taking shape on flatbed trucks and hay wagons, "sculptures" of chicken wire and banner paper. Streamers and sparkly tinsel fringe table skirts flutter gently in the breeze. The junior one has a huge fiberglass horse weighing down the back of theirs—Kimmy's worst float nightmare come true.

"Rose, what's your opinion on the role of hope in *The Great Gatsby*?"

Mrs. Ebert's glaring at me over her little pink glasses.

I manage to pull something from the depths of my brain. "James Gatz hopes that by working his butt off he can achieve the mythical American Dream and prove himself worthy of that spoiled brat Daisy. Everyone loves his parties, but when it turns out he's a bootlegger, no thanks. And then he takes the blame for Daisy's stupidity and gets murdered. So yeah, hope got him killed."

Mrs. Ebert's jaw drops.

The whole class stares at me. Everyone but Rafa. He's writing in his notebook.

Mrs. Ebert clears her throat. "Well, that's a rather macabre way of putting it, but you raise a good point about the book's theme around the American Dream."

As Mrs. Ebert popcorns further discussion questions, my eyes fall to Rafa's notebook. He's drawing a woman with long hair. His strokes are bold and confident and solid; mine are always tentative and light so they're easy to erase.

When I force myself into the cafeteria during Senior Art, Rafa's setting our box of paints on the floor in the shadow of our painting.

"Hey, you know, you can just work on your essay if you want." The ladder creaks as he opens it. "I got our masterpiece on lock-down."

"I'd rather paint."

I grab a filbert brush from the box. It's light in my hand. As I study Sparky's outline I painted at lunch yesterday, I feel it again. A tiny spark deep in my chest. Since Sparky's a demon, I'll make his face a ghoulish white with just a touch of alizarin crimson, ultramarine blue, and yellow ocher.

We fill our palettes. I climb up the ladder, dip my brush into the pasty flesh tone, and press it to the window.

Rafa's brush gently scrapes on the window with care I've never shown as he starts on the crushed timber wolf corpse.

"You missed some excitement before Great Novels," I say. "FYI, you have an Instagram friend request from Carolyn, but it was actually Kenzie who sent it."

"What?" His nose crinkles.

"They've both been crushing on you."

Rafa shakes his head like he's startled. "I guess Kenzie asked if I wanted to go bowling, but I'm not driving thirty minutes to a bowling alley, since this town doesn't even have one. But Carolyn too?"

It's hard to tell because of his darker skin tone, but I think he's blushing.

"Did you really have no idea?"

He lets out a dumbfounded laugh. "I mean, no?"

"Yeah, it was also a pretty big controversy that you didn't go to Kimmy's party."

"What, like the second day of school? I had to work." He squints up at me. "How do you know all this?"

I load up my brush with Sparky's pale peachy skin color touched with gray and start on his Superman jaw. "I let most people forget I exist, so they say all kinds of stupid crap around me."

"Carajo." Rafa shakes his head. He dabs his brush into a mix of brownish gray and reaches for the spot where the wolf head will be. "South Division's like three times the size of this school. People are always coming and going, so being the new kid wasn't really a big deal. But here . . . I mean clearly I'm like this . . ."

"Man of mysery?" I mix a little more blue into Sparky's pallid base skin tone to add some shading around his jawline.

"Apparently. Small towns are freaking weird."

"Yeah, everyone knows everything," I mutter as I brush a hint of a cleft in his chin. Am I lumped in with the small-town weirdness?

Rafa's brush falls. He glances up at me. "Crap. Sorry. I sounded like an asshole there. This just isn't exactly how I planned on spending my senior year."

I think back to how positively fricking jolly Omar was last night. Total opposite of everthing I've seen of Rafa. And we practically live together, as Rafa pointed out, so I've seen a lot.

"Yeah, I pretty much hate this school, but I still wouldn't want to go to a new one senior year," I say.

"I don't recommend it."

I dip my brush into the lighter flesh tone for the bridge of Sparky's nose. "What would your year have been like?"

He frowns as he starts painting the outline of the severed wolf head. His brushstrokes are neat and controlled, unlike mine. "I was going to be Mr. Mendoza's teacher's assistant in a freshman art class. President of the Latino Student Union—we'd even started planning this volunteer program with Centro Hispano. And *fútbol*, I mean soccer. I trained hard all summer, building up my speed, doing keepie uppies. Now that Michael graduated and Ricardo's still recovering from his torn ACL, this was going to be the year I finally made varsity."

"Holy crap. You were a super student."

Rafa's eyebrows arch as his brush sweeps the wolf's snout on the glass. "College applications are no joke."

My hand drops. "Yeah . . ."

"*¡Híjole!* I just sounded so whiny." His neat strokes slowly fill in the wolf head; he uses slightly different shades of gray to add texture to the fur.

My brush scrapes on the window as I start outlining Sparky's high cheekbones. "Is that what your painting's about? *Boy and His Horse?*"

"Uh . . ." Rafa's brush freezes. "Kinda. I didn't think anyone, you know, would notice that."

"Most of the imbeciles at this school don't even look at the art display, let alone think about what the artist is trying to convey. So your secret's safe with me."

A smile tugs at his lips. He nods.

I dab my brush into the base flesh color and swipe it around where Sparky's eyes will be. "Well, here's one highlight of your illustrious stay in Sparta, Wisconsin."

He cocks an eyebrow.

"The other day, I heard Assistant Manager Tim talking about making you the first cashier in the history of the store to earn Star Cashier in their first month of employment."

"Well, I didn't anticipate going supernova and fizzling so quickly."

"Or maybe you'll just make a new star."

Rafa's face breaks into a wide grin. I never noticed his dimples before.

"Maybe," he says.

The bell rings and our moment's over, but we walk to class together.

I try to focus in Calculus. I really do. It's a review for our first test on Friday. I force my pen to write down what Ziegler says, but his words go straight from my ears to my hand. My brain is a screen.

Because when Mom comes home, she'll probably look more like her old self. She'll be awake and alert and full of apologies. But she's proven she loves drugs enough to kill herself, even if by accident.

123

Pump, hiss, pump, hiss, pump, hiss.

And how long until I start finding the little empty packets? She'll hide her track marks under long sleeves, but she won't be able to hide her pinpoint pupils that don't respond to light. And she'll be sneaking into the bathroom, then caving on the couch. Or disappearing into her bedroom for days. But Dad doesn't get done with work for an hour after we're home, and she can't be alone with us. Guess that's where Boys & Girls Club comes in, but what about me? I just can't go home because of her? Or, more likely, she'll be off apparently fucking her dealer for drugs.

It all presses against my skin, threatening to rip me apart from the inside. I'm going to explode. I really am.

So I get up and grab the wood-block bathroom pass, which earns me eye daggers from Ziegler. I go to the pot bathroom and crouch on a toilet seat so no one can find me.

I text Dad.

> RoseMarie: So how the hell is this going to work? Cuz you are
> not home all the time.

He's working on the line and can't check his phone until noon, so I open Instagram. Nothing from Seraphina. My heart dips like when I used to wait for hours for Justin to text me back.

At the top of my feed is a picture of Misty, Gretchen's striped Maine coon, pawing along the back of their leather sectional.

Then Seraphina's latest post: a picture of dozens of little golden pagodas surrounding a larger one glowing as the sun sets. The sky is deep blue brightening to pink. I want to plein air paint that sky. Seraphina's smiling face fills the corner. Her loose braid falls over her shoulder.

The caption:

Shwedagon Pagoda at sunset — no shoes allowed. I'm
surrounded by prayers lifting me up, even though I can't
understand the words. Myanmar barely has Wi-Fi. I feel
like one of the first tourists. So many people want to take
selfies with me because they think I look like Elsa ¯_(ツ)_/¯.
Anyway, being cut off has been peaceful in a way I've never
felt because I'm truly alone with myself. XO Sera.

So maybe she just couldn't answer.

I search for Omar and find him in five seconds because he has
a public profile. The most recent pictures are of him and various
members of the football team doing stupid crap. In one, he's
sitting on Eisenhardt's shoulders draining the contents of a red
SOLO cup as a crowd cheers.

But then it's no longer Omar and a bunch of white guys. It's
a group of boys that mostly look Latino wearing blue-and-red
soccer jerseys. Rafa grins even bigger than today. The next picture
is just the two of them, arms around one another's shoulders as
sweat glistens on their foreheads. They don't look much alike.
Omar has lighter skin and a narrower face and nose than Rafa,
but in those pictures Omar's got the same little fauxhawk. In the
more recent pictures, Omar's hair is shaggier like a lot of the guys
on the football team.

It feels a little creepy, but also kind of thrilling, to get a peek
behind the curtain of Rafa's life.

A dot pops up on the paper airplane.

I press it.

Seraphina Abramsson Official: You dream big — unlike everyone
else in that town. I checked out your pics. You've got some talent.

Then I notice she liked all the pictures of my paintings.

RoseMarie: Thanks. They're some of my older works. In the process of adding to my portfolio.

A stall door claps closed next to me, and the mystery girl lets out a long, loud fart. The stench instantly wafts over. There goes my sanctuary. I head back to class.

When I walk in, Mr. Ziegler verbally accosts me. "Well, Rose, I'm glad you didn't die in there. I was about to send out the cavalry."

I stifle an eye roll and sit down.

Ten seconds before the bell rings, I'm already ramming my review packet into my backpack to flee Ziegler's impending wrath.

"Cool your jets, Miss Hemmersbach." He jabs a hairy finger stained with dry-erase marker at me.

Mike snickers.

"Pipe down, Ott. You're not the QB of the Badgers here. You also need to turn in homework."

He tucks his backpack under his arm like a football and scrambles out, leaving me alone with Ziegler's rage.

I hug my arms to my chest.

Mr. Ziegler's shaking his head as he leans on Ott's desk. "Rose . . ."

I brace myself. He was also my teacher during my last self-implosion. Literal spittle flying into my eyeballs as he hollered in my face.

But instead he sighs, because he's seen the article too. "You know what I'm going to say."

The gentleness in his voice is a hundred times worse than his spit in my eye. A lump chokes my throat as I scrape at some pale flesh-tone paint on the back of my hand.

"I know you've got your sights set on an art school in California.

Let me help you. Stop by after school." Mr. Ziegler leans down and peers past my bangs. "I'll even let you finish your review so you can get credit."

The kiddos.

"Can I come a different time? Please?"

A flush of red starts just about his dress shirt collar, slowly spreading up his hairy throat. "I am a teacher, Rose. Not an on demand tutor. You should count your lucky stars that I'm giving you a second chance at all, seeing as you've come to about fifty percent of my classes this year."

Something inside me rips. My arms fall limp as my shoulders sag. "Sure." I head for the door.

Rafa's leaning on a display case that boldly proclaims: "Dear Algebra, stop asking us to find your X. He's never coming back and don't ask Y."

"Hey." Rafa stands up straight.

"Hey."

"So"—he clears his throat as we head down the hall—"if you ever need a man of mystery for an on demand tutor, you know where to find me."

"Wow. On demand, huh?"

His shoulder brushes mine, and I wonder if it was intentional. "I mean, I already confessed that I have no life here besides school, Walmart, and helping my mom cook and clean."

"Don't forget our kickass mural, King of Sarcasm."

"Touché, Queen of Bluntness. But seriously, we can work on the review now. I've got plenty of time to work on the mural after school."

I want to paint. But exam scores make up 60 percent of our Calculus grade.

For the first time in like two years, I grab my free lunch chicken sandwich from the cafeteria. Rafa gets a chicken sandwich too.

As I'm punching in my student ID number, an arm drapes around me. "Oh *hey*, Rose. Wait, that's still your name, right? Cuz I haven't seen you in, like, days," Gretchen says. She carries a tray loaded down with her usual chocolate cookie the size of her head, slice of cheese pizza, and green apple.

Guilt picks at my gut. "Sorry, friend. Mural and work."

Gretchen's eyes sweep me from head to toe. "I'll let you off the hook this time." She turns to Rafa. "Hey, you're Rafa, right? I'm Gretchen. Sparta High's only interpreter of dreams."

Rafa maneuvers his lunch tray so he can shake her hand. "I like your cats, by the way."

"I like your jaguar warrior stabbing the conquistador," Gretchen says as she pays.

"Thanks."

How had I missed that one?

We head for the art room. "Tell you what, I'll interpret your very first dream for free." Gretchen takes a crisp-sounding bite of her apple as she balances her tray on her forearm.

"He's helping me study, Gretchen," I say as we squeeze through the crowd of Dungeons and Dragons people who always clog the steps in front of the auditorium. Anderson's gesturing wildly as he prattles on in what I think is supposed to be a Scottish accent.

"Yeah, maybe next time." Rafa's eyes linger on me instead of Gretchen. The only other time that happened was with Justin. Somewhere deep in my chest, a tiny glow tries to ignite.

Gretchen pushes up her cat eye glasses with a knuckle. "My dream interpretations are boiled down to their very essence."

"Just humor her," I say. "She's like a heat-seeking missile when on a mission."

"I'll take that as a compliment, chica." She jabs her apple at me. "But no sex dreams. Rose can't handle that."

"Shut up!" I kick her in the shin. My chocolate milk carton topples to the floor.

Rafa scoops it up and sets it on his tray. "So, in my dream, I was locked in this school then a hoard of brain-eating zombies invaded. I hid in an air duct until they killed everyone and moved on."

Gretchen strokes her chin. "Zombie dreams usually mean you feel like someone else controls your life."

Rafa gives her a side eye.

Gretchen pumps her fist. "Nailed it. Again. *Tschüß* . . ." She stretches that last word out for ten seconds as she flounces away, her leopard print poodle skirt swinging back and forth.

"Juice?" Rafa's nose wrinkles.

"German for goodbye. Was that a real dream? Cuz I cannot hang out with someone who watches everyone die."

Rafa laughs. "Ha, no. I never tell anyone my real dreams. And I wouldn't want to hang with a person like that either."

When we get to the art room, thank God Mrs. Hoffman isn't there. I can't handle the worry in her eyes again. We settle at a table lightly coated with clay dust. I yank out my Calculus folder and slide out the blank review.

"You remember how to find the derivative?" He taps the first problem with his pencil eraser.

The f(x)'s and y's and x's go fuzzy. I feel like I'm lost in the woods at night with no flashlight.

"I'm guessing that's a no."

He walks me through step-by-step, talking about limits approaching zero and factoring out h's that have magically

129

appeared, then shows me how to enter it on my graphing calculator.

"Now try that one."

As I work, the smog clouding my brain slowly clears, and it all starts to click like puzzle pieces that so obviously belong together. Because I am actually good at math, hence making it to Calculus. It always made Mom proud that I defied gender stereotypes, even though neither she nor Dad could help me in math after I started Algebra in eighth grade.

After I finish the problem, he says, "See, you don't even need me."

I knock his toe with my combat boot. Our feet stay touching while I work on more review problems. That tiny glow expands, filling the pit of my stomach. And, just like I can paint again, I can do math.

Then my phone vibrates on the table. A text from Dad.

I don't want to check it. I want to just have this moment where I can do math with the Man of Mystery. But I need to know.

I snatch it up.

Dad: Grammy's gonna help.

My fingers tremble as I type back.

RoseMarie: Yeah except she has her OWN JOB with crazy hours.

Dad's ellipsis flutters and flutters across the screen.

Dad: If she can't Maureen can go for a walk.

RoseMarie: Yeah down to the drug house shoot more of our money up her veins.

Dad: She's detoxed. Clean. Now she just has to stay that way.

This could be her rock bottom.

RoseMarie: Better be otherwise rock bottom is probably dead.
Especially if you keep giving her our money.

"Seen" pops up under the message I just sent. I wait for the ellipsis.

"You okay, Rose?" Rafa leans across the table on his book.

Biting my lip, I force myself to nod.

Still nothing. Shit, Rose, Dad's not the one who screwed everything up. God, the tears dripping from his chin. I wish I could unsend that last message.

The bell rings.

Rafa packs up his math stuff. All I can do is stare at the screen.

"Rose?"

I start, then cram my crap in my backpack.

"You work tonight, right?" he asks as we slip into the flow of traffic, heading for Chemistry.

"Yeah."

"I'll help you with parametric equations on break."

"Cool," I mutter. I just want my phone to vibrate. I want him to be pissed at me. Because if he's not . . . it's because I'm right.

Dad never messaged me back, but my life quasi-depends on finishing that stupid essay for Great Novels, so I need to focus on that. After school, I get the kiddos settled with their books and cookies, then write "Who is the loneliest character in *The Great Gatsby*?" on the top of my notebook page. Since I don't know what's going on in the book, I search that question on the internet. Common consensus appears to be all the characters.

I begin with "*The Great Gatsby* was bereft with loneliness as a core thematic element, so all characters suffered their own unique plights of intense loneliness."

Kind of like me. And maybe Rafa.

The doorbell rings. My pencil drops on my notebook. Random CPS visit? Already? They were just here yesterday. Sage's Aaron Rodgers biography claps down on the kitchen table. She stares at the door like those bunnies living under our entryway when we caught them eating the flowers in our garden.

The doorbell rings again.

Shit.

Vi gropes at my arm as I stand. I squeeze her tiny hand, then head for the door. I should drill a peephole in that cheap steel door. Rust is already eating away at the bottom of it anyway. I suck in a breath and open it.

But it's not Kristy; it's our landlord, Randy. In the nine years we've lived here, I don't think he's ever stopped over unannounced like this. Ice spreads from my heart through my veins to my fingertips.

Randy's blubbery upper lip curls as he looks me up and down. "How old are you?"

"Huh?"

"You're a senior. You're old enough." He hands me a business envelope and waddles down our sidewalk like he has a stick rammed up his huge ass to his bright red Ram 3500 Mega Cab. Overcompensate much?

I flip it over. It's addressed to Mom and Dad. Whatever, he handed it to me. I slide my finger under the flap and rip the envelope open, then pull out the contents.

At the top of the page is a heading in bold: "5 Day Notice Terminating Tenancy for Drug or Gang Nuisance." It is followed by a bunch of legalese and a date.

Everything swims around me—the apple bowl clock, the clay key bowl I made Mom, the coloring sheets and drawings covering the fridge, my brother and sisters at the kitchen table, the whole house. I'm shivering and hollow and empty, like I got a hundred shots of Novocain numbing my body.

We're getting evicted.

Because of Mom.

I can't breathe. I can't breathe.

"Roscy, are you okay?"

The world slams to a stop. Vi's looking up at me with messy pigtails as she tugs on the hem of my shirt.

"Rose, what's wrong?" Hollis whimpers. His mouth and nose are hidden behind *The Sorcerer's Stone* like it's an invisibility cloak.

"Stay . . . stay here."

I close the door. Randy's truck is gone. I press my back against the front door Mom painted robin's-egg blue three years ago. I call Dad. He doesn't answer, of course, because he's still on the factory floor.

With trembling hands, I find Grammy's number in my contacts. Tears blur our oak tree as the phone rings.

She picks up after half a ring. "Is that my Rosey Rose?" Her voice gushes with love that's been pent up for years.

"We're getting evicted."

"Well, shit." Grammy lets out a long sigh. "It's because of her, isn't it? Isn't it?"

I can't speak because tears clog my throat.

"I'm coming down. Don't you worry. We'll get this figured out."

I curl into a ball on the stoop. Stagnant heat's trapped around me, but the cold cement of the stoop numbs my butt through my jeans. I can't breathe.

The door opens an inch behind me. I scramble to my feet. Almost trip off the stoop.

"Rosey, what's wrong?" Hollis peeks through the cracked door. His face is titanium white.

I stumble into the blinding afternoon light, free of the stuffy heat that reeks of rotting wood. I can't let him see my impending tears.

Evicted.

The teal room, the peel-and-stick vinyl flooring coming unstuck by the baseboards, the threadbare brown carpet, even the entry shelter. It's ours. Or we thought it was. A black-stained tear drops onto the crab grass sprouting through a jagged crack in the sidewalk. I strangle the eviction notice in my fist. An arm wraps around my shoulders. A hint of Dad's deodorant. Hollis. Vi hugs my waist, pressing her face into my stomach. Sage's fingers weave into my limp hand.

A wave of sobs rises in my chest. The kiddos. Randy evicted these kids.

And I should be hugging them, not the other way around. I'm the big sister. I need to be strong for them.

I slip my fingers free of Sage's and scour the tears from my eyes. There's nothing to say.

The Hemmersbach brood crams on the stoop that will no longer be ours in five days. I get my arms around all of them somehow. Traci's yappy little chihuahua pulls her by our house. That witch shoots me what can only be described as a triumphant grin. I'm sure all her complaints about us to Randy dumped gas on the fire Mom started. I almost shout thanks for the free Wi-Fi, but then she might change her password.

I hear the familiar squeal of the fan belt, the rattle of his rusting exhaust pipe, before I see Dad's brown Chevy extended cab. It almost tips as he takes the turn into our driveway like an Indy 500 driver. He slams to a stop and jumps out without even turning it off.

Dad pries the eviction notice from my clammy hand. His eyes dart across the paper. His face goes bright red as veins bulge from his forehead. "Fuck!"

The kids are crying. Our hot bodies press together as I tighten my arms around all of them.

Dad whips his phone out as he paces. He's a raging bull trapped in a pen.

"What the hell, Randy, you're evicting us?" he yells. "I'll take you to court. I'll find the money!"

"What's victing?" Vi wails from between my legs. "What's victing?"

"We're getting kicked out," Hollis blubbers into my shoulder.

"He can't do that!" Sage says. "We didn't do nothing wrong!"

"Shut up so I can hear," I say.

"What do you mean, I can't . . . can't." Dad unfurls the eviction notice. He pitches his phone at the sidewalk. "Fuck!"

"Daddy!" howls Vi.

Dad turns around. His face pales. He drops to his knees in front of us. "Hey . . . hey, kiddos. It's okay." He pulls Vi to him with one arm and strokes away of Hollis's tears with his other hand. "It's going to be okay. Everything's gonna be fine."

"No it's not! Stop saying that!" I scream in his face.

Dad winces like I stabbed him. A soft cry slips through his lips. Shit.

I can't do this. Free of Vi's body heat, I jump to my feet and start walking.

"Rose, don't go. Please," Dad pleads as he pries free of Vi.

"I have to work!"

And I'm running. Running. Running. And I know he can't chase me cuz he's got the kiddos.

A memory pops into my head from when I'm like seven. Dad and I are in Grampy's rowboat going fishing on Wazee Lake. Grampy hit a rock, and his boat sprung a leak. Dad pressed a vinyl boat seat cushion on it while Grampy rowed back to shore. We were fine.

Now I'm back on that boat, but with the kiddos. And there's dozens of rocks. Every time I plug one hole, there's another and another and another, and I don't have enough fingers and toes or long enough limbs to plug them all.

Everything's not fine.

We are sinking.

My knees turn to rubber, and I don't have the strength to run anymore. I'm stuck. Frozen.

I clench my arms to my side to stop the convulsing shivers. Brakes squeal as a rusting blue van pulls to a stop next to me. "Rose?" Rafa leans across the passenger seat.

Mascara's running down my face. I scrape it away with the heels of my hands. I hide behind my hair. At least my feet can move again. I walk, arms hugging my chest.

A car door slams behind me. "Hey, wait."

Rafa jogs up to me. Through my hair, I can see his Jordans matching stride with my combat boots. I can't talk or I'll cry again.

"You okay?" His warm fingertip grazes my upper arm, and it's like he pushed pause on me. I can't move. Rafa tries to peer beneath my bangs. The bright afternoon sunlight catches bits of copper russet in his nearly burnt-umber irises. I squeeze my eyes closed.

"Hey. Rose."

His hands grip my shoulders. My knees go weak as fresh tears fill my eyes. I sink against him. And I feel his body go rigid. Face burning, I pull away.

Rafa tucks a loose arm around my shoulder. And the weight of his arm on me. The smell of lavender and lime so close. This guy I barely know who just pulled over to make sure I was okay . . .

"We're getting evicted" falls through my lips as the tears streak down my cheeks.

"¡Mierda!" Rafa wraps his other arm around me.

Shit. Shit. We're going to be homeless. CPS. Now they're really going to take us away.

Rafa's going to say he's sorry. Just like Gretchen did the times I told her about my shit. Because his mom sends dinner with him every night he works. And my mom has shattered our lives like a cheap vase. I can't handle it. He sure as shit can't.

Fuck, he's seen my cry twice in the past twenty-four hours.

I break free of his arms and walk away, scrubbing the black tar from my face.

"Hey, wait!" Rafa catches my wrist and tugs me back a step. He peels open my fist, revealing my makeup-stained fingertips, then presses his warm palm against mine. "Medal for shittiest day ever."

But there's nothing in my hand. I peek at him through my bangs.

Rafa wears a quiet smile. "It's invisible, but I swear it's totally badass. And I guess I can pass it on to you."

"Huh?"

Rafa shoves his hands into his pockets and rocks back on his heels. "A friend bequeathed it to me last year, when my mom developed kidney disease and we couldn't afford dialysis."

The breath trapped in my lungs slips out. I brush my hair from my eyes.

Rafa frowns at the sidewalk. "She has lupus. And she's okay, as long as she has dialysis and can get her treatments. That's why we moved up here, cuz rent's cheaper and Dad was able to get a better job. That's why I work so much too. And help out around the house."

The woman he was drawing in Great Novels. That must be his mom.

"I . . . uh. Oh." I can almost feel something resting on my palm. "Um, thanks. I'll give it back. If you need it again."

"Well, hopefully we can find some other sorry soul who needs it more than either of us."

I can't imagine how that could happen now. Unless someone's mom dies in a car accident. I fold my hand around this invisible medal.

"Go ahead, pump six," crackles to my right. And I realize we're standing outside Casey's General Store. Already a half mile from home.

"C'mon, hop into my glorious van." Rafa's hand sweeps toward the road. "Time to ride in style."

Rafa opens the passenger door. Sniffling, I climb in. The van may be rusting a bit on the outside, but inside it's spotlessly clean and smells like vanilla, unlike our truck that perpetually reeks of stale french fries. A little statue of the Virgin Mary watches me with sad eyes from the dashboard. The last vehicle I was in other than Dad's Chevy was that police car. I shudder.

As he drives, I check my reflection and try to scrub off the black racoon eyes caking my face. A Spanish hip-hop song plays softly on his stereo. Rafa sings along quietly, arm resting on his open window.

I can't believe I told Rafa. I probably won't even tell Gretchen. But . . . I can almost feel that silly imaginary medal in my jeans pocket.

———

Rafa trades registers with Ashlee, I think to be closer to me. While we're stocking gum, Rafa doesn't try to fill the silence like Gretchen when she figures out shit hit the fan. He's just . . . there.

Then Rafa's hand freezes as he's about to stack a pack of Orbit in a half-empty box. "Uh, Rose, is that your dad?"

I follow his gaze over the endcap. Dad stares at me from the customer service desk, thumbs tucked through his belt loops. His chin sags against his chest as he drifts over to me. Today he's not looking for my discount card.

Dad drags his eyes up from the floor. He clears his throat. "Can we talk?"

"Where are the kids?" I spit through my teeth.

"Grammy's with them," he mumbles.

I glance back at the clock over Sam Walton. "My break's not for another hour."

Dad pulls off his hat. His hair is matted chaos. "Tim said it's okay as long as it's quick. We can use his office. Please?"

I roll my eyes and shut off my light.

We walk right past Justin leaning on a stack of Crock-Pots as he checks his phone. He's got a fresh crew cut, but I no longer yearn to feel his stiff hair flutter over my fingertips. Now I don't feel anything about him.

I toss open the doors to the back room, and Dad follows.

"Five minutes, Daryl," Tim says as we walk into the tiny office.

"And Rose, don't you tell anybody, or I'll be in big trouble."

I clench my fingers around my invisible medal.

Tim flips the blinds on the door window closed and leaves us. On the wall behind the desk is a banner declaring Mr. Hansen the Regional Store Manager of the Year 2015. Dad slides around the chair in front of the massive metal desk covered with Packers and Badgers magnets to make more room for me.

"Are the social workers taking us away now?" I pick at the chipped black nail polish on my ring finger. Tonight I need to redo my nails. Because they're getting pathetic. "Pretty sure being homeless is a form of neglect."

He twists his hat in his oil-stained hands. "Kristy says they don't take kids away because parents ain't got money."

"So what happens in five days?"

"We'll live at Grammy's."

"All seven of us? In a single-wide trailer?" I scoff. "Up in Cataract."

Dad presses his fist to his forehead. "I get paid in a couple weeks. And Mom's already applied at McDonald's and Century Foods and Northern."

"Can Mom even pass the piss test? She's only been clean like a week! And where's all our crap going to go?"

"I'll figure it out, okay?" Dad folds his huge hands like he's literally praying. "Everything's going to be fine. I promise, Rosey. I promise."

I roll my eyes. "Great. I gotta get back to work."

My fingers tighten around my invisible medal as I storm back to the front end. Dad laps at my heels.

"Want me to pick you up?" he asks as I pull my register cord.

"Think I'll walk."

"I can give her a ride, sir," Rafa says as he hands a customer his receipt. Then our eyes meet. Rafa clears his throat. "I mean, if you want."

A tiny bubble pops in my heart. "Sure."

Dad's head swivels to Rafa. He looms over us like some Viking ravager from days of old, but he looks about two inches tall.

"I'm Rafa, sir." He holds out his hand.

Dad's arm is limp as he shakes it. "Daryl. And thanks." Dad gives me a weak wave before heading for the exit. The laces of his shitkickers drag on the floor as the doors part for him just like the FIB royalty.

I head for the red line, actually hoping to pull in a customer. Work. Work. Focus on work. But the aisles are empty. Wednesdays are always slow, Darlene says because of confirmation and church stuff.

Evicted. That word needles its way into my brain again. Because of *her*.

Tears fight to crack through again. I look up at the dark skylight overhead and blink them away.

Rafa bumps my shoulder.

I wait for him to ask if I'm okay. But he doesn't, because he knows I'm not. I sink against his shoulder.

On break, neither of us mention Calc, even though the test is in two days and I'm royally screwed. Rafa shares some of his food with me again. He's got twice as much as the last time. As we're eating, my foot finds his under the table like in the art room today. He tucks his around mine. Our knees press together. I clutch the invisible medal in my fist the whole time.

God, the kiddos don't have invisible medals.

I text Dad. He claims Grammy already got the kiddos in bed. I don't believe it, so he texts me pictures. And sure as shit, all three of them are already curled up in their own beds. Grammy's a bona fide sleep magician.

After Walmart closes, Rafa and I walk out together. Dozens of stars, muted by the blazing parking lot lights, sprinkle across the darkness. But I can't paint the sky tonight. All I can see is black and white. I climb into the passenger side of Rafa's van as it purrs to life. Rafa hooks his phone into the aux cord. No Bluetooth for Rafa's ancient beast either. He fidgets on his phone, then glances at me before pushing play.

A slow, somber piano melody fills the van as a violin swells in the background. Then a man starts singing. I don't know what language it is, but it's melancholy and beautiful. I've never heard anything like it. My heart rate drops.

Rafa glances at me as he grips his phone. "You know what, I'll just change it."

"Why?"

He scratches the back of his head. "Don't mean to torture you with my boring not angry music."

"Stop. What is it?"

Rafa's fingers free his phone. He checks behind him and backs out of the stall. "An Icelandic band called Sigur Rós."

"Icelandic? How'd you find them?"

As he turns on Black River Street, he says, "Power of 'watch next' on YouTube. Anyway, I listen to them when I'm feeling, I dunno, overwhelmed I guess."

"Is this what you're listening to in art?"

"Sometimes. Depends on my mood."

"What'd you listen to last time?"

"I don't want to tell you."

"Why?"

"Because you'll laugh."

I roll my eyes. "Okay, King of Sarcasm."

"I'm serious."

I flick his arm. "Consider the source. People think I eat the heads off chickens because I like Unrequited Death."

"Fine. Ed Sheeran."

I try and fail to stifle a giggle behind my hand.

"See, told you!" he says as he gives me a playful shove.

"Sorry. I'm sorry." I wipe my mouth in an attempt to stop another laugh. "No, I mean, he makes like millions of dollars, so clearly he's doing something right."

"Not light enough for the Queen of Bluntness."

"Shut up." I flick his arm again.

Smiling, he shakes his head at the windshield.

A comfortable silence falls between us as strings and a thrumming bass and steady drumbeat swells to fill the van. Strange words seep from the speakers like cold rain. I sink into it as a steady pulse of passing streetlights illuminates Rafa's profile. His little fauxhawk, slightly curved nose, and strong chin. My shoulders unfurl. I don't feel like I'm in a rusting van circa 2005. I feel like I'm floating. Like being with Rafa in this very moment is as easy as breathing. And the faraway look in his eyes, the looseness of his fingers around the steering wheel, make me think maybe, just maybe, he feels it too.

"Yeah, maybe there's something to be said for lyrics in a language you don't understand," I say. "My music just echoes my anger. This music carries you away."

This massive grin splits his face as he pulls to a stop at the stop-and-go light. "My friends Shaiti and Cristian never got that."

I bite in a smile. I feel the invisible medal against my palm.

But Dad's words creep in. We're broke. This summer, I'd saved a couple hundred bucks toward my Belwyn tuition deposit but blown the rest of my paychecks on clothes, music, art supplies, and accent pillows. Until we ran out of minutes, I hadn't realized how hard up we were. Are. And I'm sure there's a bunch of hospital bills about to flood our mailbox. If they can find our new place. But to get one, I think we'll need first month's rent and a security deposit.

"Hey, would you mind stopping at Kwik Trip?" I point to the gas station ahead. Its glowing red letters spill onto the pavement.

The clicks of the turn signal cut over Sigur Rós. Rafa pulls to a stop in front of a stack of wood bundles.

I'm shaking as I run into Kwik Trip, stick my debit card in their fee-free ATM, and drain my checking account of $160 of the $166.74 I saved. I ram the wad of twenties into my Hello Kitty wallet.

"Hiya, Rosey," Beverly calls from behind the counter. She knows everyone's name in Sparta, maybe even Rafa's. I dart out before she can ask about my parents. The cool night air wraps around me as I jog past the propane tanks to Rafa's van. My body tenses as I shiver.

"Okay, let's go." I strap in. The heat's on full blast like maybe Rafa noticed I'm cold. Sigur Rós plays on as we drive. The silhouettes of trees set against the star-filled sky droop over the empty street.

Rafa tilts his head toward me. "Which house is yours?"

I point to our little dark-blue ranch. Light spills onto the grass from the windows, highlighting the faded plastic play structure. Dad's truck sits in the driveway. Grammy's Lumina is gone.

"We've lived here since Hollis was born. Nine years," I say.

The last time I complained about sharing a room with Hollis, Dad said we need to thank our lucky stars Randy charges us only five hundred a month for a three bedroom. So maybe it'll be the four of us crammed into one room. Or me on the couch.

"If your dad needs help, I'm kind of an expert at moving things." Rafa's eyes lock on mine.

The King of Sarcasm isn't being sarcastic.

Rafa scratches the back of his head. "Unless you think that's weird, seeing as I guess, you know, we haven't known each other that long."

A smile tugs at the corners of my lips. "No, it's cool. Um, thanks."

I climb out, leaving that warm cocoon and Sigur Rós and Rafa behind. Goose bumps prickle my bare arms as I walk up the same sidewalk Randy scurried down after shoving that eviction notice in my face.

That weight crushes down on me again. My head. My shoulders. Until I'm as flat as one of Grammy's pancakes. But at least I can still almost feel my invisible medal in my pocket.

When I walk into the house, Dad's throwing dishes into boxes without even wrapping them in newspaper like I helped do last time we moved.

I fold my arms. "What're we going to eat off of the next four days?"

"We got a bunch of paper stuff left over from birthdays." Plates rattle as he slides another into the box.

There's a mountain of liquor boxes piled behind the couch. Must have stopped by Westside Liquor.

I open the fridge. No beer in there. No empty bottles by the sink or garbage either. Good.

I dig out my wad of cash and hold it out to him. The money quivers in my hand.

Dad stands up, knees cracking. The color drains from his face as he takes it in. Dad shakes his head.

"Take it." I thrust it an inch from his nose.

His hands go up like he's trying to block my tackle. "No."

"How much is first month's rent and a security deposit going to cost. Huh?" I wag the floppy bills in his face. "Huh?"

He presses a fist to his forehead. A sharp cry escapes his lips like I stabbed him.

"Take. It."

Dad lets out a shuddering sigh as his arm drops. "We'll pay you back. That and more. I promise."

Now the money weighs a ton in my fingers. "Sure. Whatever. Just get us a place to live."

Dad's hands tremble as he digs out his wallet. His loose back pocket, stretched from housing his thick leather billfold for probably a decade, is a cavernous maw. He takes the money from my fingers. His shoulders crumble. So does my rock. The wallet is empty until he slides in my money.

I want to scream.

Chapter 11

The kids are statues at breakfast. Violet's the only one eating the Cocoa Puffs from the *Frozen*-themed paper bowls in front of us. Sage didn't even build her cereal box castle. Open boxes filled with pots and pans line the wall by the front door.

I want to break my invisible medal in three and give it to the kiddos.

Dad's eyes are red and puffy. Before shit hit the fan, I'd have assumed he had a little too much to drink last night. While his coffee brews, he stares at the spot on the floor once coated with blood. God, and come Saturday morning, Mom will be at the breakfast table with us. Assuming she hasn't relapsed already.

When I leave the house, I find a mountain of baby stuff and bags of old clothes sitting on the curb. A sign attached to a high chair says "free" in Dad's messy handwriting. But it rained last night and the colors bled and who'd want that crap anyway?

That hazy, soul-crushing exhaustion fills my brain again, and getting my eyes to focus on the sidewalk is hard. I'm a juggler with too many balls: Sage, Hollis, Vi, CPS, Detective Dick, grades, mural, Mom, eviction, Walmart, Belwyn. I can't keep them all up in the air. There's too many, and I'm dropping them. But the ones I need to keep in the air are my family.

I clench my fist around my medal and drag myself to school.

Apparently we have a test today in Economic History.

Mr. Thomas watches me as I bullshit my way through an essay about the difference between micro and macroeconomics. I flip it over and draw circles, circles, circles, circles. Big and small with lines so dark and heavy they almost cut through the paper, because it seems the only form of actual art my brain can do right now is the mural.

The class is silent except for the scratching of pencils, punctuated by occasional coughs. Even Eisenhardt's flipped to the next essay question. I want to drown it out with Sigur Rós.

Because yesterday my brain could do school. Finally. Then eviction.

I get up and head past Anderson with his *Game of Thrones* Tyrion bobblehead pen and Mike with one of Kimmy's pink-and-blue ombre pens and all the other people frantically scrawling.

I lean over Mr. Thomas's desk. "I need to go to the bathroom."

He cocks an eyebrow. "Again, Ms. Hemmersbach?"

I whisper, "I think I got my period."

His eyes fill with horror as he slides his pink plastic girls' pass my way.

Gretchen and Rafa watch me leave.

I go to the pot bathroom and draw my feet up. Pull out my phone and check Instagram. I have a message.

Seraphina Abramsson Official: You'd love the MOMA and the Guggenheim.

RoseMarie: I've never been to an art museum.

To my shock, the ellipsis flutters on the screen, meaning she's sitting on the other side of the world messaging me. Me. Even though I'm sure she has some kind of entourage with her taking all these pictures.

Well, you are her niece, a voice in my head whispers. But it's Seraphina Abramsson. That's not a normal aunt.

The little ellipsis keeps flashing and I can't stand the wait, so I check her profile.

Today's picture: Seraphina floating in crystal clear turquoise water wearing a low-cut one-piece swimsuit with braid details, eyes closed, red lipstick pristine as she wears a peaceful smile.

The caption:

A few days rest and relaxation in the Maldives after roughing it in Myanmar. It's sad to think that, thanks to climate change, all of this will be underwater someday. From my overwater bungalow, I can look down and see tropical fish. My friends, you need to absolutely make it your life priority to get here before it's gone. XO Sera

I'm adding the Maldives to the list with Uluru—places I'll go someday after I Seraphina.

The message notification pops up.

Seraphina Abramsson Official: It's a crime that you've never even been to the Milwaukee Art Museum.

RoseMarie: That's why I'm getting out. Like you did. You inspire me.

Everything's Not Fine

The bathroom door opens. The slap of clunky heels echoes off the mint-green walls and matching floor tiles.

A fist rattles my door. "I know you're in there," Gretchen says in the same mom voice she used to lecture me about breaking up with Justin.

My hackles raise. "What?"

"Seriously, open the door."

I turn the lock and pull the door open with my foot. "Out with it."

Gretchen crosses her arms over her chest. "I know things are really crappy right now, chica. But . . ." Her arms fall. "You're blowing up your life. Like, did you even try on that test?"

"Okay, Mom."

She jams a finger with red nail polish in my face. "You're going to ruin your chance at Seraphinaing and end up a Walmart lifer married to some loser like Justin who gets shit-faced downtown while you sit home with the kids."

Basically Mom's life before heroin.

"Your grand plan is tech school in La Crosse. Shoot for the ground, why don't you? Worry about your own future, not mine."

Gretchen gasps, then her eyes blaze behind her red glasses. "Wow." She sucks on her teeth. "Just wow."

Her fluffy houndstooth pinup girl skirt swooshes around her thighs as she storms off.

Now I'm a pop bottle someone dropped a Mentos in and threw on a roller coaster. The pressure inside might rip me apart.

The intercom crackles. "Rose Hemmersbach to the guidance office, please. Rose Hemmersbach to the guidance office."

Screw. All. Of. This. I pull myself off the toilet and head down the English hallway because Principal Jorgenson's main patrol route is the main hall. Just outside the glass doors, tractors line the parking lot—Drive Your Tractor to School Day.

As I press the cold metal bar, Mrs. Arnold's nasal voice echoes through the empty halls again.

"Rose Hemmersbach to the guidance office, please. Rose Hemmersbach to the guidance office."

Some freshman watches me, eyes wide as she twirls a bathroom pass. She's wearing a pink Abercrombie shirt, totally something I would have worn freshman year before Rose split in two.

If I skip again, they might tell CPS, and we look bad enough already. Or what if it *is* CPS? My medal. My medal. I wrap my fingers around my invisible medal, but I can barely feel it as my feet drag me to the office.

When I get there, Mrs. Arnold's on the phone filing her nails, and Mrs. O'Neil's not standing outside the office. I let out a breath. Not CPS.

But that was a lot of trouble for another Dad-approved feelings fest with O'Neil.

When I walk in, Principal Jorgenson glowers at me as the veins pop from his forehead like the time I skipped school for a whole week. Sitting right next to him, O'Neil's lips are pressed into a firm line as she taps her pen on the table.

Well, crap. Two rounds of Seraphina intervention in a row.

"Sit. Down. Miss Hemmersbach!" Principal Jorgenson barks.

My body folds into a chair. That stupid rainbow poster mocks me from O'Neil's cinder block wall: "The same power you have to destroy yourself, you have to save yourself."

Principal Jorgenson slides on his reading glasses and holds a paper out at arms' length. "You've already skipped two full days of classes and four additional periods." He yanks off his glasses. "We've been in school for only eight days. You've skipped more than a third of it! You're halfway to being habitually truant already."

I shrink in my seat. More balls are crashing to the ground.

"You miss one more class, you can kiss that homecoming mural goodbye and say hello to lunch detention for a week. And"—he rams a finger in my face, exposing a sweat-soaked dress shirt armpit—"I'm going to require one of your parents come in for a conference."

Well, shit. Dad can't miss work, and no way in hell I'm going to let Mom show her face here.

Captain Sweaty Pits marches out, leaving me alone with Utter Disappointment.

Yeah, O'Neil could be nosy, but she got my ACT test fees waived and even convinced some of the teachers to let me do extra credit to help me escape the black hole of freshman year.

Now she just sits there in silence, shaking her head. Which is ten times worse than lectures.

I scrape at the remnants of black nail polish on my middle finger.

O'Neil loudly clears her throat. "So, you've basically done nothing all year. Does that sum it up?"

"No, I did that essay for *The Great* . . ." I start, then realize I never finished it because Randy thrust the eviction notice in my face. My head droops. "I'm doing the homecoming mural."

"Rose. You've worked so hard the last two years. So hard. And now . . ."

The heaviness of it crushes me.

"Your dad told me about the eviction, and that your mom's coming home tomorrow."

Shame burns my face as I scrape off the last bit of black on a pinky nail.

"Right now you can't see even five seconds ahead. You and your family are in survival mode, which makes it pretty hard to focus on school."

"So why does everyone keep getting pissed at me because I can't?"

Mrs. O'Neil lets out a slow sigh. "That's fair, Rose. But this is going to be a long path for your parents. Months. Maybe years. And, like it or not, it is not in your control. Whatever happens with CPS, your living situation, your mom's sobriety—it is all out of your control. And it's not fair, because it affects your whole life. But that's reality."

That's like a sledgehammer to the chest. It knocks the air from my lungs. Deflates the anger holding me up. I dig for my medal, but I can't find it.

"Now, yes, be there for your siblings. Share some money with your parents to help get a new place. But you are not the parent."

Mrs. O'Neil folds her hands on the table and leans in. "You need to focus on what you can control. School, friends, college applications, your after-school job. The rest of the stuff, you need to try and shove it into a mental box and shelve it when you're at school at the very least. Because it's not going away, and right now you're drowning in it."

I am drowning. Sinking below the surface, grasping for fistfuls of water as Belwyn shrinks further and further away. Tears fill my eyes. I shake my bangs, coated with the remnants of yesterday's hairspray, over my forehead.

"But you can still swim back up. You need to just accept where your family's at and focus on senior year so you have options for next year, whether it's Belwyn or something closer like UW-La

Crosse. You're priceless, Rose, and you deserve to follow your dreams."

The force in her voice knocks me against the plastic seat back. I gasp.

"Our experiences shape who we are. We can let them crush us, or we can rise above and emerge stronger. So do your best to shelve it while you're at school, and focus on what you can control."

Now I can almost feel that imaginary medal digging into my palm. "Okay."

I fill my lungs with eucalyptus-scented air and stand.

———

At lunch, Rafa hands me his Samsung.

I raise an eyebrow.

"I figured you'd want to use your own earbuds. So we don't mix earwax."

A bit of heat ignites in my stomach as I plug my earbuds into his phone. He pushes play, and the soothing waves of Sigur Rós fill the space between my ears.

In very un-Rafa-like fashion, he slams the nearly empty jar of red paint onto his palette, leaving only a stamp of red from the rim.

Then I remember in Psychology, I overheard Eisenhardt and Kenzie talking about the football team toilet papering Tomah's goalposts. Apparently the police showed up. Omar led the escape, claiming to have outrun the Milwaukee police dozens of times.

"Omar's never even talked to a Milwaukee cop, let alone been chased by one," Rafa had burst out, earning looks of shock from both Eisenhardt and Kenzie.

I pause Sigur Rós, take the jar from him, and tap it on the side until some paint blobs out. Then I queue up Unrequited Death's "Backstabbing Bitch" on my phone and hand it to him.

"I think you might have some repressed rage to release, King of Sarcasm."

"Yeah. Suppose so." He plugs in his earbuds and hits play. I hear the tinny, ripping electrical guitars. Rafa dabs his brush into the blood red.

I turn on Sigur Rós. This song starts with a chorus singing a cappella with the ocean crashing in the background. Then the lead singer's smooth, buttery voice joins. I let words that mean nothing to me fill my head. Carry me away.

I add shading around the demon's red eyes glowing through the shadows cast by the lip of his helmet. With this music, my brush moves slower, more gracefully, like how Rafa paints. I feel just a little bit weightless. Music in the key of Shelving It.

Below me, Rafa's attacking the neck of the wolf head—almost literally, given the ferocity of his brushstrokes. Blood red smears his burnt-sienna skin. It's the first time I've seen him get paint on himself. Rafa mixes blue into the blood color, then works on some of the sinews.

Then I feel eyes on us. I rip out my earbuds.

"Is that a severed wolf head?" a high-pitched voice squeaks.

I glance back to find Kimmy and Mike standing behind us. He's wearing his red-and-yellow home jersey, festooned with his homecoming sash. His away jersey hangs off Kimmy's small frame.

Kimmy morphs her disgust into a huge fake smile. "It's just, you know, if we have any hope of winning homecoming this year, it's going to come down to your painting."

Her eyes wander down to the crap the underclassmen lazily threw down in like an hour. The freshmen painted a stick figure cowboy lassoing a stick dog. The sophomore window had another stick guy with a Greek helmet riding a doglike creature with a speech bubble that contained "Yippee ki-yay!" The juniors tried to paint the car from *The Dukes of Hazzard* with the driver wearing Sparky's helmet, but it's a box with wheels.

"Of course *she's* gonna paint gory stuff," Mike says.

"Hey, maybe you should've painted it, then, *Hurensohn*," I spit down at him.

Mike's face scrunches up.

Fist tight around his round brush, Rafa stares up at this quarterback who has five inches on him and shoulders twice as wide. "I mean, you're the VP and QB. And volleyball, man, you're like the king. I'm sure a multitalented guy like you has lots of artistic ability."

Mike blinks at Rafa three times, mouth agape, then shakes his head and leaves.

"No, I'm sure the judges will think your mural is totally awesome!" Kimmy shines her blinding smile before chasing after Mike.

"Dang, German sounds scary. What did you call him?" Rafa taps my thigh with the end of his brush.

I poke through his fauxhawk with the end of mine. "Son of a whore. I'm shocked he didn't know, because he and Eisenhardt devoted all their minimal effort in German Two through Four to learning swear words."

Rafa's got an amused smile on his face as he steps back and studies our mural.

"You know, if I'd have known the fate of the entire universe rests on our painting, I might not have embarked on this epic quest," he says.

I climb down from the ladder. "Should have warned you."

"So if we do end up destroying the universe and devastating the reign of our trusty class president, I'm blaming it on your cloud right"—he reaches up and taps a cloud with the end of his brush—"there."

"I'm blaming your rock right there." I point to a blood-specked rock near one of the hooves. The shading is off for the light source, which is unusual for Rafa's work, but I like that it doesn't fit with the rest. No one else will notice; it's our special little rock.

"Yeah, not my best, I'd blame that one too."

The bell rings. Rafa catches my gaze. His face breaks into one of those dimpled face-splitting grins. "Hey, you got some paint on your cheek."

I wipe at my cheek but feel no grainy crust.

"No, other one."

I swipe the other cheek.

"Rose, you're kind of hopeless. Here." He cups my jaw as our eyes lock. His calloused palm is warm against my cheek. He rubs my cheekbone with his thumb. Tiny sparks rush from his skin through mine. His eyes widen ever so slightly. Did he feel it too? Yellow ocher lingers on his thumb.

My cheeks flush as I break eye contact.

"By the way"—Rafa unplugs his earbuds and holds out my phone—"I see your point about Unrequited Death. There is something cathartic about it."

I cannot contain my grin as we switch phones.

As we head to drop off our supplies, I realize I went an entire period without thinking about Mom. Maybe I could do this whole "shelving it" thing.

When I walk into German Five, Gretchen's eyes lock onto me, and then she's on a warpath.

I know I was a bitch. I know she's right. I want to scream that I want to try, but Mom's coming home tomorrow and we're getting evicted. But I don't want to see the look on her face. Or hear her say "I'm sorry."

For the first time ever, Eisenhardt saves the day. He plops down on my desk. Back to me, he says to Gretchen, "So, I hear you and Anderson had some fun under the bleachers last Friday. What do you say, Hilda? *Möchten Sie auch* sexytime *mit Adolf haben?*"

Gretchen rolls her eyes. "How about never, Hitler."

Eisenhardt, of course, has chosen Adolf for his German name every year since eighth grade.

Anderson almost literally jumps into the conversation. "M'lady, doth this uncouth jester offend thee?"

"Okay, Anderson, I can defend myself," Gretchen says.

Now's my chance. I cut through Eisenhardt's toxic cloud of Axe and walk up to Herr Wagner. *"Entschuldigung bitte, Herr Wagner?"*

Herr Wagner glances up from his book. Crumbs dot his long brown beard. *"Was willst du, Frauline Rosamunde?"*

"So I completed my packet yesterday," I lie, "and I really need to finish the window painting for homecoming. Can I go work on it?"

"There are other times you can work on that," he says in his thick German accent.

"They'll probably slaughter me if I don't finish," I whisper, then glance back at Eisenhardt and Mike, who are now laughing hysterically at something on Mike's phone. They've been the absolute bane of Herr Wagner's existence for the past three years because Kimmy isn't in German to put a leash on Mike.

Herr Wagner waves me off.

The cafeteria hums with a half-full honors study hall. Tiny freshmen are huddled around their window too.

I plug in my earbuds and stream Sigur Rós on Spotify. Rafa finished the wolf body and added more texture to the path under the horse's hooves. Spindly Kahlo trees reach for the sky. The way he used color to capture life. The amount of realistic detail in the horse's muscles and free-flowing mane. And on the worst painting surface ever. Such a contrast to the simple forms and vibrant colors, the postimpressionism style, Rafa uses to tell stories in Senior Art. It's amazing.

For Sparky's helmet, I use the trick Mrs. Hoffman taught me to mix gold for *Mother's Love*. I dip my brush into the base color.

Mom's coming home in twenty-four hours. Theoretically, she won't have used in a week and a half. Will her blue-green eyes shine bright and focused? Like when she taught me that you can eat dandelion and red clover flowers as we weeded our garden together. Will her fingers be steady and confident? Like when she showed me how to mix purple. Will her voice be strong and firm? Like when she talked me through my first breakup with Josh and told me boys should never define me.

I fight that shit back with memories of Mom's head dropping over and over again like one of those perpetual motion birds on the couch while Vi played with Barbie dolls at her feet. Screaming matches between Mom and Dad about money. The time I tried to find Oma's silver heart locket Mom had given me for my thirteenth birthday because it was the perfect complement to my outfit for the Snow Ball, only to discover she had pawned it. Mom promised to buy me a new one, even though you can't buy a new heirloom. The family drive to La Crosse to go school clothes shopping when Mom was in withdrawal. We had to pull over for her to puke. She shit herself. Finding her passed out on the toilet with a needle sticking out of her arm, drooling on the seat. Thinking she overdosed. Ha, little did I know.

And she's going to live with us again, a ticking time bomb. God, the kiddos. What's it going to do to them?

I hate her.

I squeeze my eyes shut. Shelve it, focus on the music.

I keep repeating it until the swelling violin fills my ears. My brush moves again.

Chapter 12

It's open house at the kiddos' school, and Vi's just buzzing to go. Even Sage wants to because they're raffling off some Minecraft thing. Plus maybe Principal Isensee will tell CPS we came. Bonus points.

The sun slowly sinks toward the horizon as we walk to Lawrence Lawson. I'm taking the kiddos until Grammy can get here after work. Dad's packing.

"Carry me." Vi paws at my side.

"You're in kindergarten. Kindergarteners don't get carried. Besides, you walk this every day."

"My legs hurt," Vi wails.

"Shut up, lazy ass," Sage spits at her.

"Sage! Language!" I press my fingers to my forehead.

Hollis hands me Teddy. "Tag, you're it." His fingers brush Vi's arm as his long, skinny legs carry him down the sidewalk at lightning speed.

Vi bursts into giggles and tears after him.

"Hey, I want to play." Sage sprints down the sidewalk. She tags

Vi first, then takes after Hollis, her bob bouncing as her laughter rings off the brick building. Just as her hands almost brush his back, Hollis spins away wearing a grin the size of his face.

I'm grinning too as I hug Teddy to my chest.

They're sweaty and breathless as they race into the school. But Hollis freezes at the threshold.

I pull him against my side. I swear he's grown an inch since Monday. I've worked almost every night this week, which will put a dent in first month's rent, but I've missed the kiddos.

"You okay, Holly?" I offer him Teddy.

His frowns as he hugs it. "Not really."

"Yeah, me neither. But we're in this together, right?" I give him a squeeze. His body relaxes, and we walk through the doors. Maybe if this whole mental box thing works, I'll tell him about it.

Families cluster in groups down the wood-paneled hallway adorned with student artwork and red-and-yellow banners advertising the Spartan Way. I'm the only person there between the ages of eleven and twenty-five. Vi eyes up a pile of Saran-wrapped brownies on a table decked out with baked goods. A PTO mom watches Vi like she's going to steal something. Like maybe she's read the article and knows what kind of family Vi comes from.

I want to flip off that judgmental bitch.

"Hi, Hollis." Principal Isensee leans forward, trying to catch Hollis's attention.

Good thing I didn't.

Hollis angles away. Then Principal Isensee looks at me like I'm going to burn the place down. "Your parents coming, Miss Hemmersbach?"

"Soon." I shoo the kids toward Hollis's classroom. Sage disappears into the gym. The sound of bouncing basketballs echoes over the chatter and laughter of all the happy, normal families.

When we walk into the classroom, I spot it on her filing cabinet—the daffodil I drew Mrs. Kenyon for her birthday. The paper has yellowed over the years, but she had even laminated it. A tiny spark of warmth prickles my heart.

I cop a spot against the back wall under a bulletin board papered with kids' illustrated writing. I find Hollis's. He's written two sentences, I think about cats, and misspelled half the words. The *s* in cats is backward both times and so is the one in his name. The rest of the kids wrote several paragraphs. My heart sinks. Hollis tries to sit by me, but Mrs. Kenyon tucks an arm around him.

"Hiya, Hollis!" Mrs. Kenyon wears one of those toothy teacher grins, apparently oblivious to the fact that Hollis's shoulders are hitched to his ears. "Are your parents here?"

I cross my arms. "They're busy."

"Oh. Why don't you two sit here?" Mrs. Kenyon guides us to a desk with Hollis's name on an ABC name tag. None of the other desks have one of those. She pulls a chair up next to it. "Let's chat after I talk about the math curriculum."

But I can't abandon Vi, so I wrestle her into the seat next to me in the back. I pull out my phone to stream a *My Little Pony* episode, half expecting to find a pissed off cat GIF from Gretchen waiting for me. But there's nothing.

My fingers itch to text her an apology, but my brain can't put words together to make it right. Instead my fingers coil around my invisible medal.

Then Rafa walks in followed by a tiny girl with black braids, an older girl with long hair, and his mom—that's who he drew a few days ago in Great Novels. Omar's probably at football practice. Or maybe getting drunk after the Powder Puff game while Rafa apparently cooks and cleans and gets dragged to crap like this on one of his only nights off. Their mom's black hair falls to the small of her back. She's beautiful, with the same round face and burnt-sienna skin as Rafa except for a butterfly-shaped patchy rash on her cheeks and the bridge of her nose. Is that from her lupus?

Rafa's eyes meet mine, and his face breaks into a grin. He says something to his mom, then comes up to me.

"Hey, Queen of Bluntness." He shoves his hands deep into his pockets.

"Hey, King of Sarcasm. Fancy meeting you here."

"And it continues. The practically living together."

"Who are you?" Vi gawks at him, freed from her Princess Celestia trance.

"I'm Rafa. Who are you?" He holds out his hand.

"Vi Pie!" She violently shakes his hand.

"Whoa, you're strong." Rafa massages his hand. "Vi and Pie, they rhyme."

Vi giggles. "So do Rafa and Dafa."

Rafa strokes his chin. "You know, you're right."

He's already talked more to one of my siblings than Justin ever did.

Mrs. Kenyon does that three-clap-pay-attention thing just like she did for my class. The older of Rafa's sisters darts for her desk, two away from Hollis's.

"Hey, I'll catch you later," Rafa says to me, then flashes Vi a smile. "Nice to meet you, Vi Pie."

Vi shines her gap-toothed grin up at him.

Mrs. Kenyon launches into a rousing introduction to the new math curriculum. Rafa mumbles to his mom. His mom, inches shorter than him, holds onto his shoulder as she beams at him. Mom never missed these things, no matter how high she was. Until now.

As soon as Mrs. Kenyon finishes, Rafa plops down in the chair next to me, bringing with him the intoxicating smell of lavender and lime. Is it his shampoo, hair gel, or cologne?

"So what's up?" Rafa asks.

"The ceiling."

"I would've said stars, but I guess that works too." He shoots me a lopsided grin. "So apparently our siblings spend all day together too."

"Crazy."

"You think Marisol and your brother are tag teaming some project to save the school too?"

Marisol's dragging her mom toward a bulletin board plastered with math worksheets. Their mom's eyes twinkle with pride. Hollis has wilted in his chair as he hides Teddy under his desk.

"Yeah, doubt it. Hollis is . . . shy," I say.

Marisol skips up to us. "Ooooh, is that your girlfriend, Rafa?" she teases in a singsong voice, hands pressed against her cheek.

Rafa's eyes widen. "No, *princesa.*" He tries to shoo her away, but then his mom join us.

"¡Hola, Rosa!" Rafa's mom hugs me. Her body is small and frail against mine. She smells like baked cinnamon and sugar.

It happens so fast I don't even think to hug her back. And she already knows my name? My face warms.

Rafa scratches the back of his head. "Mexican moms tend to do that. Should've warned you."

Crap, now she probably thinks I'm rude. "Uh, hi."

His mother smiles at me and then says something to Rafa in Spanish. Rafa shakes his head. She smiles at me again, then nudges him. Rafa groans, *"¡No, mamá!"*

Wait, she wanted him to translate something for me.

He rocks back his heels. "She says you're very talented."

His mom swats at him and tells him something else. Guess he left something out. She must understand some English.

"*¡Trágame tierra!*" I swear Rafa blushes as he presses his fingers to his forehead. "And she's glad she finally gets to meet you."

Holy crap, he *has* been talking about me. A butterfly takes flight in my stomach. "Uh, thanks."

Her face breaks into the same dimpled grin as Rafa's.

"Rose, you got a second?" Mrs. Kenyon homes in on me.

"Um, nice to meet you," I murmur before Mrs. Kenyon latches onto my elbow and literally drags me to the Take a Break corner, which has the same "Hang in There" picture with the cat dangling from a branch as when this room was my second home.

Mrs. Kenyon clears her throat. "It's just . . . well, your dad and I have been playing phone tag for a while. I was hoping he'd be here tonight."

"He's working overtime."

"Look, I'm really worried about Hollis."

But he's been coming to life again at home.

"The only time I can get him to say anything, if I'm lucky, is morning meeting. I was hoping he just needed some time to warm up, but it's more than that. I don't think he has any idea what's going on in class, and he just pretends to read during Read to Self because he cannot read *Harry Potter,* and he doesn't touch the books at his just right level."

She taps a blue book box with his name on a bee tag. It's filled with little skinny baby books. Most of the other kids have chapter books.

Shit. Hollis isn't at his desk. I can't see him. I get on my tippytoes and spot him on a beanbag in the reading corner cradling Teddy while the other boys pretend to shoot each other.

"Well, help him, then." I cross my arms.

"We have been, Rose. For years. It's not enough."

"What does that even mean?"

"He's gotten a bunch of extra reading support, more than all the other kids in this school that don't have IEPs, but he's still reading at only the middle of first-grade level."

"First grade?" I gasp.

"People are wondering if he might have a learning disability. Or maybe some serious anxiety. An emotional behavioral disability."

My heart drops into the pit of my stomach, leaving my chest hollow. This isn't just a tough couple weeks; this goes way deeper. And she's back tomorrow. And we're going to be homeless. And he saw her body too. All these people and no air conditioning. It's suffocating. I can't breathe.

"So, could you tell your dad we need to talk?"

"Grammy!" Vi's voice rings out.

Grammy walks in wearing her usual pastel animal shirt, grinning wide as she sweeps Vi into her arms and kisses her cheek. I head for the door.

"Rosey, what's wrong?" Grammy grabs my wrist. I catch a whiff of her Newport Menthol Blues.

"Oh, nothing, you know, except Hollis apparently can't read," I spit through my teeth.

Grammy's lips press into a frown, making the smoker's lines cut deeper into her leathery skin. "If Maureen spent half as much time teaching Holly to read as she did getting drugs, he'd be reading eighth grade books."

And I just cannot.

I leave, and Grammy doesn't even try to stop me. I want to run, but I force myself to walk down the hallway, then throw open the outside doors. The slowly creeping darkness envelops me.

Thick clouds block out the moon and stars, and the air is rich with the smell of ozone and impending rain.

"Hey, Rose!" Rafa's voice rings out.

My heart tries to skip. I stop, my hand coiled around my invisible medal.

"You forgot your phone." He holds it out.

Right, Vi had it. His fingertips brush the inside of my wrist as I take it. "Thanks."

I'm not going home, so I cut across the playground and hop up the stairs onto the play structure.

Mulch crunches behind me. "Want me to join you?" Rafa asks from the bottom of the stairs.

"Doesn't your family need you?"

"Nah, they're heading home to hear all about Omar's homecoming plans. I'll walk." I catch a hint of bitterness dripping from his voice. "So is that a yes?"

A smile tries to curl a corner of my lips. "I guess, since we practically live together."

Rafa conquers the three steps in one fell swoop. I crawl into Gretchen's and my former Tunnel of Secrets, where we talked about boys. The plastic still holds some heat from the day; I feel it through my T-shirt. The tunnel shakes a little as Rafa crawls in. He curls his body in a foot from mine.

The glow from a buzzing streetlamp spills through the tiny portholes in the tunnel, half-bathing Rafa's face in light.

"So what didn't you translate?" I ask.

Rafa's brows arch as an embarrassed laugh slips out. "So you noticed."

"It was pretty obvious."

He groans as he tilts the back of his head against the tube. "So . . . mostly she said she's glad I finally have a friend."

I laugh.

"I know, right? What am I, five?" Rafa says. "Good thing my dad's working tonight. It's like his life mission to embarrass me."

"So does that mean we've crossed into the f-zone?"

"I mean, I'm happy to keep the ruse going so my parents stop feeling guilty about ripping me away from my life. Unless, of course, we're actually crossing into the f-zone."

"I'm cool with it. I'm only one friend ahead of you, after all." I pick at the last of the black nail polish on my pointer finger; all that's left is pink and white tips. I'll paint my nails tonight, unless Dad already packed up the bathroom crap.

"Okay, cool, friend." A dimpled grin splits his face.

A few butterflies take flight in my stomach. "So the real question is, does our new status include Insta follows?"

"It's not that interesting. I promise."

"I'll be the judge of that." I hand him my phone. He fidgets on it and hands it back.

After messing on his own phone, he says, "Let the stalking commence." He leans over to witness. His hand rests less than an inch from mine, and his smell overpowers the impending rain.

I open his profile. The most recent picture is of hands with swollen knuckles wrapping something in corn husks. It's such a simple picture, but the lighting and framing make it beautiful. A work of art and love.

"That's my mom making tamales. Hers are the best. Maybe I'll bring some Sunday, since we both work the eleven to seven."

He checked my schedule. I smile. "Cool."

The next picture is of a black braid curling around a finger.

"That's my little sister Flor's hair. I'm always her human chair when it's *PAW Patrol* time."

"Ugh, don't get me started. I hear Mayor Goodway's crazy

169

voice in my sleep."

"For me it's Mayor Humdinger."

"Let Gretchen interpret the meaning of that."

Rafa's laugh vibrates the plastic tube behind us.

Next is a picture of him with a guy and girl in a cobblestoned alley with gaslight lamps. The girl is beautiful—with long, glossy black hair and huge brown eyes rimmed with long lashes—even though she has the same look of mock horror as Rafa and the guy.

"That's Shaiti and Cristian. It's dumb, but ever since sixth grade we've always pretended we're about to get slaughtered by Jack the Ripper whenever we're in the *Streets of Old Milwaukee.*"

I snort. "What?"

Rafa shifts closer to me. "Milwaukee Public Museum has this exhibit with a recreation of 1800s Milwaukee streets. We'd go on field trips there pretty much every year. And during the summer my friends and I always went on the first Thursdays of the month because it's free."

"Only museum I've been to is the Deke Slayton one." As Aunt Colleen pointed out, that's pretty pathetic.

Rafa's nose wrinkles. "What's that?"

"You haven't been?" I feign shock.

Rafa picks at some mud caked on the side of his shoe. "Haven't had much time to tourist around."

"Touché. It's the building by the library with the fiberglass astronaut outside. Deke Slayton went to Sparta High like a million years ago. His picture's in the display case by the front door. The Spartan who almost made it to the moon, but never left Earth."

The story of Mom, kind of, thanks to me.

"Cool story, bro." His knee relaxes against mine. A tiny current jumps from the contact point. There's a speck of blue paint on the knee of his khakis.

"Anyway, that museum has the space suit he never used in one of those clear mummified Lenin caskets and a real-life moon rock. And then also a bunch of old-school bikes—cuz, you know, Sparta's the self-proclaimed bicycling capital of America."

"Is that why there's that big statue of that dude riding the old-fashioned bike in that park?"

"Ben Bikin? Yep." I scoot my shoe against his. Jordans and combat boots. Not your typical combination. His folded leg is a half inch longer than mine.

He leans his shoulder into mine. A hint of warmth swirls in my stomach.

"Let me add that to the list of amazing Sparta tourism destinations for me to explore."

"Put that one at the top. Even though that tunnel on the Sparta-Elroy bike trail is pretty cool actually." I flick to another picture of a tiny shelf with a framed photo of an older lady with white-streaked black hair and dark skin like Rafa's nestled between a crucifix and a statue of the Virgin Mary.

"That's my abuela. Before she died, she had me promise to help take care of Omar and my sisters, and my parents. She lived in Mexico." He frowns at his knees. "We couldn't make it to her funeral."

"Oh . . . I'm sorry." Then I realize what I just said. "Crap!"

Rafa raises an eyebrow.

"I hate when people apologize for stuff that's not their fault." Rafa shrugs. "There's not really anything else to say."

"Yeah . . ."

Then I think back to the picture of Rafa and Omar in their soccer gear, arms around one another. "So your promise, that's why Omar gets to be Omar, and you're stuck working your life away."

Rafa's knee pulls away from mine as his arms wrap around his shins. I miss the contact instantly. "I'm the oldest. It's my responsibility," he says.

"Yeah, know about that."

"At least you don't get all the hand-me-downs."

"Touché. And teachers aren't constantly comparing you to your siblings in front of the whole class."

"Touché squared."

Through the porthole, I can see a corner of our mural on the darkened window across the street. The sounds of distant voices and slamming car doors drip into our little tube world. Open house must be ending. A slight chill invades.

"So, what happened in there?" Rafa's foot presses against mine again.

"Mrs. Kenyon told me she thinks Hollis is broken." I try to scrape at my nail polish, but there's none left. "Since Dad's literally throwing our lives away and Mom doesn't get released from the hospital until tomorrow, I've become de facto parent apparently."

"Hospital?" Rafa sits taller.

"No one told you?"

"No." Brows knit, his eyes search mine.

The words won't come. I flick through Gretchen's messages and open the link to the article. I hand him my phone. His lips purse as he skims it.

A fist squeezes my heart.

Rafa's reading about *Saturn Devouring Her Children*. His mom could have died because they couldn't afford the right medical treatment, whereas my mom's stupid, selfish choices almost killed her. And got CPS on our asses. And now is getting us evicted.

I want to snatch my phone back, but it's too late. I've stripped naked in front of him. Ripped out my soul and handed it to him. Tears burn my throat.

I crawl out of the tunnel and sit on the edge because I cannot see his face right now. I squeeze my eyes shut.

And all I can see are blue fingernails and a needle the size of Maine sticking out of her arm. Dead. Dead as a fish on the kitchen floor. She loves drugs more than her own children.

Tears roll down my cheeks. I bury my face into the crook of my elbow.

Rafa draws in a sharp gasp, then lets out a sigh. Shame scorches my face.

"So that's why you got evicted."

I press my arm into my face. "How'd you know?"

"Back in Milwaukee, we had neighbors who did drugs." The tunnel shudders as he crawls toward me. "Make room, Queen of Bluntness."

I scrub at the thick, oily makeup staining my cheekbones and then scoot over. Rafa squeezes into the round opening. Our arms and legs meet. The chill in the air fades away.

Our hands rest on our knees, fingers barely touching. Today his nailbeds have a black grime around them like Dad's after he's finished an oil change. Maybe another way he helps his family.

"God, I swear I'm not usually like this." My voice is thick with tear snot.

"Like what?"

"Crying every five seconds."

"Hell, I'd be crying, too."

I peek through my bangs. "Really?"

"Yeah. Dudes cry too, you know."

Now I've seen Dad cry, so I know he's right.

"You said she's coming home tomorrow?"

"Yep. No rehab. No jail. Just gets to come home. For now."

"Have you seen her since . . ." His eyes drop to my phone in his hand.

I shake my head. "The social worker said we couldn't have any contact. And when she comes home, we can't be alone with her."

My words hang frozen between us. God, this is so messed up, isn't it? I can't feel Rafa's medal anymore. It's gone. Cold cuts me to the bone, and I'm shivering.

He takes my fist in his hand and unfolds it. His thumb rubs the nail imprints in my palm. Our eyes meet and his stare into me, unflinching. The few times I've tried talking about the elephant with Gretchen, she either went all deer-in-headlights or threatened to rip the heads off Mom's dealers. Justin called Mom a crazy bitch.

But Rafa's staring into the abyss with me. Holy shit. Our palms press together. My fingers tighten around the back of his hand. He squeezes back.

"You must be scared," Rafa says.

"Actually, I'm just pissed." Our hands grow warm together. "I better go. I totally just abandoned the kids. Again."

Rafa kicks at a wood chip rammed into the blue metal grating. "But wasn't that your grandma with Vi?"

"That's a whole different—but related—hot mess. I better go." I drop his hand and instantly feel the nip in the air again.

Rafa jumps to his feet and offers me his hand. I take it. He helps me up, then gives me my phone. I feel a little less pressure against the inside of my skin. Like slowly opening a pop bottle. Like maybe I do still have the medal.

Rafa shoves his hands deep into his khaki pockets. "See you tomorrow, friend?"

"Yeah." I hop off the platform. My teeth clack as my feet hit the mulch. I cut across the dew-soaked grass field.

As I walk home, I can't lift my hand to dig out music. Not Unrequited Death or Nine Inch Nails or even Sigur Rós.

The cold rain unleashes, splattering the sidewalk with dark patches, soaking my hair, my middle school track sweatshirt, and my jeans. Filling the air with the smell of wet pavement. Hairspray runs down my cheeks, mixing with the hot mess of makeup.

I barely feel it.

Because tomorrow I have to see her. Tomorrow she's back. A slow-motion car wreck I can't avoid.

And I need to study for fricking Calculus when I get home. I need to.

I splash through the puddles littering the sidewalk. Now our clothes drying rack and that ancient TV/DVD player and boxes labeled "Christmas decorations" line the street too. Grammy and Dad's cars are both in the driveway. My combat boots squelch through our saturated front lawn ours for a few more days anyway. When I push the door open, I find Grammy carrying our tent under one arm and an air mattress under another.

"Now this we can use." She drops the air mattress onto the floor with a loud thump. "Hey, Rosey. Where'd you disappear to?"

Then the tears creep back up my throat. I hide behind my dripping bangs.

Dad sets down a crumbling box labeled "Halloween Costumes" in Mom's flowery writing. He brushes my bangs back from my forehead. "What's wrong, Rosey?"

Hollis stands by the half wall between the living room and kitchen. "Am I in trouble?" he whimpers through Teddy, eyes taking up his whole face.

I slip past Dad and pull Hollis against me. "No, Holly."

I catch Dad's gaze and nod toward the front door. Dad blows out a long sigh and follows me outside. I close the door.

"School says Hollis is reading at the first-grade level, and they've already given him a ton of help for, like, years." I cross my arms. "They think he has a disability."

Dad presses his fingers into his eyes. "Okay, I'll fix this. Get him a tutor. Or maybe Boys & Girls Club has one."

"Okay, sure." I roll my eyes. "Just call the school back so they stop harassing me."

"I'll call tomorrow," he says through his hands.

Right, he can, because he's taking the day off to pick up Mom.

My eyes wander to the mountain of our stuff lining the street, now drowning in rain. "Are we really just throwing everything away?"

Dad's hands fall. His gaze follows mine. His brows furrow. "Storage unit ain't that big. Beds and clothes, that's the priority."

My logical brain agrees. My heart does not. Because I want to keep that stupid fricking teal pillow.

I head inside. Hollis is braced against the half wall, shoulders shaking as Grammy pats his back.

I coil my arm around Hollis and guide his trembling body to our bedroom. It's still exactly the same . . . so far.

Hollis crawls into my unmade bed and rolls to face the wall. "She told you I'm dumb, didn't she?" He chokes on a sob.

"No, Holly." I weave my fingers into his sweaty hair and rub the back of his head. He needs a haircut. "She told me you're kind and gentle and have the biggest heart ever." I kiss his hot, salty cheek and then stroke his forehead just like Mom used to do.

The door creaks open. Vi scampers into bed with us and cuddles up against Holly like she's the big spoon.

Then Sage pads in too. "Fine, you can have my Shining Mew." She plunks a Pokémon card on his face.

My jaw literally drops.

Hollis sniffles as his fingers find it. "But it's the best."

"Just shut up about it," she mutters.

Hollis wipes his face and pulls himself to sitting, holding the card like it's a Rose Bowl ring.

"Sage, it's bad to say shut up. My teacher says so," Vi says.

Sage sticks her tongue out. Two weeks ago she would have shoved her and told her to shut up again.

I wrestle Sage into a hug she can't escape. Finally her solid body sinks into mine and I kiss the top of her head, breathe in the mix of grass and watermelon. Her body relaxes.

I love these kiddos with my whole heart.

Chapter 13

Today's the day. Less than nine hours from now.

As I wait for the morning bell to ring, a feverish fog afflicts my brain and I can't see or think five inches ahead. I twist my shaking hands in my lap. Maybe it's good Dad didn't tell the kiddos Mom will be home after school, because I don't know how even I'm going to make it through the day.

"Can you believe Rachel is actually going with Max?" Carolyn's voice cuts through.

The world snaps into focus.

Red-and-white homecoming sashes flash around me. I forgot tonight's the game.

And shit, the Calculus test is today.

"I mean, he's kind of weird, but he's not, like, the worst," Kimmy says.

"Dude said he was gonna eat a frog heart in Bio Two last year." Eisenhardt. "I mean, c'mon, at least grill it."

Obligatory laughs.

All the yelling and laughing and bodies and overdone Axe mixed with Bath & Body Works. It suffocates me. Nope. I can't do this. I am going to explode. Flip my desk. I need to go.

But then Rafa walks in. The soft look in his burnt-umber eyes strikes me deep in my chest. He stared into the abyss with me yesterday and didn't look away.

He tosses a folded triangle of loose-leaf paper on my desk.

I pinch the paper between my fingers. "I didn't even know people still passed notes."

"I'm old school."

I unfold it. It's a drawing of a black medal with a skull and crossbones hanging from a blood-red ribbon. Scrawled in Rafa's perfect penmanship: "Dear f-word, research suggests it does possess the property of repelling further bad luck, if kept on your person 24/7."

"You pretty much nailed it. Except for the devil horns," I say.

"Silly me." Rafa shines me a dimpled grin as he snatches it and a pen from my desk. While sketching, he says, "I may have needed to bust out a little more Unrequited Death on my walk to school."

"Omar the Magnificent again?"

Rafa pops the cap back on my pen. "He's doing too much. Fighting with our dad because he wouldn't give him money to buy a corsage for his homecoming date. Sorry. Not a priority."

"Yeah, no." I fold the medal back into a triangle.

Mrs. Ebert rushes in, late as always. "Okay, so let's talk about the hollowness of the upper class in *The Great Gatsby*!"

Rafa ducks into his seat, but I still feel the connection, like a cord connecting us. And maybe he feels it too, because I keep catching him looking at me. When I do, he gets that cute little smile. Now I have the strength to shove my shit into a box and shelve it. For now.

———

As we swing by art to grab paints for our mural, Gretchen turns her entire body away from me. I hate this canyon between us. My fingers curve around my folded triangle medal in my pocket. I need to find a way to fix it.

When we get to our window, Rafa's jaw drops. "When did you get the helmet done?"

"We pretty much never do anything useful in German Five."

"It's awesome."

I study Rafa's wolf. The brownish grays he mixed for his wolf are perfect; the way he used different tones to shade and highlight makes the fur pop off the window.

"Hey, Rafa?"

"Hey, Rose?"

"It's amazing, how much texture you can create on a window."

"And your demon face, it kinda gave me nightmares last night." An adorable grin fills his face. It's impossible to fight the contagion effect. The bright morning light piercing through our painting highlights the copper flecks in those puppy dog eyes framed by long lashes.

Right then, being so close it him, it smacks me in the middle of my forehead—Rafa's hot.

My face flushes.

"Did I embarrass you?" Rafa taps my combat boot with the toe of his Air Jordan. "How does your face get so red?"

"Shut up!" Giggling, I shoulder bump him. He presses right back. Sparks flutter from my arm through my chest.

Silence falls as Rafa adds the final details to the rocks at the horse's hooves. I add a few last touches to the helmet and clouds. We work in silence, no earbuds even, but it's a comfortable silence like I've never felt with anyone else.

Until a voice echoes through the cafeteria. "Hey, butt kisser!"

Omar saunters up with a nonchalant smile, kitted out in a red-and-yellow home football jersey that hangs loose on him. His thick body spray gags me.

"You coming to the game tonight? Watch me smash all these white boys?" He kisses both of his relatively small biceps.

Rafa turns back to the window. "Can't, manito. Gotta work."

No he doesn't.

"But it's homecoming!"

"So? You'll have other games."

"Dude, it's your senior year! All you ever do is work and homework. And I guess this creepy-ass mural. You're so boring now."

The brush snaps in Rafa's fist. He chucks the pieces onto the ground and shoulders past Omar. *"Me vale."*

Omar's face scrunches like Rafa punched him, which I probably would have done if I were Rafa.

"What's shoved up his butt?" Omar mutters.

"Dick move," I say as I climb down the ladder.

Omar squints at me. "Who are you?"

"Rose."

I head out to find Rafa. Where would he even go? Pretty sure he's never skipped a class. And he probably wouldn't go back to art. Gretchen mentioned he was on Mrs. Petrowski's good side. She might look the other way if he hid in the LMC. I push open the heavy wooden door. The library security system quietly clicks as I walk through and am enveloped by the musty smell of books. And perhaps our brains really are connected, because I find him at the table behind a display of the "decade's hottest" young adult fantasy books. He's spinning a little golf pencil that usually lives by the library computers.

I sit next to him. He glances up at me and shifts in his seat.

I dig the folded triangle out of my pocket and drop it on top of a pencil scratching that says "Gabby sucks dick" in front of him.

Rafa waves a hand. "Please, crap with that *mocoso* doesn't even compare."

"Just because my life is *Titanic* meets Chernobyl right now doesn't mean that you also don't get to harness the power of the medal." I slide it closer to him. "So what are you really doing tonight?"

Rafa spins the folded triangle on the table. "My family will be at the game, so whatever I want."

"So what does one Rafa, Man of Mystery, do with his free time here in Sparta?"

He spins it again. When it stops, one of the corners points directly at me. If we were playing Spin the Bottle . . .

"Maybe I'll hit up the bike astronaut museum," he says.

"Sorry, that closes at like four thirty, my friend."

A smile tugs at the corner of his lips, adding the slightest dimple to his cheek. "Guess I better take up deer shining or whatever Buddy and the tech ed guys were talking about in the locker room yesterday."

"What?"

"Kidding."

"Yeah, you don't seem the type."

His brow arches as he spins the medal again.

I could ask him to do something. Neither of us probably has the gas money to drive to La Crosse where there's actually stuff to do, like Olive Garden and Grandad Bluff. But Rafa likes photography, so maybe I could take him to the FAST Fiberglass Mold Graveyard. He might think the huge old molds of octopuses and frogs and devil heads are Instagram-worthy.

But I can't. Because it's Family Intervention Night. And we have less than two days left to pack and clean. My shoulders cave.

"Hey, want to study for Calc?" Rafa asks. "We can add the finishing touches to the mural at lunch."

"Yeah, thanks."

And, even with the shit going on, today I have room to fit some stuff about parametric equations into my brain.

When the bell rings, Rafa slides the medal back to me. "I'm good now."

I slip it into my pocket. The corners dig into my thigh. It grounds me.

But when it's test time, my brain dissolves into a pile of muddy mush.

The first question: "Draw a graph of $f(x)=2^x$ and $g(x)=(12)^x$"

My fingers death clench my medal as the letters and numbers swim before my eyes. I'm pretty sure it's an exponential function, but the file on how to solve it is missing from my brain. And I'm standing on the shore watching Belwyn drift away with no boat to catch it. Just like Gretchen, interpreter of dreams, foretold.

A loud throat clearing draws my attention. Rafa catches my gaze. "You okay?" he mouths.

Biting my lip, I shrug.

His brows knit.

"Eyes on your own paper," Mr. Ziegler proclaims like we're taking the ACT as he strolls down the aisle between Rafa and me. Rafa shoots a glare at his back.

No. I can do the derivative ones. I flip to those, and my brain retrieves the stuff that Rafa taught me. But that's like three problems out of twelve.

Erase and scribble, erase and scribble. My dream circling around the drain, about to get sucked in as Carolyn and Kimmy and Rafa and even Mike plow through their tests.

I want to scream.

I flip over my test and draw an anime picture of myself walking off a cliff. But hey, it's the first art I've been able to create besides the mural in almost two weeks.

The bell rings.

Mr. Ziegler's hairy fingers snatch my test from me. "Is this a joke?"

"No, I worked really hard on it." I grab my backpack and storm for the door.

"She doesn't belong here anyway," Mike snickers.

I flip him off over my shoulder as I walk out.

"The only reason you're here is because Kimmy does your homework, *pendejo*."

Holy crap, was that Rafa? But my feet keep moving.

Rafa catches me by the wall aquarium of Mississippi River ecology. He's violently shaking his head. "Well, I thought your drawing was amazing."

"I know, right?"

"You ready to finish our masterpiece?"

Shove it into a box. Focus on what you can control. Gretchen. I need to try and fix it with her. "First I got to do something."

"I'll go finish up the rocks."

The corners of my medal dig into my palm as I follow the cacophony of instruments flowing out of the band room—scales and bits of the school song and "Eye of the Tiger."

As I walk in, Anderson elbows Gretchen. She now sits at the end of the second row, meaning she's first clarinet in addition to drum majorette because it's band geek canon that only first chairs can sit there, even at lunch.

Gretchen locks onto me and folds her arms across her short-sleeved checkered shirt. "Look who my Maine coon dragged in."

Even the sound-absorbing material lining the walls—the same stuff as in that interrogation room the night Mom almost killed herself—can't absorb the anger saturating her voice. What if I've finally gone too far?

I head for the hallway, hoping she'll follow.

Gretchen closes the door, muting the music.

I grip my upper arm. "I'm sorry, okay?"

"For. What?"

"You know. Yesterday."

"See, here's the thing." Gretchen jams her browning apple core in my face. "I'm your best friend in the whole world. When people care about each other, they push them to live their best lives. And you're not doing that.

"I'm happy with my plan to be a vet tech. I don't want more. You do, and I won't stop pushing you to go after it." She adjusts her cat eye glasses, pink today. "So deal, or we don't need to be friends anymore. I mean it this time."

It's overwhelming, how much she cares. I throw my arms around her shoulders and breathe in her Juicy Couture.

"Uh, okay then." She hugs me back. "Now go finish that mural. Seriously, chica. The fate of beer at our first class reunion hangs in the balance."

I laugh. "Well, I guess I don't want to become the senior class's bringer of doom."

On the way to the cafeteria, I feel lighter. Less alone. I sneak into the bathroom and check Instagram.

I have a message from Aunt Colleen.

Seraphina Abramsson Official: Once I'm back in New York, you absolutely must come visit me. We'll tour all the museums, I'll take you to *Hamilton* on Broadway and then we'll have dinner in Chinatown. I'll even cave and take you to see Bethesda Fountain in Central Park even though it's uber touristy. I want to show you what your life can be.

Oh my God. No. Fricking. Way. Me in NYC? I squeal.

Seraphina Abramsson Official: I'll fly you out because I'm sure your parents are broke.

So broke we're homeless. And Colleen doesn't even know about the overdose. Should I tell her? No, I'd rather focus on NYC.

RoseMarie: OMG that'd be amazing.

———

Rafa and I manage to survive the totally cliché homecoming pep rally together, then head to the cafeteria to do our final mural inspection. The fate of the universe depends on it.

Afternoon light filters through the darkness that is our masterpiece. Sparky the Spartan rides his gray Clydesdale through the gangling, bare trees wearing a dented and blood-spattered suit of armor. A Greek helmet bathes his face in shadow. His eyes glow red as he holds the timber wolf head high, blood dripping from its neck. The horse is mid-canter as he crushes the body of the wolf under his hoof, mane flying free. Flames curl out of his nostrils. At the top in muddied red and yellow, "Apocalypse Now: Tomah's day of reckoning."

"Your horse," I say, "the way you captured the shading for the muscles, the hooves. The mane looks like it's in motion. I'd never be able to do that."

"Well your knight . . . I mean . . . . Yeah, you're great." His face breaks into a lopsided grin that rocks my heart.

"You're pretty great too." I lean my shoulder against his.

He leans back. "Better take some pictures for Belwyn."

"Oh, right." I take out my phone and snap one.

Rafa juts out his hand. "No, no, no. Give that to me." He snaps a million photos from all different directions. "You gotta get the angle and light just right. That's what makes it art." He flicks through them, deleting as he goes. "This one. Send this."

I take my phone back. He hearted it for me. "Thanks."

He snaps a few with his own phone. "So they announce the winners at the homecoming dance. Um, you got any plans to go?"

"Yeah, no."

"Right." Rafa waves his hand dismissively. "I get it. You know, with everything . . ."

I scrub at a stray drop of gold on the tile with my boot. "I mean, I do want to know if we win."

"Okay, I'm just going to say it." Rafa practically shoves his hands through his pockets. "I know it's short notice, but do you want to go . . . with me?"

And I'm dumbfounded.

Rafa's eyes widen, and I swear he blushes. "¡Mierda! Forget it, stupid idea."

A glow fills me up to the brim.

"No, I mean, yes! I want to go with you, but . . ." I can't leave the kiddos with Mom already. I don't care who's there to supervise. My chest cracks, and the glow leaks out.

"Look, how about we say maybe? See how things go."

"Okay. I better go get the kiddos." Even a box made of tungsten can't contain my feelings about this reunion.

Rafa's fingers weave through mine, and it lifts my heart a tiny bit. "Can I walk you to the crosswalk?"

"Sure." I press my fingers between his knuckles.

As we walk outside, we're enveloped by the sticky remnants of heat from a slowly dying summer. The sky is heavy and boiling and gray, about to unleash pounding rain. My favorite clouds to paint. Rafa's thumb caresses mine, and I remember the little folded triangle in my pocket.

French ultramarine and burnt umber, mixed with titanium white. These gray clouds have a slight purple hue, so I'd add a tiny touch of alizarin crimson.

I don't have a box for Return of the Mother, but I can paint the sky in my mind again. Proof that my brain's not so broken anymore.

"Rose!" Gretchen snakes behind me through the kids lining up for the busses. "I know you don't work. Come to the game. It's our last homecoming."

Then her eyes drop to our linked hands. She squeals.

I exchange a glance with Rafa. "So, we might be going to the homecoming dance tomorrow. Can I borrow a dress?"

Gretchen jumps up and down. "Oh my God, yes, yes, yes! And you're coming to the game tonight, chica."

Rafa looks to me. "Hey, if Rose goes, I'll go."

"Wait, what?" I stammer.

Rafa's face splits into a smile that belongs in *Seventeen* magazine. "Well, the space bike museum's closed, after all."

Gretchen's nose wrinkles as she looks between us.

This meeting can't take all night, and if I bring the kiddos with, then we don't need to worry about the supervision thing. And I don't have to be around *her*.

"I'd need to bring my siblings," I say.

"I got the van tonight." Rafa lifts our hands and presses them to his chest. Our bare forearms connect.

My heart skips. And I can't believe it, but I want to go to a football game more than anything. "I'll ask my dad."

"Well, that's the only way you're getting your homecoming dress, chica." She winks at me.

The bell rings across the street.

"Crap, I gotta go get the kiddos."

Rafa walks me to the crosswalk. He squeezes my hand. "I hope I get to see you tonight."

"Me too. I'll message you."

"And"—his eyes drop—"I hope it all goes, well, I guess the best it can."

"Yeah." My shoulders sag.

The crossing guard heads into the street holding up her flashing stop sign.

"See you later," he says.

Our fingers slide apart. I dig in my pocket for my little folded medal.

I just have to get through Mom.

Chapter 14

I walk to our meeting spot by the dog-eared Lawrence Lawson sign. As I wait, a huge V of Canadian geese honk overhead. Mom, oh God, Mom. She's home. Right now. Panic crushes my heart. And it's back. Her limp, lifeless body's on the kitchen floor. It's back. It's a black hole sucking in everything except the scorched spoon and the syringe.

"Is she breathing?"

Pump, hiss, pump, hiss, pump, hiss.

Her face bone white and bloody with blue lips.

I squeeze my eyes closed and breathe until the images go away.

What will she look like? I don't know what would be worse, if she has the bright smile and glowing eyes like in the wedding picture plus a few years . . . or pinpoint pupils and fresh scabs on her face.

Mom always wants to apologize and smother us with kisses whenever she sobers up for five seconds. But there aren't words in English or German or Spanish or any other language that can delete the memory of trying to find your mom's pulse. I don't want to hear her stream of guilt-fueled apologies that will become meaningless when she starts asking for a little food money with shifty eyes, when little things start going missing from around the house. Or when she starts sneaking something into her purse to return later with a receipt she found in the Walmart parking lot.

Rafa was right last night. I'm scared to see her.

I'm a pop bottle thrown off an airplane without a parachute. I wish I could migrate south with those Canadian geese.

Focus on what you can control. Anger. Rage. That's my shield.

I make a mental list of all the things I hate about her.

Neglecting the kiddos.

Getting us evicted. Leading to most of our lives being thrown out.

Her actions triggering the fricking article documenting my family's tragedy for time immemorial. That everyone's seen.

Being a criminal.

Being fired from the place she'd worked at for my entire life because she was shooting up in the bathroom.

Stealing from Grammy to the point that Dad had to choose between his wife and his mother.

Stealing from Dad. Guilting him into giving her money by threatening to fuck Jeremy or kill herself, to the point that we couldn't pay for our cell bill.

Stealing and pawning the PS4 and tons of other stuff from our family.

Stealing and pawning the heart locket she gave me.

Stealing from my place of employment while I'm working.

Giving up everything we had together: painting, stargazing, gardening, doing my hair and nails, baking snickerdoodle cookies, walking to Culver's for frozen custard just the two of us. Because now her entire life is shooting up, sleeping, and questing her next high.

Overdosing and almost dying right before my eyes. And Hollis seeing it and probably being scarred for life.

Choosing drugs over us to the point that the kiddos haven't been able to even speak to her in almost two weeks and none of us can be alone with her.

Then leaving us to pick up the pieces while she's in the hospital.

Numbing her pain, and the perpetual guilt of failing as a mother, with drugs while we can't escape it.

Lying. Lying. Lying. Promising to get clean. Then relapsing. Because she loves heroin more than us.

And I could list dozens more. Heat broils through my blood.

I'm screaming all of it in her face; that's something I can control. Because I don't give a fuck. I hate her for what she's done to us.

Now I'm strong. My anger makes me invincible.

Sage and Vi race toward me laughing, tagging each other back and forth as their book bags bounce off their backs. Hollis lags behind, head down, sans backpack.

"Can't catch me, Holly Wolly!" Vi yells over her shoulder, and bolts past me.

Hollis looks up. A slow smile spreads across his face. He hands me Teddy. His bony legs pump faster and faster as he closes the gap between him and tiny Vi. He wraps her into a hug, and she explodes into giggles.

"I'm the tickle monster!" She jumps on his back and tickles his neck.

"You're the stinky monster!" Laughing, he tries to pull her off.

Sage gets Vi good in her armpits and she loses her grip in a fit of giggles.

"Okay, kiddos, let's go home," I say.

Sarah J. Carlson

Vi skips up to me, her golden locks flying. "I counted to twenty today. My teacher gave me this!" She points to a rainbow kitty sticker on her Pinkie Pie shirt just above a ketchup stain from lunch.

"Kitties are stupid." Sage bats at the back of her head.

Vi pouts.

"Stop being a bully!" Hollis shoves her.

She shoves him back. Hollis wrestles her into a headlock.

"Ow! Stop! Stop!" Sage cries. "Rose! Make him stop!"

I let it go on a second longer, just to remind her that he actually is bigger than her. And because he's actually alive.

"All right, Holly, let her go."

Hollis drops her.

Red-faced, Sage stomps ahead to the stop sign.

Hollis's chest puffs out. I give him a side hug and kiss his head. Maybe they'll be okay.

Well, until we get home anyway. And the kiddos have no idea what lies in wait. My fist crushes Teddy's head. That's not fair.

"Huddle, kiddos," I call.

We form a herd outside Anytime Fitness.

The freewheeling glee all nine-year-olds should have evaporates from Hollis's face.

I let out a slow sigh as I grip my backpack straps. "Look . . . Mom's home."

"Mommy's home! Mommy's home!" Vi claps and dances in circles.

Hollis's eyes go wide as his brows pinch like in Caravaggio's *Medusa*. A silent scream. I haven't seen that look for days, but now it's back. He's seeing her body again. The needle sticking out of the inside of her elbow. The Western-embellished belt around her upper arm. I'd give up Unrequited Death forever if it meant I

193

could suck the image from his brain. Instead I hand him Teddy, then my fingers dig for the paper triangle in my pocket.

I expect Sage to go nuclear. But instead her head hangs low.

"Is she just gonna be home? Forever?" Hollis's voice cracks.

"I don't know. We're having a family meeting with that social worker when we get home."

Sage kicks at a cracked section of sidewalk over and over again. "Whatever, she'll just start doing drugs and sleep all day again anyway. Maybe really die this time."

Tears fill Vi's eyes. "Die? Like go to heaven with God like Goldie Pie?" The goldfish Dad won her at Butterfest last year.

"Yes!" Sage screams in her face and stomps toward home.

Hollis walks with Teddy pressed to his nose. I wrap an arm around him and the other around Vi.

Anger. Anger. My shield. My Sparky Spartan armor. This is all her fault. *Saturn Devouring Her Children*. I death grip my rage with both fists.

A block from home, I see the curb out front is empty. Now all that stuff is in the dump. Dad's truck is parked in the driveway, meaning they're home.

She's home.

My heart beats faster than hummingbird wings, pumping tingling adrenaline through my veins.

Sage snatches her baseball off the grass and chucks it at the oak tree Dad used to help me climb. A chunk of bark flies off. She snatches up the ball again.

Vi sprints for the door but freezes before her hand touches the knob.

The door swings open, and Dad's massive form fills the entryway. His eyes wander to Sage. Dad sighs.

Just past his broad form, I see her through the kitchen sitting on the couch, craning her neck to see us. She really is alive. A rush of relief pours through me. My throat thickens.

No.

Blue lips. Blue nails. Desperately searching for a heartbeat. Her fault. Her fault. Her fault.

They're coming. The apologies and empty promises. The excuses and unfinished sentences meant to stab me or Dad or Grammy with guilt. My fingernails cut into my palms.

Dad slips past me through the entry shelter then skulks over to Sage.

Violet bolts through the open door. "Mommy!"

I grab for her arm but she escapes.

Mom practically runs into the kitchen, arms open as she sinks to her knees inches away from where I found her. Violet crashes into her. Mom scoops her up and hugs her tight, kissing her cheeks over and over again. Violet melts against her. Mom's long dishwater-blonde hair falls over her face and Vi's shoulder.

Shit. Vi's unsupervised with Mom. What if CPS comes right now? *Rose, Dad's just outside*, a voice in my head says. But it's not just that. I don't want Vi alone with her.

I harness my anger and march into the kitchen. Today it's eighty-five, and even the humming mega box fan does nothing to fight back the heat absorbed in the couch, the carpet, the soul of our home. But goose bumps prickle my arms.

"I missed you, Vi Pie." Mom's eyes are closed, and she has the exact same love-filled smile as in *Mother's Love*. There's yellow bruising under her eyes and around her nose. She must have broken it; maybe that's where the blood came from. But the scabs she always picks on her face and arms have faded from red to very light pink. From her frame hangs a pink T-shirt that generically says Paris, even though the farthest she's even been from Sparta is Chicago. When Mom OD'd, she was wearing that T-shirt from the Dells, but that got covered with blood. Dad must have brought her new clothes.

In my head, she became this massive monster, a supersized Godzilla smashing everything. Saturn taking up the whole canvas.

I forgot she's actually two inches shorter than me and weighs less now too.

The heat slowly leaks from my body as my palm sweat soaks into my little folded triangle. I grasp for that massive list of shit she's done to us, but it's slipping through my fingers. Mom's eyes open. And there's a focused glow in her blue-green eyes, like when she used to tell me the names of all the ditch flowers. Her cheeks are flushed with life like after she gave birth to Vi, when her heart allegedly grew bigger so she could still love all of us the same. She looks so much like Aunt Colleen, sans red lipstick.

Other than those fading bruises, there's no sign that less than two weeks ago, she was dying where I'm standing now. Or that she had to have surgeries to drain pus from her lungs.

She just looks like Mom. And she's so close I can almost smell the Vanilla Field I got her for Christmas.

The anger holding my chest open deflates like a popped balloon, and I'm left shivering and empty as a tidal wave of ice rushes through me. Steals my breath.

"Holly, I swear you got even taller," Mom's voice wobbles as she braces Vi on a hip and opens her arm. The bruise that had been on her hand from missing the vein is now gone.

Hollis hugs me tight, squeezing the air from my diaphragm.

Mom's eyes lock onto me. A smile brightens her eyes like she's seeing me back when I was seven—her Rapunzel—and it was my job to pour the chocolate chips into the pancake batter.

I shake my hairspray-crusted bangs over my eyes. Mom's

brows knit as tears track down her cheeks. "Rosey. I . . . I—"

Grammy walks in. She shakes her head at Mom and pulls a pack of Newport Menthol Blues from her huge studded hunting camo purse.

Mom's head droops. A wilted daisy.

"Hey, Mindy," Kristy calls from outside, "why don't you wait out here a second?"

Grammy shakes her head one more time before she leaves. Dad pulls Sage in by her upper arm. Kristy follows.

Chair legs scrape on the kitchen floor as Dad drags some chairs to the living room. "Let's get this party started," Dad says.

My feet carry me to the couch. Mom sits in one of the kitchen chairs across from me. Vi curls at her feet. I want to scream at Vi to stay back, because she's just going to let us down again, but the Queen of Bluntness has no words.

Hollis climbs into my lap, clutching Teddy for dear life. His body is hot and sweaty, but today he smells kind of like Dad because he remembered to put on his deodorant. His feet sit on top of mine, and his knobby knees jut out.

Sage plops down right next to me as she stares at her Mine-craft game on Dad's old phone. She's a coiled spring. I tuck an arm around her; her body relaxes.

When I catch a surprised look on Mom's face, her eyes fall to her lap. She twists a glossy brochure that says "Gundersen Lutheran Behavioral Health Residential Addiction Services" in her hands.

A kitchen chair creaks as Dad sinks into it. Kristy sits next to him. Now the only one missing from this *Intervention* scene is Grammy.

"So Maureen and Daryl." Kristy pulls out some paperwork from her file. "I'm going to need you both to sign releases of information for Grandma Mindy to be here. It's valid for a year from today, but you can revoke it at any time."

She hands one to Dad. The tinny music from Sage's Minecraft fills the silence as Dad scrawls his chicken scratch.

Now the Blu-ray tower is gone, revealing a crayon picture of Batman Sage drew on the wall when she was four. Mom tried everything to get it out. Now it would be painted over. All the magazines are gone from the coffee table. A few pink splotches of nail polish dot the wood from before Rose split in two.

Proof of a time when Mom's love for us was boundless. Uncontainable. When I used to help her rub Sage's and Hollis's backs while she read from the Chronicles of Narnia because I wanted to hear, too, but didn't want to be a baby.

When she loved us more than drugs.

Something wobbles in my chest like a spinning top about to fall.

Kristy hands Mom a paper to sign.

The buck head presides over this menagerie with dead eyes. I brace myself for her to rip it up and scream that Grammy's a "judgmental old bitch" like the last time we were all together, when they were probably fighting about Mom pawning Grammy's prized silverware from Germany to buy drugs for a few more days. But Mom's fingertips go bone white as she clenches the pen and signs. Without looking up, she slides it across the coffee table to Kristy.

"You got any other family around?" Kristy asks. Her eyes settle on Mom.

Mom shakes her head. Last I heard, her mom and stepdad were somewhere in Nevada, and Aunt Colleen . . . I guess I'm the only one who's had contact with her.

"Okay, well, this won't be anything too formal. More a chance for me to get to know you all as a family." Out comes Kristy's yellow notepad. "I'll take a few notes."

The screen door claps closed behind Grammy as she comes back in. The strong odor of fresh menthol cigarettes follows her as she settles into Sage's usual armchair. Grammy folds her arms across her massive bosom. Her left eye twitches like when she threatened me with the wooden spoon for ninja climbing her Precious Moments curio cabinet and breaking the crawling baby boy she got after Dad was born.

"They should make a Precious Moments figurine for this," I mutter to Grammy.

Grammy bursts into a knee-slapping guffaw. "Kid of my heart."

"So Daryl and Maureen, you both grew up in Sparta?" Kristy cuts in.

"I grew up in Cataract," Dad says.

"Uh, yeah, Sparta." Mom's hands choke the brochure.

Hollis shifts in my lap. My thighs are going numb under his weight, but I hug him tighter.

"You both graduated from Sparta, right?"

"In 2001," Dad says.

"Any education past that?"

"I was going to go to Western Wisconsin Technical College." Mom's brows knit.

Then I feel it watching us, Mom's painting from before I was born, the pure-white dove breaking free from black tendrils. Mom follows my gaze. Her lips press into a tremulous line, deepening the wrinkles around the corners of her mouth.

"We got pregnant with Rose our senior year," Dad says. "Crazy to think we were only a few months older than you are now, Rosey."

Holy crap. I never thought about that before. And I literally cannot imagine being pregnant. Having a kid.

"And you had that football scholarship to Stout, Daryl. Don't you forget that." Grammy fans herself with a church bulletin she dug from her purse.

"Thanks, everyone, for highlighting how I shattered your dreams."

I peel Hollis off me and storm out, slamming the front door behind me. Indecipherable arguing leaks through the door and fills the tiny porch clustered with cobwebs where the kiddos sat for hours while Mom shot up so much heroin she almost killed herself. My teeth cut into the inside of my lip and I taste tangy, salty blood as tears burn holes in my eyelids. *Don't cry, Rose, that'll smear your eyeliner.*

Screw this whole family except the kiddos. But now I have my anger back. My shield. I can sit taller.

The screen door creaks open and claps closed. Dad sits next to me. He doesn't smell like sweat and raw metal mixed with Old Spice today, because he had to take off work to pick Mom up from the hospital.

Dad grabs my shoulders and turns my body toward him. "Rosey, you were the best part of my senior year."

I roll my eyes. "Sure, Dad."

"You were. When I held you for the first time, so tiny you could almost fit in my hand, I cried because I never felt so much love for anything in my entire life. I wouldn't change a thing. Not one damn thing." Dad wraps his huge arms around me. "I love you, Rosey, more than all the fish in the sea."

I press my cheek against his chest. He kisses the top of my head. His five-o'clock shadow itches as his breath warms my scalp.

He's my rock.

"Kristy's gonna go over what's happening next." Dad's rough fingertips graze my forehead as he brushes my bangs from my eyes. "You want to hear?"

Sniffling, I nod. I push myself to standing.

Mom watches me as I cut across the kitchen where I found her. Tears rimming her eyes, her lips part like she's going to say something, but then her head drops.

Hollis climbs back into my lap. He wraps his arms around my neck. His shaky breath tickles my throat. I hug him tight.

Grammy takes Sage's spot next to me. Menthol fills my nostrils.

"Rosey, I'm sorry. You came when your mom and dad were young, but you were the most loved baby in the whole world." Grammy squeezes my elbow, her palm rough from a lifetime of washing dishes in scalding water.

I sniffle and nod.

Kristy clears her throat. "Gundersen's hospital social worker hasn't been able to line anything up for you yet, Maureen."

"She gave me this." Mom hands Kristy the brochure. "But there's a wait list."

Kristy lets out a slow sigh as she shakes her head. She hands it back to Mom. "We'll keep working on that. For now, we've got a lot of stuff to talk about. Maureen, I know this isn't going to be easy to hear. But we need to know where we're at to know where to go."

Mom's chin trembles as she nods.

"I'll finish up my paperwork and complete the initial assessment in the next week or two. Then I'll file a CHIPS—a Child in Need of Protection or Services—petition with the court for all the kids. There will be a court hearing a few days after that. Probably do the initial appearance and the plea together since you're cooperating. You'll be facing the drug charges and charges for child neglect. The case against you will be substantiated."

Tears stream down Mom's cheeks.

And even after everything, I don't like seeing her cry. I fight to find my anger, but it slips through my fingers again.

Dad sucks in a sharp breath. He presses his fist to his forehead. But he doesn't move to comfort her.

"Maureen, you'll have a court order saying you have to do random drug tests and counseling, other stuff too. You might need to do some time."

Grammy's eyes shoot daggers as she shakes her head, visibly busting at the seams to speak.

"Like jail?" asks Sage.

Right, the kids didn't know that part.

"Mommy might go to jail? But that's where the bad guys go!" Vi squeaks.

"Don't you get it, stupid? She *is* a bad guy!" Sage screams. Dad's phone falls to the floor, screen up. The Minecraft block people are still moving around.

"Shut the hell up!" I yell at Sage.

Mom lets out a choked cry. All I can think about is Mr. Smith's stupid joke. The psychologist worrying about helping *the mugger* while the innocent dude is bleeding in the street.

Vi jumps to her feet. "You're not supposed to say stupid! That's what Mrs. Kennedy says!" She screams back so high-pitched it shreds my eardrums.

Hollis peels himself from me. He scoops up Vi and pulls her into his lap. She blubbers into Teddy. And now Mom is all alone, tiny and broken and sobbing in that chair.

I feel weightless and cold without Hollis.

Kristy clears her throat. "Your mother's not a bad guy, Sage. Being a drug addict isn't a moral failure, it's more like a chronic disease. Heroin changes how your brain works."

But if she wouldn't have taken heroin in the first place, none of this would have happened.

"Which is why, Maureen, you're the perfect candidate for drug court. You make your appearances, stay clean, and do the court-ordered therapy and meetings, you might be able to avoid jail. You consistently pass your drug tests, you may be able to get unsupervised time with the kids."

The brochure slips through Mom's fingers and lands on the brown, matted carpet.

"You'll have twelve months to get it together," Kristy continues, "or we can move to terminate parental rights."

Mom buries her face in her fists like the sorrowing old man in Van Gogh's *At Eternity's Gate*. Her wedding ring hangs looser than it used to.

"What does that mean?" The words slip past my lips.

Kristy's eyes move to me. Her gaze softens. "That the court feels it's in your best interest that Maureen no longer have custodial rights over you."

"Like she won't be our mom?" Hollis's arms fall from Vi.

My head is spinning, spinning, spinning. I'm a pop bottle tossed into the Gravitron at Butterfest. My skin itches and burns.

"Just that she can't take care of you anymore, or decide things for you."

"How does that affect Daryl?" Grammy asks as she tucks a cigarette between her lips.

"It doesn't. Daryl, you just need to follow the safety plan— make sure the kids aren't left unsupervised with Maureen, no drinking while you're watching the kids, and keep answering my phone calls. And, just so you know, Mindy, we'll be doing random home visits wherever the children are living."

"And I got no problem kicking Maureen out, if that's what

needs to be done," Grammy says around the cigarette pinched between her teeth.

Dad lets out an exasperated sigh as he presses his fingers to his forehead. "Mom."

I'm standing in her blood. Blue lips and a needle hanging out of her arm. Skin bone white.

I jump to my feet. "Then she'll just go live with fricking Jeremy over in that drug house with all the other junkie losers!" I shout at Grammy.

A strangled cry leaks through Mom's hands like I stabbed her.

"That's enough. Both of you!" Dad's on his feet shouting across the coffee table.

Sobs rack Mom's body. And I want her to spew meaningless apologies and promises she'll break in two days. But she doesn't say anything.

My rage dissipates like a puff of smoke. My knees go weak, and I fall back into the couch again.

"Give her a chance, Mindy," Kristy says quietly, almost pleading. "Daryl, how many days until you need to be out?"

Dad's chair creaks as he sits back down. "Two."

"Thanks to McKinney-Vento, Sage, Hollis, and Violet can continue to go to Lawrence Lawson for as long as you are looking for housing this year, and the school has to provide transportation. Rose, you'd go to the high school no matter what, but you'll ride the bus."

Ugh.

Dad stares at his hands draped between his knees. "How will the other kids get to school?"

"Taxi probably."

Mom and Dad exchange a glance for the first time in this whole lovely family meeting.

"Now I don't like that idea," Grammy says. "Donny drives for Sparta Taxi, and he's a pedophile."

Dad blows out a long breath. "But that's a lot of gas money. Maybe we should just send them to Cataract. It's where I went to school."

"But doesn't it go to only third grade?" Mom's voice comes out quiet and weak. It's only the third thing she's said this whole time.

"We wouldn't go to the same school?" Hollis's arms around Vi go limp as tears rim his eyes.

"I am not going to a new school!" Sage shrieks.

"And when we move back to Sparta, cuz I am not living in Cataract forever, you're going to make them change schools *again*?" I say.

Mom's hands tighten in her lap.

"We can get you a couple gas cards." Kristy scribbles on her yellow notepad. "Can't promise it'll be a regular thing, but at least to start off."

"Thank you." Dad gets up and shakes her hand.

"Why don't we take a quick tour, then I'll be on my way."

I checked every room before school; that's about all I can control. Still my hands shake as I pull out my phone and check Instagram. Rafa tagged me. I press it. He posted a picture of our mural.

The caption:

@RoseMarie and I created a masterpiece of Rivera and
Kahlo proportions.

It has thirteen likes. I skim the comments. A few are in Spanish, but then I see comments from his two besties.

FutureCristianoRonaldo: Stop painting that creepy shit and
ditch that basurero.

GoddessShaiti: Glad you're still alive and still have A PHONE.
Rafa . . . I cannot with these freshman in Latino Student Union.

Another comment pops up.

Seraphina Abramsson Official: Painting on a window like that
takes true talent.

Oh my God. She publicly acknowledged me. And appreciated
my art. I cannot contain a smile, even after that family meeting. I
like her comment.

"Good luck with the move," Kristy says as she walks back into
the living room. Dad, Mom, and Grammy trail behind. Grammy's
ready to spit nails.

"And I'll get those gas cards," Kristy says as she tucks her
notepad into her computer bag.

"Thank you, Kristy." Dad takes her hand in both of his and
shakes again.

"Thank you," Mom mumbles to the floor, face half-sheathed
in her long hair.

Is that what I look like when I hide behind my bangs? It's
almost enough to inspire me to never do it again.

The door clicks closed behind Kristy. It's like some extrater-
restrial being pressed pause on the whole room. Mom's trembling
chin is the only thing that moves. The only sounds filling the void
are the humming box fan and the annoying music from Sage's
game, still on the floor. The apple bowl clock that we've had probably since I was born is gone now.

No one says anything. Not "I've missed you" or "I hate you"

or "I love you" or "I'm sorry" or "It'll never happen again." Mom just stands there in a puddle of tears.

A tiny part of me wants to say something—anything—to break the silence. Because right now the elephant fills every square inch of the house, asphyxiating us all.

But the only thing my brain can think to say is happy birthday, and my mouth is choked with cotton, and I can't even remember the last time I told her I love her.

Mom will be in court soon. What if she does go to jail? Or what if she gets into treatment next week and climbs up from the bottom of the pit she's fallen into? But what if she relapses? Tears blur the coffee table with the splotch of pink nail polish. What if she overdoses again and dies this time?

Can't someone say *something*?

My fingers fail to grasp onto any tiny shreds of anger, so I clench my little folded triangle instead.

Rafa. The game. And the kiddos are all staring glassy-eyed at the floor.

Something I can control. I pull a Grammy and say it like it is. "I'm taking the kids to the homecoming game."

Dad drags his head up. He squints at me. "You serious?"

"Yep. My friend Rafa can give us a ride."

A smile twitches on Mom's lips.

Sage prostrates at Dad's feet. "Please, please, please!"

Vi skips around the couch. "I'm going to be a cheerleader."

Hollis jumps up. "I want to see the halftime show."

Dad and Grammy exchange a look while Mom twists that brochure in her hands again. Some of the ink is rubbing off.

"Well, I suppose the kiddos'll probably make a bigger mess than they're helping," Grammy says.

"Okay, then." Dad throws his hands up, but he's smiling a

little too.

"Here, let me give you some money for concessions." Grammy digs in her purse and hands me a twenty. I fight back the urge to hand it directly to Dad for our new place.

I message Rafa on Instagram. The flashing ellipsis pops up instantly, like he's been sitting there with the app open. I bite in a smile.

Rafa: Give me like 15.

"Maureen, let's run to the dump again," Dad says. Mom's shoulders practically drag on the floor as they leave.

As soon as the door claps closed, we all can finally take a breath.

"Well, I'm gonna get started on cleaning that kitchen," Grammy says. "Clearly Maureen hasn't touched it in ages."

"Dad is perfectly capable of cleaning too," I say.

"Maureen ain't had a job in months," Grammy fires back.

And I have no retort, especially since I shocked myself with my quasi-defense of her.

"Hey, you guys gotta show your school spirit for homecoming," Sage says. "Wear red and yellow."

"I got a Badgers shirt," Hollis says.

"And I know where Vi's Minnie Mouse shirt is," Sage says. She eyeballs me.

I roll my eyes. "Please, I don't own red."

"Yes, you do." Hollis darts for our room.

Then I remember we have a roll of yellow streamers in the junk drawer from Sage's sixth birthday. I dig it out. Hollis skips into the living room holding up my faded red eighth-grade marching band polo like it's a Super Bowl trophy with the biggest grin I've seen on his face in months. He's drowning in Dad's old Badgers shirt.

"No. Just no," I say.

Sage and Vi race in wearing their red shirts too.

"You gotta wear red." Vi plants her hands on her hips as her chin juts out.

"Or what?"

Sage pounces first and wriggles her fingers into my armpits.

"Ah, stop!" I cry between giggles.

Then Hollis gets the backs of my knees. My secret ticklish spot. Vi goes for my stomach.

I'm laughing so hard tears roll down my cheek. Breathless, I concede defeat. I change into the stiff, musty band shirt that's been buried at the bottom of our closet forever, then tie streamers around their heads like Rambo bandannas.

And I feel surprisingly okay.

Chapter 15

"He's here!" Hollis climbs down from his post on the kitchen chair by the window. Teddy lays abandoned all the way on the couch.

Butterflies dance in my stomach. "Thanks for taking care of Vi today," I say to Hollis as we walk down the sidewalk toward Rafa's ancient van.

He grins. "I was just trying to be strong and brave like you."

Brave? Me? "I'm scared too."

"You are?" He looks at me like I'm Captain America.

"That's what it means to be brave. Doing something even though you're scared." Holy crap, where did that wisdom come from?

Hollis ponders, then nods. He walks taller.

"Love you, Holly." I pull him in and kiss into his mop of hair.

He crushes me into a hug. "Love you too."

Rafa gets out of the van and jogs up to us.

"Everyone, this is Rafa. Rafa, this is Sage and Hollis." I tap each on the head in order. "And I'm sure you remember Vi."

"Is he your boyfriend?" Sage looks him over.

Rafa smirks. "And I thought you were the Queen of Bluntness, Rose."

"Apparently it's genetic."

"So I guess the real question is, where's your yellow bandanna?" Rafa pokes my arm. Heat spreads from where he touched.

"Coming from the guy wearing a black shirt to a red-and-yellow team's homecoming game." I play punch his arm.

"Yeah, and Tomah's colors are black and yellow," Sage says.

"Good thing I don't have a yellow bandanna, then." Rafa winks.

Sage laughs.

Rafa helps Vi and Sage into his sisters' booster seats. Then he looks Hollis over. "You're tall enough you don't need one, right?"

And that may be one of the sweetest questions I've ever heard someone ask.

Hollis looks to me.

"You'll be fine." I tuck a few tufts of hair back under his streamer bandanna.

Beaming, Hollis climbs past the girls into the back.

I get into the front seat. "God, it's like we're Mom and Dad heading off on a road trip."

"Crap, if I'd a known, I'd a googled some Dad jokes."

"I think that just was one."

Rafa shoots me a wide dimpled grin.

"But seriously"—I glance back at the kiddos—"thanks for doing this."

"Guess you're lucky the space bike museum is closed." He starts the van.

God, he's kind of perfect.

"Okay, so where do they even play football games here?" Rafa asks over his shoulder.

"Memorial Park!" Sage busts out.

Rafa puts on some pop music, and the kiddos, even Hollis, are dancing in their seats. Rafa taps along on the steering wheel.

I direct Rafa there, texting Gretchen on the way. The clouds have been vanquished by evening sun dripping melted butter over the houses. Memorial Park's parking lots are clogged with cars—the entire student body and half of Sparta must be here. At least Walmart won't be too busy, seeing as two of its fastest cashiers are here. Tomah's bus is already parked in front of the public pool. On their windows in black and yellow is "Suck it Sparta." Clearly they didn't appreciate Omar and the football team's goalpost decorations.

Rafa cops a spot by the ancient brick building that used to be an orphanage. Probably starting next week, kids from the Boys & Girls Club will transform it into a haunted house like every year. Maybe the kiddos will get to help, thanks to Kristy. Sage would love it.

I take Vi's hand as we cut across the parking lot with a hoard of middle schoolers garnished with patches of red-and-yellow temporary hair color spray. The ends of the kiddos' streamer bandannas flutter in the light breeze. The air buzzes around us with laughter and conversations. Music blares from car speakers. The smell of freshly popping popcorn wafts from the concession stand. Stadium lights beat back the twilight.

A few kids wearing black-and-yellow letter jackets jog past us.

"Go get your people." I give Rafa a playful shove with my free hand.

Rafa shines a smile at me. "I'm with my people."

That lights up my whole body.

As we close in on the fence around the stadium, Sage and Hollis belt out, "Sparta High, Sparta High, that's the school we're standing by. And we'll boost you, we'll boost you along!"

Vi doesn't know the words, so she shakes her little butt; it's pretty adorable. I grip her hand tighter until our feet touch grass. I spot Gretchen's white drum majorette uniform through the garment bags hanging from the fence. We flow with the crowd to the small, red-roofed Gridiron Club Fieldhouse—"Home of the Spartans" according to the sign on the side. Since it's homecoming, the ticket windows are shuttered. Free admission, meaning more candy money.

Loud voices echo around us in the tiny red-and-white hallway. Stadium lights backlight the cutout letters over the gate on the other side: Spartans spelled backward. In one of the display cases, I spot Dad's tiny picture from his senior year, flashing his million dollar grin in the same football uniform the players wear tonight. The headline: "Hemmersbach smashes Sparta record for most completions in a single game."

What would have happened if Dad had been able to take that football scholarship to UW-Stout? Guilt pinches my gut.

No. He said he wouldn't change a damn thing. I shake it from my head.

We emerge into the cooler night again. A huge fiberglass statue of Sparky the Spartan threatens us with his drawn sword as I hand the twenty to Hollis. "One candy each. And we'll be sitting in the band section."

He nods solemnly and takes it like I'm handing him the *Mona Lisa*.

"I'm getting M&M's. They're the best," Sage says as they head for the concession stand under the stadium. Now she holds Vi's hand.

"You can get M&M's anytime. But you can't get Fun Dip at Walmart," Hollis says.

"Well, I'm gonna have Baby Ruth!" Vi says.

"Gross!" Sage and Hollis cry.

Candy can be pretty damn important.

Rafa strokes his chin. "I gotta agree with Hollis."

"Ugh, no. It's too messy," I say as we head for Gretchen in the sea of red uniform jackets. "Baby Ruth all the way."

"Seriously?" Rafa wrinkles his nose. "Now I can't talk to you anymore." His hand slips around mine. Warm bubbles fill my chest. "By the way," he glances back at Sparky, "yours looks way more badass."

I laugh. "Yeah. That Sparky's skirt belongs on a cheerleader."

As we navigate the obstacle course of black hatboxes littering the grass, the cacophony of band people in various states of dress warming up their instruments surrounds us. A few color guard girls twirl their red, gold, and black flags.

"Get ready for the most amazing rendition of 'Bulls on Parade' ever," Gretchen says as she rams her red feather plume into her white hat. Today she wears her red glasses to complement her uniform.

"You guys are not doing Rage Against the Machine," I say.

"Oh, we are. I saw to it." She winks at me. "No 'Build Me Up, Buttercup' this year."

I laugh. "That alone makes coming to this game worthwhile."

"This year, the band will outshine both the cheerleaders and the football team as they plummet into defeat like every other homecoming ever."

"Defeat is not certain this year, *fräulein*," Anderson says in a crappy German accent as he buttons up his red-and-white uniform jacket. The stadium lights reflect off his glasses. "Thanks to this *herr*'s brother." He claps Rafa on the back.

Rafa squints at him. "Who are you?"

Switching to an Australian accent, he holds out a hand and says, "G'day, how ya going, mate? I'm Anderson."

Eyebrow raised, Rafa shakes his hand. "Rafa. Knock 'em dead, or whatever you band people do."

"We march around like we have drumsticks shoved up our *Ärsche*," says Anderson as he plugs the mouthpiece into his trumpet.

"In formation," Gretchen says through the reed she's sucking on. "And your German accent's the worst."

"Yeah, stick to British." I turn to Rafa. "Anderson here aspires to be an audiobook narrator."

"Didn't know that was a life path," Rafa says.

"They even have their own version of the Oscars called the Audie Awards." Anderson blows a short blast into his trumpet.

"Don't get him started." Gretchen rolls her eyes.

"Don't slam my passion," Anderson says.

Anderson and Gretchen start pretend jousting with their respective instruments.

"Band geeks are so weird," Rafa whispers, so close his voice vibrates my eardrum. I can smell mint on his breath.

I cup my hands and whisper back, "At least us art geeks don't have to wear feathers on our heads."

Rafa chuckles. His fingers curl around mine. Gravel crunches under our feet as we head to the band section. The kiddos catch us as we climb the stairs to the bleachers.

"I want to sit by Rosey!" erupts Vi.

"No, we're sitting here," says Hollis as he points to the bottom bleacher. "Rosey needs some privacy."

"So she can kiss her boyfriend!" Sage makes kissy faces.

"Shut up, Sage." I smack her arm as heat blooms across my face. I catch Rafa grinning at me, and I know exactly why, which just makes my face burn hotter.

Sage sticks her tongue out as she drags Vi next to Hollis.

Hollis is rising. Maybe so is Sage.

Rafa and I end up sandwiched between Gretchen and some freshman band girl who looks very confused by my faded middle school band shirt.

Us in a sea of red as our thighs touch. Bugs swarm the buzzing stadium lights over us. Orange goal post streamers gently twist in the breeze. Kimmy, Kenzie, Carolyn, and the rest of the cheerleaders launch into that "Alligator, Alligator, Eat 'Em Up" cheer in front of the bleachers next to us.

From in front of the stands, Mr. Paulson belts out "Final Countdown" and flails his conductor baton. Gretchen, freshman girl, and all the other people around us stand, knocking Rafa and I together. The band bursts into a deafening out-of-tune rendition. The pages of freshman saxophone player's marching band folio music holder flap in my ear. Through a gap in red uniforms, I spot Sage dipping her finger into Hollis's Fun Dip as he dumps some of her M&M's into his mouth. Vi's flapping a little pom-pom around with so much gusto I can't even question where she got it. I grin.

The music dies, and the girl's saxophone bumps my thigh as she sits.

"Sparta Spartans!" roars through the speakers. "Are you ready to roll over the Timberwolves?"

Everyone around us jumps to their feet and screams. Rafa and I make eye contact. Grinning, he jumps up and screams. And now I have to too. The roar of our side drowns out the boos of the smaller stand on the Away side, even though Tomah's three-deep along the fence too.

Mr. Paulson cues up the school song. A kid I don't know pounds on the quads from the front row. Sharp snare beats reverberate in my chest. Toby on the tuba blares right behind us as we walk down the sidewalk toward Rafa's ancient van.

The cheerleaders form a red-white-and-yellow miniskirt tunnel, shaking their pom-poms over their heads. It must be VP QB Mike who dives through a huge red paper circle held by the water boys, followed by the rest of the team in their red-and-yellow uniforms and helmets. Omar brings up the rear. I'm only sure it's him because he's small compared to the rest of the team, and he's the only kid who isn't white. He saunters onto the field raising his hands up and down. Our side breaks into explosive cheers. Mike and Eisenhardt—I can tell because only he'd wear tropical-themed football cleats—clap him on the back.

Anderson leans around Gretchen and says in his actual voice, "How long has he been playing?"

"About a month and a half," Rafa says.

Anderson's jaw drops.

"All he has to do is hold onto the ball, run fast, and dodge. He learned that playing real fútbol—soccer," Rafa mutters to me as he watches Omar and the rest of the team jog to the sidelines.

We all sit as the game starts. Rafa's staring at his hands. I dig in my pocket and pull out my medal. I hold it out on an open palm.

He shakes his head. "Please."

"Hey, I survived my shit today. Your turn."

Glancing at me, he takes it. "How'd it all go?"

"Haven't decided."

His fingers close around the medal. "So that's a nice shirt you've got there. Didn't think you owned anything but black."

"The sacrifices we make for kids."

"When did you quit the life of a band geek?" His arm presses into mine.

I stare across the field at the sea of black and yellow. "Freshman year, when I imploded. After I found out about Mom's . . .

217

extracurriculars."

He nods once as he stares across the field too. "Confession time."

I raise an eyebrow.

"I was in show choir freshman year."

"Really?" I try to picture Rafa with a cheesy smile and bow tie doing jazz hands.

"Scout's honor." He holds up a hand.

"Sing for me, then."

Rafa lets out an embarrassed-sounding laugh. "Did you know if you say 'watermelon' on repeat it looks like you're singing everything?"

"So if you didn't sing, why were you even in it?"

"My 'girlfriend'"—he throws in air quotes—"freshman year. And the air quotes are cuz all we ever did was group dates."

"Ha, sounds like my freshman dating life. Josh and I were frequently a part of the three rows of obnoxiousness at the Sparta Cinema."

Rafa's face scrunches. "You and *Josh*?"

"Shut up, Jazz Hands." I try to laugh it off, but it falls flat.

"Carajo. You're never gonna let me forget. Just don't tell Ashlee, or she'll do it at me every time I'm ringing up a customer." Rafa leans his shoulder against mine. His smile sags. "Josh is such a cookie cutter jock. Doesn't seem your type, but I guess I never knew Pink Rose."

"Maybe she would have been a cheerleader tonight." I don't have any nail polish left, so I pick at a string hanging from the tear in my jeans.

Rafa's fingers weave into my fingers. He pulls my hand to his knee. "Good thing I like art geeks."

"Touchdown, number twenty-three!"

The crowd goes wild. Sage cues Hollis and Vi to cheer. Rafa jumps to his feet, eyes on the end zone.

Omar spikes the ball, rips off his helmet, and chucks it at the ground, then shakes his tiny ass at the Tomah stands.

Our crowd goes wild. "Go, Paco!" some guy—a sophomore, I think—shouts from the front row a few people away from the kiddos.

Rafa's fists clench as his jaw tightens. He climbs past Gretchen and Anderson to the center aisle and heads for the bleacher stairs.

"Hey, wait!" I call, but he probably can't hear me over the lingering cheers. I scramble past Gretchen.

"Go get 'em, Tiger!" She smacks my ass so hard it stings, but my eyes stay locked on Rafa.

"His name is Omar!" Rafa shouts at the guy. Dude stares at Rafa's back slack-jawed. I hop off the last stair and follow.

"Rosey, you okay?" Hollis calls as I pass.

"Fine, just watch the kiddos."

He nods like I told him to save the world.

As I jump off the bottom bleacher stairs, I spot Omar on the sidelines. All the football players are pushing him and cheering.

I find Rafa behind the bleachers pacing like a caged bear.

"Hey," I say as I walk up to him.

Rafa stops. He glances at me, then shakes his head. Crap, what if he wants to be alone?

"He doesn't even care when people call him that," Rafa spits through is teeth. "Just laughs it off."

The band launches into "Party Rock Anthem," muted by the bleachers and bodies above us.

I sit on the cement base of a bleacher post. Coolness seeps through my jeans.

Rafa sits next to me. He leans back against the post. Our

shoulders meet. Stadium lights spill patches of light onto the dirt at our feet through cracks in the bleachers and legs over us. Empty pop bottles, stray popcorn, and candy wrappers litter the ground around us. People wearing Sparta and Tomah school colors walk by, but under the bleachers we're in our own special world.

"We played in this Mexican soccer league since we could walk." His shoulder blade vibrates against mine as he talks. "I've always been jealous of his fútbol skills. I think too hard instead of trusting my instincts. But Omar, he made varsity his freshman year."

I think back to that Instagram picture of them together, grinning in their soccer uniforms.

"But we move here, I can't even join the soccer team because I don't have time—and trust me, I'd look like Messi, I've seen them practice—but then Omar chooses football?"

"What's with that?" I crunch a clump of dirt under my toe.

"Luis told him only losers play soccer here, and he wants to be *el mero mero*. Because he was nothing special back at South Division." Rafa kicks at a rock buried in the dirt, soiling his pristine Air Jordan. "The night before we drove to this shitty town in the middle of nowhere." His eyes jump to me. "No offense. Anyway, we made a pact that we'd be in this together. But the first day, he's off with all his new football friends."

I turn my body toward him. Our thighs touch.

"And meanwhile, you're the one working at Walmart to pay for your mom's medication and helping your parents."

Rafa's eyebrows arch. He lets out a long sigh through his nostrils. "I mean, all that, yeah, it sucks. But I'm the oldest. That's how it is in my culture. Family first. And I want to support Omar. He's *mi sangre,* my blood until the end. But I don't even know him anymore."

"So your brother doesn't exactly seem like the King of Maturity here. Does he realize he's being a grade A dick?"

"Probably not."

"Tell him."

Rafa brushes the dirt off his shoe. "Gotta maintain the peace."

"The elephant. Yeah, know about that."

"Elephant?"

"When everyone pretends everything's cool, but it's not. In my family, it crushes us all. Sounds like, in yours, you're trying to carry it all by yourself. And how's that working for you? Clearly not super well if your mom's desperate for you to have a friend."

Rafa crushes the medal in his fist as he shifts away from me.

Shit, maybe I went too far. I hide behind my bangs.

He exhales slowly. "Well, guess you just proved you're the Queen of Bluntness."

"Yeah . . . I get it from Grammy apparently."

I peek at him through my bangs. Our eyes meet.

"Maybe you have a point," he says.

———

Sparta wins the homecoming game for the first time in a decade, thanks in large part to Omar's three touchdowns.

As Rafa drives us home, Vi's passed out with her pom-pom precariously close to slipping from her loose fingers, but Sage and Hollis are all hopped-up on sugar and belting the school song on repeat. "For it's hi, hi, hee! It's Sparta High for me. Shout out your colors loud and strong. Red gold!"

"Well, at least now I know the words." Rafa winks at me.

I laugh.

Rafa pulls to a stop in front of the home we'll have for less than two more days. Both Grammy's car and our pickup sit parked in the driveway. And crap's just piled on the curb again. Light from the humming streetlamp spills light through the tree onto the sign that says "free." Mom's handwriting this time. A baby crib, Mom and Dad's dresser, Dad's now-empty gun case, that copper bald eagle table lamp Grammy gave us when we first moved in, boxes of books and blankets. Sage's throne.

The car falls silent.

Warmth envelopes my hand—Rafa's palm against mine.

"Um, thanks for the ride." My hand slides out of his. I grab Gretchen's dress from in between us, then peel Vi out of the booster seat. Her limp, sweaty body drapes against me.

Rafa gets out. "Here, let me carry the dress." He jogs around the van and takes the garment bag from me.

"Thanks," Hollis mutters to Rafa as he climbs out. He rips off his streamer bandanna and drops it into the gutter. Sage drags her feet behind us.

Our front door pops open, spilling light and shadow across the grass. Dad's huge form fills the doorway, a silhouette against the brightness. As he takes Vi from me, I'm almost knocked over by the stench of his sweat. But I don't smell any beer on him, even though we've been gone for hours and he's allowed to drink when he's not watching us.

"Thanks." Dad gives Rafa the dude nod he never once gave Justin.

Rafa hands me the dress. "Well, they won for apparently the first time in forever. Maybe I'm a good luck charm."

A smile fights to crack Dad's face. "Rosey tell you I was the quarterback back in the day?"

"No, sir."

Then Mom peeks past Dad's shoulder. Her cheeks are flushed,

potential evidence that she's been working hard too.

"Hi, ma'am." Rafa gives a little wave. "Nice to meet you, Mrs. Hemmersbach."

Mom's gaze drops. "Nice to meet you too."

And now Rafa's seen her. That punctures a hole in my happiness and collapses my chest. The garment bag crinkles as I hug it.

"C'mon, kiddos. It's time for bed," I mutter.

Rafa peels one of my hands from the garment bag and presses something into my palm. The medal, now a little damp from his palm sweat. His eyes search mine. "See you tomorrow?"

My shoulders wilt. "I'll let you know."

His fingers tighten around my fist. "If you can't, I'll IG Live them announcing it, so you'll practically be there."

"Okay, cool."

I pull my fist free and head inside. As soon as I close the door, I'm surrounded by an overpowering smell of lemon cleaning product.

The kitchen literally glistens, even the inside of the open, empty fridge. The counters are bare, and the cabinets are open and empty too. The kitchen table and chairs are gone. When I was like thirteen, I stuck a bunch of glow-in-the-dark stars under the table. Hollis and I used to charge them with flashlights, then turn off the lights and pretend we were under the stars. Now I don't know if our stars are in storage or at the dump.

The garment bag slips through my arms and falls to the ground.

"Randy better give you the security deposit back," Grammy spits past the unlit cigarette clenched between her lips as she scrubs the baseboards under the cabinets. Had she found any more blood?

"We're not sleeping here tonight, are we?" I say.

Dad hoists Vi a little higher. "It's easier if you guys stay with Grammy this weekend."

That steals the breath from me.

"So I don't get to sleep in my room ever again." Sage's voice doesn't even sound angry. It trembles.

Mom presses her fingers to her forehead.

Grammy groans as she stands, then tries to hug Sage.

"No! Don't touch me!" she shrieks, and bats her away.

I take Sage into my arms. She presses her face into my stomach. I tuck my fingers into her bob and rub the back of her head. Her yellow bandanna falls off.

"What's this?" Grammy's knees crackle as she kneels and unzips the garment bag. Inside is a seafoam-green dress. "This for homecoming?"

I can't abandon the kiddos tomorrow. Not when we've just officially become homeless. Tears burn my eyes. "Nothing!"

Mom's fingers fall from her face. Her blue-green eyes are clear and focused. So she hasn't lurked off and shot up yet. "Rosey . . ."

"No!" I shout, and storm for my room. The couch is gone. Did they even take a second to check under the cushions for treasure? They sure as shit didn't give Vi a chance to. I slam my door probably for the last time. The sound ricochets through the house like a gunshot.

The walls are empty; darker rectangles spot the wall where my paintings hung—archeological proof that I was once here.

My medal slips through my fingers.

Our empty dresser drawers hang open. My clothes have been packed in clear plastic tubs. My easel's been taken apart and tossed into a paper shopping bag with my brushes, blank canvases, and paints. All of my paintings sit in a box. *Mother's Love* lays on top of *Justin in My Mind*. If only I could travel back to when that was my biggest problem. I snap the frame over my knee, relish the burst of pain, and drop the carcass on the floor.

I curl into a ball in the spot where my bed once was and dissolve.

A knock comes on the door. "Rosey?" Dad calls.

"Screw off!"

"Now, Rosey, we're not doing this." Dad opens the door and comes in. He towers over me. "You're going tomorrow night, and that's final."

"Oh, I'm sorry, Dad, but pretty sure the entire world is falling apart around us. I'm not getting turned into a Barbie doll and going to a stupid dance."

Mom grips the doorframe.

At least she's not shooting up to numb the pain and guilt yet. Cuz none of the rest of us can.

Dad sits next to me with a grunt. "Now, Rosey, I know you're not a kid, but I won't take homecoming away from you."

I roll my eyes. "This place needs to be packed and cleaned, and *someone's* gotta be with the kids."

Grammy comes in too. "I ain't working tomorrow. And Maureen, you can clean this whole damn place tomorrow. Least you can do."

Mom's shoulders shrivel like dying daffodils. A tear drips from her chin.

And I grit my teeth. Do you have to be *such* a bitch, Grammy?

"Mom, that ain't helpful." Dad runs a hand through his sweaty, tangled mass of hair. Dad says. "She's worked her ass off today, even though the doctors said she needs to take it easy."

Grammy chomps down on her unlit cigarette.

Mom brushes her tears away and drops to her knees. She picks up my medal. "What's this?"

"That's mine." I crawl across the floor and take it from her. My fingers almost brush hers. The medal is still damp, and now the blue lines are smearing. I'm not sure if it's sweat from my hand or Rafa's. Rafa . . . That shy, awkward smile on his face as he asked me to go with him.

I want to be there with him in that seafoam-green dress. I fold into a ball against the barren wall again, pressing my medal to my forehead.

"You can go to a dance for a few hours, and Grammy's house will still be standing. You're going tomorrow night, Rosey." Dad declares with certainty as rock-solid as opening weekend for gun deer hunting being the weekend before Thanksgiving.

"Fine. Whatever." I get up. But a tiny piece of my heart soars. And I feel a little guilty.

Mom withdraws when I'm ten feet from my door. I don't look back as I walk through the living room, the kitchen, and out the front door. Maybe I'll regret it someday, because this could be my last time in this house, but I just can't.

Grammy makes me sit in the front seat because legally I'm the only one old enough, so—just like the ride in the cop car after Mom's overdose—I can't even comfort the kiddos crying in the back seat. Her car smells exactly the same as I remember, menthols mixed with vanilla. As she drives away, Mom and Dad, draped in shadow, watch from the doorway. As if God wanted to perfectly frame this heartbreaking moment, rain speckles Grammy's windshield.

"It's just a building. Home is where your family is." Grammy rolls down her window. Cool, moist air leaks in. She lights the cigarette pinched between her lips, draws in a puff, and blows it out the window. The stink of menthol laces around me.

"I want Mommy!" Vi sobs.

"It's all her fault you're homeless." Grammy sucks on her cigarette.

Hollis presses his face into Teddy and lets out a choked cry.

"You know, Grammy, she already feels guilty enough!" I snap. "Shaming her even more isn't going to help her get better."

Grammy's brows arch as her cigarette almost drops from her lips.

As we leave Sparta behind, it's a black hole outside because there's no streetlights, no moon, no stars. Just the headlights reflecting off the white line paint a few feet ahead of us, glowing through drops of rain. I watch the rivulets running down the window, distorting the black silhouettes of trees whizzing by.

An oncoming car crests a hill, its high-beams blasting us. I squint against the brightness.

"Turn off your brights, asshole!" Grammy flicks her high-beams at the car. The inside of our car dims as they switch to their low-beams. The sound of tires squelching on wet pavement fills the silence as the car passes.

Grammy blows another puff of smoke out her cracked window. "You know, Rosey, you're wise beyond your years. You got that from me too."

"Thanks," I say. And I kind of mean it. I tuck in my earbuds and stream Sigur Rós, then message Gretchen and Rafa.

Gretchen: I'm picking you up at eight in the morning to start the transformation.

Her insta-response suggests she's been waiting with bated breath for my response.

RoseMarie: I'm at Grammy's up in Cataract. You can transform me up here.

Gretchen: Okay, what's the address?

Maybe I can tell her about the whole eviction thing tomorrow. I check Instagram again. I have a message.

Rafa: You made my week, Queen of Bluntness.

Even though I'm kind of officially homeless, I can still smile.

RoseMarie: You made mine too.

I check my feed.

Aunt Colleen posted a picture of herself releasing a floating lantern up into a void of blackness filled with dozens of glowing lanterns. She's the picture of beauty as she watches the sky in wonder.

The caption:

It's amazing how much love you can find, even when you're all alone. Especially in Chiang Mai, Thailand.

Vi lets out a cute little mewl from the back seat. Hollis strokes golden curls from her cheeks as he stares out the window. His profile is starting to look so much like lady-killer Dad's back in the day. Sage holds Vi's hand.

And I'm just so overwhelmed with love for all of them.

Aunt Colleen's not alone. She has all of us. We've been here all along. Does she even know about the kiddos? She hasn't asked about them, so maybe she doesn't. I don't think Mom and Dad have talked to her in like a decade. And how could you *not* want to know them?

I snap a picture of them in the back seat and edit the photo to make it brighter.

RoseMarie: Did you know about my brother and sisters? Hollis is 9 and he's the sweetest boy ever. Sage (8) is a punk, but she's strong and brave. Violet (5) is so silly and cute. They'd love to meet you too.

I send her the picture.

I clench the medal in my fist. All I can grasp onto is the promise of tomorrow.

Chapter 16

The next morning, Gretchen shows up at 8:00 a.m. on the dot. Grammy lets us set up shop in her bedroom so we can have a semblance of privacy. She brings us plates of warm snickerdoodles and fawns over us during our horror movie fest while Gretchen accosts me with curling irons and bobby pins and probably a whole bottle of hairspray. For makeup, just a dab of silver eye shadow and light mascara. Now my eyes look huge. Cleocatra watches the whole thing unfold with a bored disregard only a cat can manage.

Freshman year, before Rose split in two, I'd been 99 percent sure what's-his-name, the upper classman who'd been flirting with me in band, was going to ask me to homecoming. Mom even started planning a dress shopping trip to Eau Claire and how to do my hair and make-up. For Tim's wedding and my eighth grade completion ceremony, Mom had turned me into a work of art. Freshman year, I couldn't wait to see what she'd do for homecoming.

But then . . . the Big Fight.

Almost three years ago today when the truth came out. Mom had been hauling Vi to drug dealers' houses to buy poison and then shoot it up her veins in front of Vi. Before then, I'd noticed there were times when Mom seemed really tired and acted kind of weird, but Vi wasn't sleeping much, and Dad had just gotten arrested for that DUI. I'd had no idea.

But now that I'm actually going to homecoming, a teensy piece of me wishes Mom was here to orchestrate my transformation.

As the clock ticks to 6:30 p.m., Gretchen pulls me through the tiny kitchen to the front door.

Grammy pauses *The Lion King*. "Well, Rosey, you look very nice. Don't she, kiddos?"

I feel like an alien.

Vi squeezes me so tight it forces the air from my lungs. "You look like a mermaid Barbie princess."

Gretchen did her hair today, too, and gave her some pink eyeshadow. "Well, you look like a princess yourself, Vi Pie." I kiss the hairspray-sticky top of her head.

Sage and Hollis watch me too. Guilt digs in its claws. This is so selfish.

"I won't let anything happen to them." Grammy squeezes my shoulder. "Now here's your donation to get in free. Lord knows I ain't got anywhere to put all that food your dad bought." Grammy chuckles and hands me a bag of canned goods.

"Holly, you take care of Vi, okay?" The bag handles cut into my palm as I lean over to stroke his soft cheek.

He sits up straight and nods.

"What about me?" Sage pouts.

"Help Grammy with the air mattress."

"Chica, we're going to be late!" Gretchen pushes me toward the door. The bag of cans clatters against my leg.

Outside, the encroaching night is warm and filled with the smell of Grammy's neighbor burning garbage in a barrel. I've kind of missed that smell. The creek Mom and I used to go frog hunting in tinkles behind the trailer.

The sound of tires crunching gravel grows louder as the Chevy emerges from the tall, skinny pine trees. Mom and Dad are both inside. Dad pulls to a stop next to Grammy's car. As they climb out, some twangy, upbeat country song plays quietly from his radio. Their clothes are filthy. Mom pulls her hair out of its disheveled ponytail as she walks across the grass toward us.

Dad lets out a long, loud whistle. "Rosey, you look beautiful. So different."

"Thanks to Gretchen."

Gretchen stands next to me clutching her kitty bowler purse full of Rose transformation tools to her chest like armor. Apparently she's found something fascinating in the grass.

"That dress is the perfect color for you, Rosey. You look so much like Colleen." Mom's voice comes out quiet, like an apology.

I glance up at her.

Mom's lips press into a tremulous smile. She's too far away to smell for Jeremy's secondhand smoke, but her eyes are focused, and her pupils aren't pinprick tiny. So she's still clean. For the moment.

But then her lips turn blue. Her skin goes sallow.

Pump, hiss, pump, hiss, pump, hiss.

No pulse. I almost lost her.

I squeeze my eyes closed. My throat tightens as I hug my arms to my chest. The sequined bodice scratches my skin.

"I ever tell you about my senior homecoming, Rosey?" Dad cuts in.

My eyes pop open and we're surrounded by towering pine

trees again.

I clear the tightness from my throat. "You were the home-coming king and Mom was the queen and you threw seven touch-downs to beat Tomah."

"Yeah, that was back before people got so uppity about being PC and they were the Tomah Indians. I tell you me, Travis, and Tim snuck over to Tomah and burned 'Tomah sucks' into their football field with gas? Made the *La Crosse Tribune* even, and we never got caught." Dad guffaws.

"Only about ten hundred times, Dad."

"What about you, Gretchen?" Dad asks.

"Yes, Mr. H," Gretchen mutters. Finally she looks up, but she's now found something interesting in the pine tree over us.

"Daryl, they got a dance to go to," Mom mumbles.

"Yeah, we better go." Gretchen practically bolts for her Prius. As I pass, Mom says, "Have fun, Rosey."

In Mom's back jeans pocket is the folded brochure for that treatment place.

Her arm twitches like maybe she wants to take my hand and weave her pinky around mine. Our special way of holding hands that she never did with any of the other kiddos. Part of me wants her to. But my hand is too heavy to lift so instead I grab a fistful of my dress because I don't have a pocket for my medal.

"Thanks," I say to her over my shoulder before I pull Gretch-en's car door closed.

As Gretchen speeds down the long driveway, she fumbles on her phone for her perfect homecoming playlist. Gretchen couldn't even look at Mom. She can't stare into the abyss like Rafa. But it's a pretty deep abyss, so it's a pretty big ask.

"Okay, even you'll appreciate the first song!" Gretchen chirps with forced cheeriness. Her shoulders visibly relax after we turn onto Highway 27.

Some upbeat Linkin Park song fills the car.

"It's not the worst," I say.

I rest my forehead against the window. Milkweed pots bursting with white fluff and dying Queen Anne's lace curling in on itself sprout through yellow bird's-foot trefoil. Mom taught me all their names.

This is the longest she's been clean since she started using. And this time, there hasn't been any begging for forgiveness, self-deprecating apologies, or grand promises to never use again.

The brochure in her pocket . . .

This time is different. Because if you almost die, something has to change. It has to. Like that dove in her painting, escaping from the blackness. And I cannot deny her love for us, her desperation to have us back.

What if . . .

What if this time I can finally have her back?

I squeeze my eyes shut.

No. Nope. Don't even. Box that. Mom is not invading homecoming. I won't let her.

I draw in a slow, cooling breath and check Instagram. Rafa's posted a new selfie of him and Omar wearing black suits with a blue-and-gray chevron shower curtain as a backdrop. Omar raises one eyebrow as he tilts his head back like Luis just crop-dusted them, fingers adjusting his purple tie. Rafa wears a red tie and this beautiful grin that can be described only as teen heartthrob movie star. Their arms are around each other like in that soccer picture.

Maybe things are better between them. I hope so.

I heart it.

Oh God. He's coming. This is really happening.

Then I get a message alert. I press it.

Seraphina Abramsson Official: Cute that they're named after plants in honor of Oma. But I don't really do little kids.

I gasp.

How could she not want to meet her own flesh and blood? She's on a quest for love.

Nope. Boxing and shelving that too. I close my app.

I stifle the urge to text Grammy about the kids and instead look out the window. The setting sun drips amber across cornfields and barns tucked back into coulees cutting into the rolling ridges, occasionally broken up by straight lines of pine trees. Grammy said the trees were planted by the Civilian Conservation Corps during the Great Depression. Apparently one of my great-grandpas helped. Wispy clouds near the horizon glow in gilded light that fades to rich purples and pinks. Long, thick strokes cast oranges to yellows to pale blues to deep, rich ultramarine violet. If Gretchen hadn't spent a half hour on my hair, I'd roll down the window and breathe it in.

Gretchen pulls into a spot near the back of the packed parking lot. Her black lace sleeveless Audrey Hepburn cocktail dress swishes as she jumps out of the car.

"Let's show you off, chica. You're my masterpiece tonight."

I climb out. "Thanks for objectifying me." And turning me into Seraphina. After she totally dismissed the kiddos, I don't know how I feel about that. *Nope, Rose, shove it back into the box.*

My bag of canned goods rattle as Gretchen pulls me across the parking lot through other cupcake-frosting-colored dresses and black suit jackets.

Muted DJ music echoes through the main hallway from the big gym. Through the open doors, colorful flashing lights reveal the dancing crowd. Kimmy and her pack of homecoming-sashed cheerleaders swathed in pastel all turn and stare at me like I'm Pennywise the Dancing Clown. Mike's jaw drops.

This was a mistake.

I hug my arms to my chest as I fight the urge to rip my bangs free of the bobby pins. I'm a fricking mermaid Barbie, not Rose Marie Hemmersbach. And my silver heels look just like that snobby FIB lady's.

Gretchen grabs my arms and wrestles them to my side. "Rose, you look way more spectacular than any of those girls. Act like you believe it."

I square my shoulders like Dad used to when he saw an impending tackle and try out some more of Mrs. O'Neil's words. *You're priceless.*

Tonight, right now, I kind of believe it. "Let's find Rafa."

Omar rushes through the doors carrying a bag of cans, some pretty girl on his arm. On her wrist is a red rose corsage, even after the drama Friday morning.

"*¡Báilale!* Don't be a total lame ass tonight, *carnal!*" he calls back at Rafa as a pack of football players surround him.

"Try to not be *puerco*, manito," Rafa says. He takes my breath away, even though I got an Insta preview. In one hand is a bag of cans and the other a little plastic box with a corsage. For me?

Dozens of butterflies flutter from my heart to my fingers.

"Go talk to him!" Gretchen pushes me. I almost trip over my stupid heels; the straps are already cutting into my skin.

Rafa looks me up and down, eyes widening. "*Rose?*"

My face flushes, which, of course, makes him grin as he smooths his little fauxhawk. With my heels, I'm a little taller than him. Would that bother him?

"How'd I do on Rose here?" Gretchen winks at me.

He scratches the back of his head. "You just look . . . so

different."

I rub at a scuff mark with my sparkly toe. My sequin dress flaps against my calf. "Is that bad?"

Rafa shakes his head twice, then holds out the box. In it is a white rose. "I, uh . . . it's totally cliché, I know, but it's short notice and . . ."

I'm grinning so wide my cheeks hurt. I pop open the box and take out my rose. It's ornamented with off-white pearls and seeded eucalyptus. "It's perfect."

He slides it on my wrist. The delicate touch of his fingertips on the inside of my wrist sends chills up my spine. The grunge that was staining his nailbeds earlier is gone, evidence of the effort he went through to look his best for tonight.

"You got a corsage for Omar's date, too, didn't you?"

Rafa tosses the box in the garbage can by the display case with *Boy and His Horse* smack in the middle. "It's his first homecoming, and he kicked ass last night."

"Touché. I suppose our siblings deserve nice things sometimes. Like candy and corsages."

"Touché."

Rafa takes the bag of cans weighing down my arm, and we head to the ticket table. Blue-haired Mrs. Petrowski has a rarely witnessed smile for Rafa as he drops our bags into a bin already half full with canned corn and peas and beans.

We walk through the open gym doors into the hot loudness. Red and yellow streamers drape from the bright yellow walls. A huge "Ride over the Timberwolves" banner hangs on the pushed-in bleachers.

The floor is packed with people dancing to hip-hop music. The beat vibrates in my chest. Little freshmen-sized boys chase each other, chucking red and yellow balloons. Omar twirls his date—I think her name is Chelsea—and laughs as he dips her. Can Rafa move like that?

"Show off." Rafa watches his brother, smiling as he shakes his head.

"Show him how it's done, then." I press my arm into his.

"Well, I did teach him almost everything he knows."

He grabs my hand and yanks me through the circle of spectators. "Shit, I didn't mean with me!" I try to pull back. "Last time I danced with someone other than Dad at a wedding was eighth grade."

Rafa pulls me against him. His breath tickles my ear as he whispers, "Do you trust me?" His smooth cheek grazes mine. The delicious smell of lavender and lime makes my head swirl.

"I guess?"

His burnt-umber eyes burn into mine, catching bits of colored light. "I've got this. Just follow along."

And then he's spinning and twirling and dipping me. His arms are surprisingly strong for how skinny they look. I have no idea what's going on, but I let him carry me away and it's amazing. I'm breathless and weightless and laughing, and we're the only two people in the whole world. And it's so graceful and natural to him, like breathing. It's magic. And our eyes stay locked the whole time. When the song ends, we cave into one another. The sparkles in his eyes just fill me up. I'm drunk on him.

Then I realize people are clapping. I look around. It's Kimmy and Kenzie and Mike and Eisenhardt and lots of other people, all circled around us. Even Omar and Chelsea are off to the side clapping. My face blazes hotter than the sun as my heart flutters. Laughing, Rafa hugs his arm around me and guides me out of the circle to Gretchen and Anderson.

"So did we show him up?" I ask.

"Who cares?"

I sink against him. Perfect again. "So it's just the singing part of show choir that you can't do, huh?"

Rafa does some jazz hands.

I bust out laughing.

Gretchen races up to us. "Squee! That was the most beautiful thing, like out of a Molly Ringwald movie."

Rafa tips his head against mine. "Who?"

I press back. "No idea."

"Hats off to you, governor!" Anderson says in a British accent as he removes his literal top hat and bows to Rafa. He wears a three-piece suit and purple old-school bow tie.

"Jeez, Rose, I didn't know you could dance!" Ashlee's floor-length hunting-camo and blaze-orange dress swishes around her legs as she charges us. "And Rafa, you gotta give my Bobby some lessons."

Bobby lumbers up too. A camo vest stretches across his huge gut. "No, thanks. I don't dance."

"Well, if you change your mind, free lessons in the back room," Rafa says.

Bobby guffaws.

"Boot Scootin' Boogie" comes on next.

"You know this one!" Ashlee pulls Bobby out onto the floor.

As they get started, Bobby's kick ball change is positively sprightly.

Rafa nods like he's impressed. "I could probably teach him to bachata at the very least."

I giggle. "Now that would be YouTube worthy."

As the song plays on, it takes me back to countless dart nights—because they always play that one—and Shirley Temples and Schwan's deep-fried cheese curds and Mom and Dad flirting and kissing, slow dancing to "I Couldn't Leave You if I Tried," their prom and wedding song.

"C'mon, Rose, I know you love this one." Gretchen tugs me toward the floor.

I manage to get my fingers around Rafa's wrist. "Embrace your inner redneck, Rafa."

"Mierda, too soon!"

I kick off my heels. Now I don't have to worry about being taller than Rafa. Gretchen and I get into a line. I follow along with the dance, hands on my hips as I sidestep, then stomp backward and forward.

"Man, if Shaiti and Cristian could see me now." He lets out one of his sidesplitting laughs as he tries to copy my stomp, stomp, kick, kick ball change.

By the last do-si-do, we're both laughing uncontrollably, crashing into each other. One of Rafa's beautiful, face-consuming grins radiates as rainbow lights dance around us.

The music stops.

"All right, Sparta Senior High School," the sunglasses-wearing DJ hollers into the microphone, "can we get the homecoming court up here? It's time to announce your homecoming king and queen!"

Carolyn bumps into me on her way up. "Ope, sorry!" Glitter sparkles on her flushed cheeks as she does a double take. "Oh, Rose! Wow. That's a good color for you."

"Uh, thanks," I say before she takes off for the stage. The dress is almost the same color as the shirt she bought me for my fourteenth birthday because it complemented my eyes.

The senior class's best and brightest (or maybe not so brightest in Eisenhardt's case) line up onstage, spotlights on their perfect smiles like they're in a beauty pageant. Kimmy in a pink dress and

Mike with a matching pink tie, because so perfect.

"Drumroll, please . . ."

Some underclassman taps on a snare drum, squinting through the blaze of the spotlight.

"Kimmy Martin and Mike Ott!" DJ Sunglasses yells.

The crowd goes wild. Kimmy cries as they perch the cheap rhinestone crown on her head. Eisenhardt grovels on his knees before Mike.

"Barf." Gretchen does a slow clap. "Rafa, here's another shocker—they were the prom king and queen too. I didn't even know you were allowed to be both."

"And now, the homecoming competition," DJ Sunglasses proclaims with gusto. "You all were competing for a five-hundred-dollar contribution to your class funds, generously donated by Century Foods and Northern Engraving."

My heart speeds up.

"You all know the seniors won the shout competition yesterday," DJ Sunglasses says.

Hollers erupt around us. "For the skit, the judges were unanimously in favor of the sophomores and their *Jeopardy* skit!"

Omar and his friends jump and scream. Their ties had all become *Rambo* bandannas, even the clip-on ones.

"I'd have voted for them too. Kimmy and Mike's thing was a misogynistic piece of crap," Gretchen says.

"The float competition is a little more fierce, folks. But the juniors came out on top with their fiberglass horse with . . . I guess you'd call it a scarecrow Spartan." Another roar of cheers.

DJ Sunglasses raises his hand and quiets the crowd. "Now, the window paintings were a much tougher decision. I'm told there were some . . . unique entries."

I wring my hands. Whatever. Maybe I don't want to win. At

least the mural proved my brain isn't broken. And I have a unique collaborative piece for my portfolio.

Somehow Kimmy and Mike lock on to us. Kimmy chews on her glossy lip. Mike glowers as his fake velvet red crown trimmed with fake leopard print slips down.

"A five-year-old could have painted that other crap." I adjust my corsage. The tips of the petals are already turning brown.

"Guggenheim, that's where yours belongs," Gretchen says.

"It only matters what Belwyn thinks." Rafa presses his elbow into mine.

"And the winner of the window painting competition . . . is . . ."

"¡Ándale!" Rafa mutters.

"The . . . seniors!" DJ announces.

I jump up and scream. So does Rafa. So loud it rattles my eardrums.

"Oh my God, we did it! We did it!" I throw my arms around him.

"I knew we'd win. That was practically a Van Gogh." Rafa's chest and stomach press against mine. Our bodies fit together like two puzzle pieces. Excitement rolls down my spine.

I pull away, grinning from ear to ear. "We make a pretty good team."

"Yeah, we do." Those puppy dog eyes, that smooth smile, fills me to the brim.

A hip-hop beat rattles out of the huge speaker towers, reverberates in my chest. "That means the seniors claim victory for homecoming. Congratulations, seniors!"

Eisenhardt grabs the mic from DJ Sunglasses, Burger King crown adorning his head. "Know your role, shut your hole! Know your role, shut your hole!"

Rafa laughs deeply and richly, his whole body unrestrained. It's beautiful.

Principal Jorgenson huffs onstage, red-faced and sweating through his blue dress shirt. He snatches the mic from Eisenhardt, who jumps off the stage and runs through the crowd.

"Eisenhardt!" Jorgenson growls loud enough for the mic to pick up.

But it's too late.

"Know your role, shut your hole! Know your role, shut your hole!" The chant rises around us. Even Gretchen screams it. Boos break out from all the underclassman, but even three classes united together can't beat us.

Some twangy Florida Georgia Line song interrupts the chant. A bunch of people belt out the lyrics.

Kimmy rushes up to us. "Oh, my gosh, you guys are amazing!" She adjusts her sparkly crown. Her huge smile is contagious.

Mike saunters up behind her. His suit jacket strains against his bulging arm muscles as he crosses his arms. "Yeah, good job."

"We totally owe our victory to you!" Kimmy grabs my hand.

"We better get a special plaque in our honor at the five-year reunion," I say.

Rafa bursts out laughing behind his fist.

Kimmy's smile vanishes.

I laugh. "Joking."

Kimmy's smile re-forms as she giggles. "Right! Thanks again, guys!" She grabs Mike's hand, and they cut through the crowd to rejoin Carolyn and the rest of their homecoming-sashed friends—minus Eisenhardt, who vanished into the night.

Another hip-hop song blares out of the speakers.

The flashing colored lights catch glitter hovering on my skin in my peripheral vision. It glints off bits on Rafa's cheek too. Glitter from me.

"Hey, Anderson!" Gretchen winks as she abandons me again.

"Hey, it's so hot and loud in here," Rafa says. "Want to grab some fresh air?"

"You have no idea."

He grabs his jacket and hands me my shoes.

I head for the gym doors, gripping Gretchen's heels by the straps.

"Aren't you going to wear those?"

"Nah, they're killing my feet. Gretchen insisted it wouldn't be ironically cute for me to wear my combat boots."

"I don't know, I think it would have been Rose."

I grin at him. He gets me.

It's about twenty degrees cooler in the hallway, but that doesn't touch the heat between us. I take off through the glass doors to the parking lot, grabbing a handful of dress before it catches.

A wave of fresh air brushes my bare shoulders, perfumed with a hint of burning leaves, my favorite fall smell, mixed with a tiny hint of rose from my corsage. I jog across the parking lot, the cement cold and rough under my bare feet, but I barely feel it. The parking lot lights catch bits of sparkle on my dress. Rafa chases me up the stairs to the practice football field, laughing as his red tie dances from side to side. He catches me at the gate. Rafa's fingers tighten around mine.

I pull him through the gap in the fence. Dew-covered grass snakes between my toes. I plop down on the fifty-yard line.

Rafa drops down next to me. "Aren't you worried about the pretty dress?"

"Nah, Gretchen said she'll never wear it again. You worried about your fancy pants?"

Rafa brushes some white line paint off his knee. "No. Pretty sure they don't fit Luis anymore."

So we both borrowed tonight. It's flawless.

Rafa's eyes wander to the sky. The moon's just a sliver—waning crescent, I remember from Physical Science. Stars and reddish Mars spread across the sea of purplish black over us. Muffled beats come from the gym, a few people laugh in the parking lot, but up on the football field it's just me and Rafa and the stars. He sits close enough for me to feel the heat radiating from his arm through his dress shirt.

"Alizarin crimson, ultramarine blue, mixed with some burnt umber. Add a little yellow to lighten it at the horizon," Rafa says.

"You do that too? Mix the sky in your mind?"

Bits of light fill his dark eyes with stars. "Yeah, all the time. There's so much raw power over us."

"Exactly." My heart somersaults.

The cool night seeps into my skin, and I can't fight off the shiver.

Rafa holds out his jacket.

"Won't you get cold?"

"I'll be all right."

I carefully take off my corsage and slide my arms through the wide sleeves, silky on the inside and still warm from Rafa. His smell wraps around me like a blanket.

"The stars are one of the good things about Sparta. In Milwaukee you can see like five. Here you can see hundreds."

One of the good things . . . I bite in a smile. "Mom and I used to sit in the backyard sipping hot chocolate under the stars." I draw my legs to my chest and rest my arms on my knees. "We'd make up stories about alien worlds filled with flying purple cows and princesses who fought the dragons to protect the princes."

Rafa hugs his knees too. Our elbows touch. "I can totally

picture you as my knight in bloody Greek shining armor. Hopefully sans red demon eyes."

Chills prickle my arms, and it's not from being cold. "Sometimes I look up there and think about how huge the universe is, and how I'm not even a grain of sand in it all. That all my problems are nothing. I am nothing. Not really."

A frown dimples Rafa's chin as he brushes a strand of hair that somehow Houdini-ed free of the hairspray from my forehead. "But you *are* something, Rose."

Literally the most perfect thing anyone has ever said to me. Ever. Maybe I really am a little bit priceless.

Rafa's fingers slip across my palm and slide through mine. My synapses sizzle. Our eyes meet again. My heart races as I get lost in the star-speckled darkness. He's beautiful. Can guys be beautiful? God, those full lips are so close, just inches away. I ache to feel them against mine. Does he feel the same thing?

His thumb caresses the skin between my thumb and pointer finger. "So, how are things with your mom?"

My heart dives to the pit of my stomach. Our perfect moment crumbles.

"Not like I expected." Tears well in my eyes. I press my fingers to my eyes to shove them back in. Rafa tucks his arm around me and pulls our bodies together. "I want to hate her. But she's just so small and broken. And I miss my mom."

Rafa takes my fist and pries it open. He strokes the fingernail imprints in my palm. "She's your mom. You love her."

I push out a shaky breath. "Yeah. And that scares me shitless, because . . ."

"She might relapse and hurt you even more. Or die."

Warm tears track eye makeup down my cheeks. I can't stop them, even though they're ruining Homecoming Rose, the Barbie mermaid princess. Rafa cradles my chin in his hand and thumbs my tears away.

"The social worker said addiction changes brain functioning. Like it's not as easy as waking up one day and deciding to quit. Drugs almost killed Mom, and she's still on a fucking wait list for treatment. Maybe it'd be better if she was in jail, because at least we'd know where she is and that she's clean. And she can't overdose.

"And the scariest part of all is I know, *know*, guilt makes her use. So she can numb herself out and escape it. Now that her overdose has taken almost everything, her guilt's the size of Mount Everest."

Guilt makes her use.

My words echo through my ears. It crashes into me like a wave. I'm falling through an ocean of ice. Drowning.

"Rose, talk to me."

Through the ice, I feel a warm finger stroke my cheek.

"The day it happened was her birthday." The words escape my lips. "I was supposed to help the kiddos make her a cake cuz it was Dad's dart night, but instead I hung with Gretchen. And the kiddos . . . The kiddos . . . "

My heartbeat hammers in my ears. All the white lines and stars whirl around me, and my stomach plummets like when the floor drops out from under you on the Scorpion's Tail at Noah's Ark.

"Oh God. I'm so selfish. They're home with her, and we just said goodbye to our house, and . . . and . . . I gotta get home." I scramble to my feet.

"Rose, stop! Slow down, you're not making any sense." Rafa wraps me into a bear hug. I try to break free of him, but his hold on me tightens.

"If I'd been there that night, maybe she wouldn't have felt like a discarded cigarette butt. Maybe she wouldn't have used so much. And the kiddos wouldn't have been trapped outside for hours with no food and Hollis wouldn't have seen her dying and CPS never would have gotten involved and Mom wouldn't be maybe going to jail. And we wouldn't be getting kicked out of our house. Guilt makes her use, and I still haven't said more than one word to her."

"Wait, are you blaming yourself?" Rafa loosens his hold on me and grips my shoulders. His nose is inches from mine. "Rose, you can't blame yourself. That's crazy."

That last word shanks me in the gut. I frantically scrape the trails of tears and makeup off my cheeks. "Did you just call me crazy?"

Rafa's hands fly up. "No! What you're saying is crazy, though! You didn't stick that needle into her arm."

Record scratch. His condescending tone raises my hackles.

"Wow. Did you not hear what I just said? You really don't get it. See, this is why I don't tell people my shit."

Rafa doesn't flinch at my anger. He stands taller. "Well, you chose to tell me, and now I'm telling you that you can't blame yourself for this."

"You've been talking to me for, like, a fucking week! You don't get to talk to me like that!"

"¡Órale! You didn't have a problem telling me how to handle my shit last night," he fires right back.

"Oh my God! You can't even compare the two!" I scream right in his face, so close our noses almost touch. I rip off his jacket and chuck it onto the grass next to the dying corsage. My dress, damp with cold dew, clings to the backs of my legs as I sprint for the gate.

"Where are you going?"

"Leave. Me. Alone!" I shout, and slip through.

As I cut across the parking lot, this time I feel each pebble cut into the soles of my feet. Because, shit, I left Gretchen's shoes up there. The heavy bass and beats from the gym are gone now, replaced by a cacophony of voices and music blaring from car stereos. Pastel fabric swishes into vehicles as people head for after-parties. The air is now thick with exhaust.

But the scent of lavender and lime lingers on my skin.

I can't even walk home, because it would take like a day to get to Cataract.

I need Gretchen. Her Prius is still hanging out at the back of the emptying parking lot. The halls are empty now, except for the night custodian. One of his cleaning cart wheels squeaks as he pushes it toward the gym. But voices echo from the direction of the band room. I head there and find her and Anderson making out in the corner while a couple other band geeks pretend not to notice.

"Gretchen . . ." I croak. And saying just that one word almost unleashes another tsunami of tears.

Gretchen's and Anderson's bodies part. Her cheeks are flushed as her eyes sweep me up and down. "Hey, chica . . ."

"Oh, my gosh, you and Rafa are so cute. Are you, like, a couple?" Mandy, who was the second chair clarinet freshman year, asks with her hands clutched to her chest.

I flip her off and storm out of the room.

"What's going on, Rose?" Gretchen's voice rings out after me as her clunky heels echo through the halls.

"Just drive me home. Fuck. To Grammy's. Please."

Gretchen's face scrunches up. She pushes up her cat eye glasses. "Seriously, what's going on?"

Shit. Our conversation earlier about letting people in. I choke on a sob. "I can't right now. Please, just take me to Grammy's."

Gretchen's eyes widen. Right, the last time she saw me cry was after Rose split in two. "Uh, okay then."

She doesn't talk the whole fifteen-minute drive. When she pulls up in front of Grammy's trailer, Dad's truck is gone. Where's Mom? Is she with him or inside?

I can't see her. I can't. Because if she asks how homecoming went, there's nothing I can say. Because she ruined it. Or, rather, my own failure ruined it. And Rafa too. Everything's ruined.

When I get inside, I find the kiddos sprawled on the air mattress staring at an infomercial for Ginsu knives while Grammy snores on the couch. And this is exactly fricking why I can't leave the kiddos.

No sign of Mom. For all I know, she's pawned her wedding ring for heroin.

Or maybe fucked Jeremy for her next high.

I cry myself to sleep.

Chapter 17

A burst of light makes my eyelids glow red. Bobby pins dig into my scalp. I rub my eyes. Salty residue coats my cheeks. And I remember I cried myself to sleep.

I peel my eyes open. Grammy's dust-coated ceiling fan hangs overhead motionless. Hollis and Sage both sleep with their backs to me. The air mattress sinks a little as I push myself to sitting. The Disney-themed fleece tie blanket I made Grammy slips from my chest, releasing the warmth. Vi's curled up at our feet, eyes closed tight as her pink lips hang slightly open. Her hair still has half the updo Gretchen did. And I'm still wearing the seafoam sequin dress.

Mom and Dad are supposed to sleep on the couch, but it's empty. The curled, folded residential treatment brochure lies on the coffee table shoved against the Precious Moments curio cabinet. They weren't here for Vi's night terrors last night either.

Maybe Mom already skipped off to shoot up with Jeremy and Dad went to chase her down. Or maybe they really did spend all night cleaning and packing.

The air mattress reels as I crawl over Hollis to the couch. I snatch my phone from the center cushion.

I text Dad: **Where's Mom?**

She's made it only a day—two tops—when she's "quit" before. This time, sure, it's been over a week, but she was also in a hospital where she couldn't get drugs and where maybe they were giving her some kind of painkiller.

I squeeze my phone between my fingers.

Now she's free. And Grammy's being a total bitch to her and Gretchen couldn't even look at her and she's been cleaning out our home that she got us evicted from and she can't even be alone with us anymore. And I've said like a word to her, and it wasn't "I love you" or even a belated happy birthday.

As I hug my legs against my chest, I catch a whiff of lavender and lime on my skin. That uncontainable grin as Rafa dipped me last night, our lips almost touching. But that's over now. Pretty sure. Sickness rips at my gut like I'm hungover.

Shit, we both work the ten to seven today.

I need to get rid of the smell of him. I lock myself in Grammy's tiny bathroom and rip all the bobby pins from my hairspray-crusty hair and make a pile of metal on the narrow sink ledge. I yank off the dress. A few sequins speckle the floor. I scrub off Seraphina's trademark red lipstick as I fight back the tears clawing to get out. How can I even have room to cry about that?

And why the hell hasn't Dad texted me back?

Because she's already relapsed.

Then my tears are mixing with the hot water pelting my face. I ball up sobbing in the corner of the shower away from the warmth.

My phone vibrates on the bathroom floor.

I fumble for it, but it slips through my wet fingers.

Gretchen: Ok, you have to tell me what's going on. Please.

I text Dad again.

Now even breathing hurts. And I can't see Rafa; how am I supposed to go to work today?

A fist pounds on the door. "Hurry up! I'm going to pee myself!" Sage shouts.

I find the strength to reach out and unlock the door. The sound of her peeing cuts over the shower. I press my hand to my mouth to stifle my sobs.

You have to be strong for the kids. You already failed them once.

After she leaves, I pull myself up. Dry off. Pull on clothes.

"Rosey, I got some pancakes ready." Grammy's voice drips sunshine as I squeeze past her and Sage—Sage—cooking in the kitchen. "Your favorite, chocolate chip with a little bit of vanilla. Purple sprinkles. You have fun last night?"

The smell of melting chocolate mixed with a dash of frying bacon makes my stomach pitch and roil. I might puke. I climb across the air mattress and sink into the couch next to Vi. She lays her head on my lap. I stroke her lingering hairspray-sticky curls as my limp, dripping mess of hair hangs in my face.

Why hasn't Dad texted me back? I press my phone to my forehead as I bite in a cry. And I hate that I wish I had my medal right now.

"Rose?" Grammy calls.

"I'm fine."

Finally, my phone vibrates.

Dad: Sorry, couldn't find my phone for a bit there. She's been with me the whole time. We were up most of the night cleaning.

RoseMarie: How's it going?

Dad: There's a lot left to do.

We have to be out at noon today. I steal a glance at the clock with the white-tailed deer over the TV. It's already almost eight in the morning.

"Are you okay, Rosey?" Vi looks up at me. Her eyelids are still a glittery pink.

"Everything's fine," I grumble.

RoseMarie: I'll come help.

Dad: That's me and your mom's job.

RoseMarie: I am not a kid.

Dad: How are you going to get here?

"Grammy, can you take me to Walmart early?" I call into the kitchen. "I've got homework to do, and I can focus better in the break room."

"Okay, Rosey, let's just eat some breakfast first."

I call in sick for the first time ever. At least now I don't have to see Rafa.

⸻

We're all crammed in Grammy's tiny car again. She's belting out Queen's "Somebody to Love" as she sways in the driver's seat.

She turns the music down. "You kids wait till this Thanksgiving. After we mash the potatoes for lefse, we're going to that Christmas tree farm again. I already started making your ornaments. Figure I got a few years to make up for."

Three Christmases ago, she made me a bead and wire angel

with a gold crown. Last year, we never got around to putting a tree up. And now Mom and Dad had to throw away all our Christmas decorations.

Mom will almost definitely have relapsed by then.

"What's lefse?" Vi chirps from the back seat.

Grammy looks at her in the rearview mirror. "A special kind of potato pancake. It's a lot of work, which is why we make it only on Thanksgiving. I learned to make it from my great-grandma, who learned from her grandma. The one from Norway, not the one from Germany. I still use her potato ricer."

And I have missed warm lefse with butter and sugar—the taste of Christmas. It breaks my heart that Violet doesn't remember it.

A slow sigh leaks through Grammy's wrinkle-lined lips. She steals a glance at me. "It's not all on your parents, Rose. I was stubborn too. And it's you kids that got hurt the most. I'm sorry." A tear streaks down, trailing her deep wrinkles. She wipes her eyes, then digs out her Newport Menthol Blues. "We got some time to make up, sure, Rosey. But the most important thing is now we got the chance."

It's hard to see more than a day ahead, but I hope we do get to chop down that Christmas tree.

Grammy drops me off at Walmart with a peanut butter and jelly sandwich and an apple in a brown paper bag.

As soon as her car rattles away, I walk home. Well, home for three more hours.

Bags and bags of garbage line the street in front of the house. One particularly large pile is crowned with Dad's prized buck head. Along with Vi's collapsing Barbie doll house, which used to be mine, and the caving box for Chutes and Ladders with Dad and my tournament tally tucked inside. We can't just buy that stuff back someday.

The screen door cracks closed as Dad jogs down the front sidewalk. He's wearing the same buck-antler Mathews Solocam T-shirt as yesterday, but I swear there are new wrinkles in his fore-head and between his eyebrows.

"It's just stuff, Rosey. We'll fill our new place with better stuff." His heavy hand rests on my shoulder.

I brush it off and force myself to stand taller because I have no other choice. "What do you need me to do?"

"If you could get cleaning the bathroom, that'd help a lot."

"Daryl, don't make her do that," Mom says from the doorway. She's wearing the same purple T-shirt as last night.

"Well, I gotta take this shit to the dump, and I can't leave you alone with her!" Dad snaps.

Mom flinches.

"Stop being a dick, Dad!" I shoulder past him.

Mom's brows knit as she watches me.

I sniff for Jeremy's secondhand smoke as I slip past her. I don't know a ton about cigarettes, but I know it smells different from Grammy's menthols. All I smell is rose-scented deodorant fighting to cover up her BO.

Light pours unfiltered through the window over the sink onto the spot where I found her unconscious body because even the curtain is gone now. I don't know what our house usually smells like, because it's home, but now all I can smell is lemon and it's all wrong.

The house is completely empty except for a small mountain of bags and a few tubs of clothes. The walls are covered with greasy handprints a few feet off the floor. Now that all the furniture is gone, I can see a few more crayon drawings of princesses and cats and Hollis's name. The dent in the fridge door from when Sage tipped her chair over and gave herself a concussion. More archeological evidence of our lives here that can't easily be thrown away.

Nope. Don't go there. Box it up, focus on what you can control. I fight to swallow the lump choking my throat.

As I head for the bathroom, my combat boots echo on the floor, making the house sound five times bigger. The contents of one garbage bag catch my attention. Pressed against the white plastic is the double wedding ring quilt Grammy made Mom and Dad. "You're throwing this away?"

"No, that's going in storage," Mom answers from the doorway. Something tells me she's lingering there so Dad can still see her while he's outside.

Whatever. The cleaning stuff waits for me in the bathroom.

I tuck in my earbuds. I kind of want to listen to Sigur Rós, but that'll just make me think of Rafa. So I blast Unrequited Death, and now, bonus, it doesn't make me think of Justin. I attack all the mildew from in between the shower tiles with a worn-out toothbrush. Then I assault the soap scum and old toothpaste and hair crusting the sink.

Over "Death Punch," I hear Mom and Dad come back, but thankfully they leave me alone. I drop to my knees and scour the piss and pubic hair around the base of the toilet with a wipe. My fingertip brushes something crinkly on the back of the basin. I peel it off.

It's a tiny square of wrinkled aluminum coated in a sticky black residue.

Pump, hiss, pump, hiss, pump, hiss. My heart hammers against my rib cage as adrenaline rips through my veins. Makes my head dizzy and my arms and legs tingle.

Her stupid fucking dove painting. The black tendrils reach off the canvas, coil around her, and drag her back into the maw.

And I'm screaming. Screaming. Screaming. Then I'm sobbing against the toilet seat, like I'm puking my guts out after drinking too much.

Dad's face is in mine. He's talking, but I still have my earbuds in. I rip them out. "She's already relapsed! She's only been home two fucking days and she's already relapsed!"

"Rosey, that's not possible." Dad puts up his huge oil-stained hands. "I been with her the whole time."

I thrust the empty heroin packet in his face. "Doesn't take long to shoot up. Especially when you're a pro like her!"

Dad's face pales as his eyes take it in. His furrowed brows etch gorges into his forehead. Then his face goes blood red as his eyes bulge.

"Maureen!" Dad roars so loud it rattles the foundation of the house.

"What?" She slinks to the door, gripping her upper arm.

"What the fuck is this?" He points to the little empty packet still pinched between my fingers.

Her face deforms into the same expression of white-eyed horror the woman wore in Goya's *Monk Talking to an Old Woman*. A cry slips out. "No, no! It's . . . it's old. It has to be. I haven't used. I haven't!" Mom holds out her arms. She still has old purple scars and track marks on the insides of her arms, but I don't see any new bruising.

"Plenty of other places you can shoot that shit into your veins!" I say.

Mom recoils like I slapped her. She presses her hand to her forehead. She still has her wedding ring, so at least she didn't pawn that.

Dad's seething as he slowly shakes his head.

"Daryl, I haven't used. Where would I even have gotten the

money? And we haven't been apart for more than five minutes. I'm never touching that stuff again. Ever." Mom's blue-green eyes jump to me. "Cross my heart and hope to live."

Bingo. There it is. And stab me with a knife and twist it, she even busted out the promise we used to make because we agreed hoping to die was weird.

"When I called 911, they had me check your pulse, and I couldn't find it for like a minute!" I scream in Mom's face. "I thought you were dead!"

Mom's eyes widen. Tears spill down her cheeks.

Dad's crow's-feet deepen as his eyes tighten.

"Now that you're home, I spend every second worrying that your guilt is going to drive you to use again. Because you can just shoot that shit up your veins and feel nothing, but we have no escape. And we have to deal with all the consequences. And there's not a damn thing I can do about it.

"And . . . and now all I can think about is, that night I abandoned the kids to hang out with Gretchen," I choke out through my tears. "And that if I would have been here. If I would have said happy birthday. Made you a card. If I hadn't yelled at you to get a job. Maybe you wouldn't have overdosed.

"And in spite of all that, I just want my mom back!"

Now she's Frida Kahlo in *The Broken Column* with tears covering her face as she mourns her broken body. Broken brain. The nails all over Frida's face become needles and scabs. Mom chokes on a sob and falls to her knees.

Dad buries his head in his hands, strips of blond falling through his fingers. A strangled cry followed by a tremulous breath. His shoulders start shaking.

And I can't. So I run. Leave home for the last time ever.

My combat boots pound the pavement as I run to West Side

Park. And thank God, it's empty. I climb into my castle and hug my body into a ball on the wooden planks.

One thought plays on repeat in my brain: what if I just guilted her into relapsing?

My skin tingles with thousands of bee stings.

———

Ominous clouds slowly build in the sky as the day moves on without me. I think they're probably rather spectacular, but I can't paint the sky today. I can't remember the names of the colors.

It's well past noon, so our home is no longer ours. Meaning I don't know where Mom and Dad are, and I forgot my phone so I can't text them. I don't know how I'm going to get up to Cataract.

The kiddos.

The kiddos have enough to worry about already, and now Mom's just going to be there all the time because she doesn't have to help remove all traces of us from the building formerly known as home anymore and she doesn't have a job.

The thought of life going back to how it was festers in my head. Mom drooping on the couch trying to act like an engaged parent like we don't all know, shooting up while pretending she's going to the bathroom, inventing things to "buy from the store" so she can escape the house and steal shit or get more drugs, begging and arguing and guilting Dad into giving her money we don't have so she can shoot it in her veins.

Waiting and watching for the first signs that it's starting again, then finding more of those empty packets and scorched pop can bottoms and used syringes.

And what if a new landlord won't take us because Mom's now a fricking drug criminal?

Exhaustion cuts me to the bone.

I need to protect the kiddos. Be a buffer. A distraction. Something. So they don't have to feel what I do right now. Yet here I am in my wooden castle being selfish. Again.

I could call Dad from Walmart, but I can't exactly just stroll in there now because I'm "sick" and Rafa's working and I can't see his face.

So I'm frozen. My fingers itch for my medal, but I have no idea where it is and am pretty sure it doesn't work if the person who issued it now hates you.

I'm trying to catch all the falling pieces, but I can't. My hands aren't big enough. And I can't make sense of all the feelings tearing me up inside and how they can all coexist without destroying one another.

And then the rain unleashes. Cold, fat drops that instantly penetrate my hair and my Unrequited Death shirt. Run down my bare arms and cheek. I'm shivering, but I don't have the energy to move, not even to get under the platform I'm on.

Then I hear the distant squelch of shoes plodding through wet grass.

"Rose? Rosey?"

I peek through the gaps in my castle wall. Dad's form cuts across the huge field like a knight in flannel armor. Rain drips from his limp hair.

"Rosey, please!" Dad's voice cracks.

I find the strength to pull myself to my feet.

Dad locks onto me. "Oh, thank God!" He runs across the field, water spraying up from his shitkickers with each impact. He climbs into my tower and pulls me against him. I scream into his wet chest. He hugs me tighter, cradles the back of my head in his huge hand. Dad trembles too.

261

"Rosey, oh, Rosey, baby girl." He kisses the top of my head over and over again.

And I'm shivering and sobbing and snot is pouring out of my nose and I'm soaked.

"Let's get you in the truck. Let's get you warm."

But I still can't move. I don't have the strength. Because where is she right now? And what if I pushed her to use? And it might not be another overdose that kills her. It could be a heart infection or hepatitis or even AIDS. Or maybe police will find her body discarded in the woods with a bullet in her head, like that mom and dad a bunch of years ago, murdered over drug money.

Dad sweeps my feet out from under me and carries me across the soggy field like he's Knight Daddy rescuing Princess Rose from her tower. He sets me in the passenger seat and buckles me in. My door closes. I slump against it. The window is cold against my cheek.

Dad's door creaks open. He reaches across the front seat and tucks that stinky old Packers blanket from his truck bed around me, then blasts the heat.

My eyes stare out the rain-speckled window, but my brain can't see anything as we drive. Warmth slowly soaks into my skin, and all I can smell is wet dog.

I hear his voice. "I found her. We're coming home."

But we don't have a home.

Grammy said something yesterday that made me feel a little better, but I can't remember it. I can't reach that far back.

Dad lets out a slow sigh. He finds my hand under the blanket and squeezes it so tight it might hurt but I just feel numb. I think he's crying again, but I'm not sure because I can't move my head.

I must fall asleep, because I open my eyes and Grammy's brown-and-cream trailer with the bright-red metal chairs flanking the door is in front of us. A few of her aspen tree's leaves have turned golden since yesterday.

Dad's still squeezing my hand. My hair is still damp and stringy, but water no longer drips from the ends.

"Rosey, I don't know what I'm doing with all this, and I know I've screwed a lot of things up. What you had to see . . . What you had to do . . ." Dad's voice comes out like broken glass. "I'm sorry. I wanted you to talk to the counselor, because I was too chicken-shit to talk to you myself. Because it was *me* who should have been there to protect you."

"Where's Mom?" I ask.

Dad lets out a shuddering sigh. "She's been here with Grammy the whole time. And Grammy won't even let her pee with the door closed."

I throw the door open and sprint through the pouring rain into Grammy's house.

Hollis puts his hands on my shoulders and looks right into my eyes, just like Dad does. He takes my hand and pulls me to the couch. Sage wraps the hunting quilt around me.

Mom's eyes fill with tears as she watches me from the armchair. I know it's still the same size as always, but she looks like a tiny child sitting in it. Mom pulls herself up, drags herself through the narrow kitchen, and droops on the kitchen table. Because this trailer only has a bedroom, a living room, a bathroom, a kitchen, and a tiny laundry room. There's nowhere for her to go. Harder to shoot up in secret. Bonus.

The brochure of Gundersen's treatment program stands like a little tent just inches from Mom's elbows.

"Let me get you some dry clothes, Rosey Rose." Grammy heads through the kitchen and past Mom. I wait for a cutting comment, but instead Grammy just squeezes Mom's shoulder.

"Mom and me made snickerdoodles, Rosey!" Vi skip hops into the kitchen and returns with a plate piled high with golden cinnamon-caked cookies. She watches me with huge, expectant eyes like Pinkie Pie when she delivers a cupcake to Twilight Sparkle.

Now I have to take one. I pick one off the top and take a nibble. The white chocolate chips are still melted. Mom's recipe. Also my favorite cookie in the world.

I catch Mom watching me through the kitchen, brows knit with a hand pressed to her chest. Her tears break free. I still hate seeing her cry.

I take another bite.

Chapter 18

When Dad drops me off at school on Monday, the first thing I notice is all the homecoming murals are gone. Literally the only thing I've done this entire school year, besides writing half an essay in Economic History and answering three problems on a Calculus test.

I don't want to see Rafa and those teen heartthrob eyes today. Or ever. I want to hide in the bathroom, since I need to physically be in the building, but then I'll still get marked absent and that means parent meeting with Captain Sweaty Pits. But Dad cannot miss work, and since Mom can't be alone with me, I'm not sure she counts right now.

I head to my locker because I don't have the energy to carry a backpack today. When I get there, I find another fricking locker tag stuck to it.

"Rose Hemmersbach! Riding over the underclassman to victory!" in those same girly, perfect letters with a construction paper paintbrush with pom-poms coming out of it.

That was ten years ago.

I rip off both locker tags and throw them to the ground.

I drag myself down to Great Novels because I need to be there when Mrs. Ebert takes attendance. When I walk in, Rafa actively turns away from me and buries his face in his sketchbook. I sink into my desk. This hollow sickness spreads from my gut and sucks everything out.

And I hate how I want to steal at glance at Rafa to see if he's looking at me.

So I bury my head in my arms. I hear Ebert talking about a new book, but my ears can't string the sounds into words. My brain's a pile of mush leaking out of my ears, and my body aches because sleeping on an air mattress with three kids who kick and push all night long might actually be worse than sleeping on the floor. And I had to keep one eye on the couch to make sure Mom didn't sneak off and use.

"Rose!" Someone's shaking me.

I peel my head up from a small puddle of drool. I fell asleep. Mrs. Ebert's frowning at me, but not because she's pissed. Her brows knit like she's worried. Like now she knows we're homeless too.

"Bell rang," she says.

Rafa's gone. So is the rest of the class. I wipe the lingering spit from my chin and drag myself up. Sit in the bathroom for art because I cannot face Gretchen and Rafa; I don't care what happens. And my brain only has room to contain one thing. Mom. Dad and Grammy both work today. Meaning she's all alone. All day. Sure, in Cataract, but Jeremy has a car. She can still get drugs.

A voice from the intercom echoes off the bathroom tiles: "Rose Hemmersbach to the main office, please. Rose Hemmersbach to the main office."

Shit. I cannot deal with Principal Jorgenson.

I head for the side door to the parking lot.

"Rosalinda!" a voice echoes through the halls.

There are no Rosalindas at this school, and I'm the only Rose. I glance back. Force my scratchy eyes to focus. Omar's jogging toward me, swimming in his football jersey. The hero of homecoming.

"Are you talking to me?" I ask.

He stops a few feet from me, panting. "Dang, you were on a mission."

"Aren't you supposed to be fast?"

He shrugs.

"What do you want?"

Omar scratches the back of his neck like Rafa does when he's nervous. "So what's with all the weirdness, Rosalinda?"

"Okay, so my name is Rose."

"I know." He shines a roguish grin I could never in a million years imagine on Rafa's face. "Rosalinda's one of the people in our mom's favorite telenovela."

I cross my arms. "Get to the point, Mr. Football Hero."

"Okay!" He throws his hands up. "I teased Rafa about sneaking off with you at homecoming, and he told me to fuck off."

"Okay?" I set off for the office.

"He never says that. And after he comes home from Walmart yesterday . . . Well, he pretty much always just locks himself in our room and does homework or draws or whatever he does since we moved here. But last night he didn't even come out for our tía Laura's mole."

"Okay . . . ?"

"Don't you see, Rosalinda, that's his favorite food ever. And then he left for school before I was even up. So what's wrong with him?" He dramatically strokes his chin with an eyebrow cocked.

The intercom cuts in. "Rose Hemmersbach to the main office,

please. Rose Hemmersbach to the main office."

"How the hell should I know? He's *your* brother." I leave.

When I get to the main office, Dad's wringing his hands. Why isn't he at work? Sage stands next to him. The remnants of dried tears stain her cheeks.

Dad pulls off his Packers hat. "Just here to take you guys to the doctor appointment."

I squint at him.

His eyes dart to the secretary.

I turn on my heel and march out of the office. Dad catches the door before I let it slam and follows me into the hall.

A frown stretches the deepening marionette lines around the corners of his mouth. "Sage destroyed her classroom and hit Mrs. Krause. Two teachers had to restrain her."

That's a bucket of cold water to the face. "What?"

I look past him through the wall of windows at that tiny girl hunched over in a chair that's too big for her, legs swinging. If I'm drowning, she's burning alive.

"She's suspended. Grammy's working, and Mom can't be alone with her."

I realize what he's asking. "What if CPS finds out you're taking me out of school for this?"

Mrs. Ebert walks by with a stack of copies in her arms. She shoots Dad a side-eye because, fact, she's seen the article. Dad frowns.

"Rose, please." He folds his hands like he's begging. "Please. If I don't go back, they might fire me."

"Whatever, I don't want to be here anyway."

Dad signs me out. I don't even bother to grab my backpack before we leave. Through the passenger window, I see Mom's head drooping like a dying rose, her face hidden behind a sheet of dishwater-blonde hair.

"So you and Sage go up to Grammy's. Mom's going to stay in Sparta. Pick up some job applications," Dad says.

I glare at a dandelion sprouting in the sidewalk crack. "Or some drugs."

Dad tips his Packers hat up and digs his fingers into his forehead. "I'm doing the best I can here, Rose."

I roll my eyes.

"Just pick the kiddos up from school, then here"—he pulls some cash out of his wallet—"take them for some ice cream at Ginny's until I'm done working."

I shove it against his chest. "Rent money."

Dad's hands shake as he crams the twenty back into his wallet.

Mom climbs out of the truck. Brows knit, she reaches for Sage's cheek, but Sage bats her hand away. I sniff for any hint of Jeremy's secondhand smoke on her. Nothing. Yet.

"Let's go, Sage," I say.

Sage climbs into the back seat.

Mom slinks away. Her arms hang limp as the cuffs of her ancient flared jeans drag on the sidewalk. She looks even smaller than yesterday. And now she's going to be left to her own devices. In Sparta. All day.

What if this is the last time I see her clean? What if she overdoses again and there's no one to call 911?

I haven't hugged her in months.

Numbness prickles down my arms to my fingertips as my body caves from the hollowness inside me. I don't even feel pressure anymore.

"I'm sorry, Rosey." Sage shrivels in the back seat. "I won't do it again."

"We're all a little screwed up right now."

Dad climbs into the passenger seat. He watches Mom walk away, and I know he's thinking the same thing I was. I turn the key. The engine thunders to a start and fumes puff out of the exhaust pipe. The fan belt screeches as I back out of the parking spot. I haven't driven Dad anywhere since probably beginning of junior year. Now I feel like a little kid in a booster seat as I hold the huge steering wheel. On the drive to Northern Engraving, I wait for him to tell me to ease off the gas. To keep my hands at ten and two. To flick the turn signal on when I'm half a block from turning instead of a quarter. But when we pass our old house, there's already a tilted "for rent" sign in the front lawn.

Dad twists his hat in his lap as we drive through Northern's packed side parking lot toward the sprawling puke-yellow one-story building. One stall right at the front is empty. Probably where the truck was before the line manager had to retrieve Dad. After dropping us off at school, he must have gotten to work like an hour early.

I pull to a stop in front of the open gate in the chain link fence running the length of the building. The low hum of dozens of industrial roof-mounted exhaust fans fills the silence. Dad steals a glance at me before he climbs out. He tips his hat on his head, then his long legs drag him through the gate to the ruddy-colored entrance. His shoulders droop.

I head for Grammy's. The Chevy struggles up the slight hill, exhaust pipe rattling as I press the gas pedal to the floor.

For the first time in her life, Sage is absolutely mute for over a half hour. By the time we get to Grammy's, the truck's down to a quarter tank. I hope Kristy's got some gas cards coming our way real soon, or the kiddos won't be at school tomorrow. I'll have to ride the fricking bus. God, how can I keep working at Walmart? That'll be an extra trip every night I work.

But that's too far into the future.

My phone vibrates on my thigh, but I don't even have the energy to care anymore.

I park in the grass next to Grammy's spot. Soon there will be two rectangular patches of dead grass.

As I climb out, my feet weigh more than the truck. I plop Sage in front of the TV and turn on *Family Feud*. I should probably make her scrub the floor with a toothbrush or something, but I don't have the energy for that either. Yet even though I feel empty, this pressure pushes against the inside of my skin again.

She's using. She's using right now. Because she's not strong enough to deal with all this. Hell, I'm not, and my brain hasn't been ravaged by drugs. I can feel the needle pierce her vein.

What if she's dead under the bridge by Sparta Greenery where Rafa got my corsage, on that mattress where everyone knows junkies shoot up? Or in one of those dirty rooms in that drug house with Jeremy?

"Rose, I'm hungry." Sage touches my knee.

I pull myself up and throw together a peanut butter sandwich.

A knock rattles Grammy's door.

"It's that social worker!" Sage rasps, hand gripping the curtain as she looks out the front window.

"Shh!"

"Look, I know you're in there," Kristy calls through the door. "Truck's outside, and I saw the curtain move."

My heart stutters. Shit. My hand shakes as I turn the knob and pull the door open. Kristy nods at me as she carries her yellow notepad inside. Her eighties curled bangs have fallen limp in the humidity.

"I'm sorry!" Sage bursts into tears. "It's all my fault. I got suspended. Don't take us away!"

I crawl across the air mattress to the couch and hug Sage. She presses her tear-soaked face into my stomach; her shuddering breath warms my skin through my shirt.

Kristy pulls a chair in from the kitchen. She looks to me. "Your mom here?"

My arm tightens around Sage. "Nope. Dad left her in Sparta for the day so he could work."

"Seems like a good day for a random drug test." Kristy digs out her phone.

That's something we can agree on.

"How's that work?" I ask.

"She'll get a notification and has to report immediately. Then we'll report the results to the court."

"Will you tell us? If she fails?" I ask.

Kristy sighs as she leans on her thighs. "I know that would give you peace of mind, but that's not how it works, hon. It'll be documented in the court report. Her case will be reviewed every three months at the minimum. If she gets into drug court, more than that."

My heart sinks. "And if she relapses?"

"She could go to jail. On our end, if she keeps failing tests, she's not going to get back unsupervised time with you kids."

"But we won't know," I mutter.

"I think you can tell when your mom's used." Kristy gets up.

Sage sits up, tears still staining her cheeks. "I bet she's high right now. Cuz she loves drugs more than us."

All this time, we've held on to the same thought. It shouldn't take my breath away, but it does. And that twists my gut just as much as Hollis's flashbacks.

Kristy crouches on the air mattress in front of Sage. "Trust me, Sage, your mom loves you kids more than herself. We've never doubted that."

"Then why didn't she quit a long time ago?" Huge, fat tears roll down her cheeks. "Why did she almost kill herself?"

And I want to hear the answer too. Because what if the threat of losing us isn't enough to make her stay clean?

"I believe her when she says she wants to quit." Kristy sits criss-cross applesauce on top of the fleece blanket. "But drugs change the way your brain works, hon. It tells your brain lies to get you to use again, like 'just this once' or 'I can control it this time.' And after you quit, it takes your brain a long time to get better. It usually takes a couple tries. Your mom's going to need some help with that, and that's part of why I'm here. That's what drug court's for. To help her get what she needs to get better."

"So why can't she get into fucking treatment?" I spit through gritted teeth.

"I know how wrong it feels." Kristy meets my gaze. "That she's trying so hard to get in, she needs to get in, but she can't right now. It's not fair. Wait lists. Insurance issues. Deductibles and copays. It's hard."

Shit. I hadn't even thought of how much treatment would cost. Even if she got in, what if we can't pay for it? Hot tears spill down my cheeks. "Isn't that what insurance is for?"

Kristy squeezes my hand. "We're exploring payment options and scholarships, and other approaches too."

"Why does it have to be our mom?" Sage's body quakes with sobs. I wrap both arms around her and pull her into my lap.

"There's lots of moms who are addicts, even moms of other kids at your school, but no one talks about it. Your mom needs to learn how to deal with all the bad stuff that happened to her a long time ago. And how to deal with her feelings now," Kristy says as she pats Sage's knee. "Drugs have messed up her brain, but she still loves you. Her addiction can drive her to make horrible choices, choices that hurt you, but she still loves you. And that's why you can love your mom, even if you hate her addiction."

Such a simple dichotomy. It clicks into place, and now I can make sense of my feelings, put them into boxes.

"And the thing for both of you girls to remember"—Kristy's eyes flash up to me—"is that your mom's addiction is not your fault. The choices she makes because of her addiction are not your fault. You didn't cause it, you can't control it . . . Rose. It's times like this I wish we had an Alateen group closer than Rochester."

"What's that?" I ask.

"A group for teens with parents who are addicts, so you can see you're not alone. But I'm working with your dad to get some family therapy set up."

Maybe that would be good. I pull in a breath and scrub the tears from my face.

"Uff da." Kristy grunts as she fumbles her way off the air mattress. She digs a Kwik Trip gift card from her pocket and hands it to me. "Hopefully it'll get you through the week, then we'll see what we can do."

"Thank you, Kristy." And it's weird, but I kind of want to hug her.

"And Rose,"—she jabs her yellow notepad at me—"if you continue holding your breath waiting for her to relapse, you'll suffocate. Your life must go on."

The edges of the card dig into my palm as I clench it. Focus on what I can control, box everything else, like O'Neil said. At least at school. I nod.

The door slaps closed behind her.

I text Dad and let him know. And another message waits from Gretchen. I ignore it.

Sage and I snuggle on the couch. I stroke her tangled hair. Now *The Price Is Right* is on. Rafa and Belwyn and Gretchen and Mom on her own in Sparta and drug tests flit around my brain like tennis balls. But I catch them and shove them into the box.

Because sometimes you do have to ignore the elephant and go on with life.

And maybe you Seraphina and run as far as you can, then cut off that part of you, even though it's a limb that's just broken, not gangrenous.

Before she became Seraphina, Aunt Colleen was trapped too. She escaped and left Mom with their stepfather who abused her and their mother who looked the other way. And that probably just made Mom feel even more worthless. Unlovable. And look how that worked out for Mom. Aunt Colleen abandoned Mom to pursue her own dreams. Would things have been different for Mom—for us—if she'd stayed?

Aunt Colleen didn't even want to know Hollis, Sage, and Vi.

For a second, the haze that's blocked me from seeing more than five minutes ahead dissipates like steam, and I can see myself plein air painting the soaring snowcapped Sierra Nevada Mountains.

Even if I can resurrect my grades, it's thirty hours to Merced, California, by Greyhound. At Belwyn, I'll be thirty hours from Hollis, Sage, and Vi. Hollis has been rising into being a big brother, but he'll be too young to shoulder this burden, even in a year. And what if we're still trapped at Grammy's? What if Mom's in jail? What if she's lost parental rights because she can't stop using? What if she's dead?

Or maybe she'll be three hundred and sixty-five days clean with a job and she can be alone with us again.

You're allegedly priceless. So are Hollis, Sage, and Vi. So was Mom. But Aunt Colleen didn't care about that when she just left her and never looked back. Ice pumps through my veins. I send Seraphina Abramsson a message.

RoseMarie: Do you ever think about Mom?

"Seen" instantly pops up under my message. But she's not typing back.

I close the app so I can't see either way.

I can't Seraphina the kiddos.

———

A knock comes on the door at 2:07.

My heart jackhammers against my sternum, because maybe it's a police officer coming to tell us she overdosed again. Sage's shoulders inch up to her ears. She's thinking the same thing.

But we have to know.

I move her off my lap and open the door.

Gretchen . . . and Rafa stand on Grammy's front steps.

"¡Bendito!" slips through Rafa's lips as he s my face.

"You don't just go MIA on your bestie for almost forty-eight hours after all the shit you've gone through!" Gretchen shoves me.

Sage springs up and charges for Gretchen. "Don't you touch my sister!"

"Let's not hit two people in one day." I grab Sage's shoulder and wrangle her back.

Gretchen rams a pink-and-black fingernail in my face. "I'm sick of it, Rose, that the only way I can find anything out about my best friend's life is from other people."

I glare at Rafa.

Rafa steps back and almost falls off the stoop. "Uh, sorry. I was just really worried, and I didn't know how to find you."

"And I don't even care that you told Rafa, even though I've been your BFF since kindergarten," Gretchen yells in my face. "I just wanted to know that you were okay. Cuz here's the thing. You've spent the past three years pushing people away. The only one you let in was Douche-tin because you knew he didn't give two shits about your life. Then Rafa cares enough to have a hard conversation with you, and you push him away because you don't want to hear it."

I look to Rafa. He has bags under his eyes and his hair lays flat, not his usual fauxhawk. His brows knit as he shoves his hands into the kangaroo pouch of his South Division soccer sweatshirt. He's been worried. About me.

I was kind of a bitch to him.

"Just let people care about you, Rose," Gretchen says. "And maybe let us take care of you every once in a while."

Something inside me trembles. The stars twinkling overhead. The smell of him clinging to his suit jacket. The feel of his warm, rough hand in mine. Tears sting my eyes as it rolls me over, how utterly alone I've been. And now they're both standing right next to me staring into the abyss.

Gretchen pulls me into a hug. I sob so hard my gut slices with each heave, until I feel weightless, like I've cried everything out and can just float away, and I have nothing left and my side aches.

Gretchen's arms release me. I scrub the tears away with my sweatshirt sleeve. I didn't have the space for makeup today, so at least my face isn't a total mess.

Rafa pulls his gaze up from the crooked wooden step under him. His puppy dog eyes search me from head to toe, and his brows knit as if asking permission to speak.

I miss my medal. I knot my fingers together. "So you skipped school? To see me?"

"First time I ever skipped. But I was afraid you wouldn't come to work tonight." His voice cracks.

Shit, forgot about work.

"But what are your parents gonna say when they get the robo-call?"

"Well, it'll be in English, so . . ." Rafa glances up at me. "And I told Omar the situation, so he knows to cover for me."

I hug him. He tucks his arms around me, surrounding me in lavender and lime that I can barely smell through all the snot and tears. I rest my head on his shoulder. His fingers massage the back of my head.

"Ew, you're not going to kiss, are you?" Sage asks.

Rafa lets me go, scratching the back of his head.

"Shut up, Sage. You're the literal worst," I say.

She sticks her tongue out at me.

I check the clock. "Crap, I have to pick up Vi and Holly, then Dad, then figure out how to find Mom. And apparently go to work."

But I want to stay with Rafa.

"So, how about this," Gretchen jumps in. "Peter Rabbit, why don't you ride back to Sparta with me and I'll buy you a McFlurry. You can drive Rafa, Rose."

"Deal!" Sage holds up her hand, and Gretchen slaps it.

I hug Gretchen. "You're the best."

"Remember that the next time you're pissed at me."

I half smile. But our relationship has shifted now. For the better. I'm not going to cut her out anymore.

Sage races Gretchen to her Prius, bits of gravel flying from under her gym shoes.

Just me and Rafa.

"Give me a sec." I scramble over the air mattress for the jeans

I wore on Friday, in a pile by the Precious Moments curio. I pull out my medal and shove it into my pocket. The edges dig into my thigh.

Rafa and I climb into Dad's truck.

"Now this is truly riding in style." I turn the key, and the engine roars to life. The fan belt screeches. And, because it's Rafa, I don't feel utterly mortified by the ancient food wrappers littering the floor or the clumps of dirt from our shoes or the thick layer of dust on the dashboard. Because I know he won't care.

Silence hangs over us as I pull down the gravel road through a tunnel of towering pine trees.

I clear my throat as my fingers constrict around the steering wheel. "So was it really bad yesterday without me? Noon Packers game and all."

"Walmart was saved by the record holder for highest Items Per Hour." Rafa's attempt at teasing lacks its usual luster.

"Uh, you mean me?" I say as I turn onto Highway 27. Gretchen's Prius follows behind. In the rearview mirror, I can see Gretchen and Sage are both laughing.

"What's your record again?" he asks.

"Five sixty-eight."

"You're looking at five hundred eighty-one now."

"Hashtag lifetime achievement."

"Hashtag haters gonna hate." Rafa's smile doesn't quite light up his eyes.

We pass Cataract Mart with the giant wooden Leinenkugel's chair out front. Unleaded gas is $2.59 a gallon. The truck's gas gauge dips down to an eighth of a tank, but Cataract Mart doesn't exactly take Kwik Trip gift cards. I chew the inside of my lip. We'll be able to make it to Sparta.

Rafa sighs. "Look, I'm sorry. You're right. It's not fair for me to compare."

"No, my garbage doesn't give me a get-of-jail-free card for being a dick."

"Well, Queen of Bluntness, if it makes you feel better, you were kind of right about the elephants. I talked to Omar, and we . . . figured some stuff out." Now his smile reaches his dark-brown eyes dripped with radiant copper.

"Guess that explains why he stalked me this morning."

"Stalked you?"

I tell him.

"*¡Chin!* The food even?" Rafa runs a hand down his face. "I'm gonna kill that *flaco*. Guess that's karma for telling Gretchen some of the stuff you told me. I really didn't know I was the only one."

"Yeah . . ."

"Why me?" he asks.

I shrug. "I guess because we're both invisible."

"Yeah, about that. Hate to burst your bubble, but our dance now lives in legend. And, uh, it's on TikTok."

My face flames. "Oh my God."

"I didn't know how easy it is to impress these small-town people. Hope I didn't ruin your reputation."

"No going back now."

He laughs.

"But it's okay you told Gretchen."

"Still though, I broke your trust." Rafa takes my hand. Shocks tickle up my arm and activate my nervous system.

"We're cool, f-zone."

Our hands rest in the middle seat.

I put on Sigur Rós as we crest a ridge and pass through a roadcut through layered sandstone. Violin and piano and sounds I can't even name swell and mix with Icelandic.

Rafa breaks out a full-on dimpled Prince Charming grin. "So I converted you?"

"Added to my repertoire."

"I'll take it."

I crack my window. The crisp smell of pine fills the air, thickened by the dying summer heat. The warm breeze kisses my cheek. Rafa rests his arm on his open window and watches the world pass us by.

The bright-blue sky, barely streaked by wispy cirrus clouds, peeks through the slowly shifting leaves and branches over us. A brilliant cerulean blue mixed with radiant turquoise to lighten without cooling it. I'd use a fan brush to lightly dry sweep clouds across the sky.

I feel lighter. Like someone's slowly opening the cap to that pop bottle and letting the pressure out.

"Okay, I'm not going to lie. It's pretty out here in the country. Pastoral, John Constable style," Rafa says as he watches fields of corn starting to turn golden, weaving into tree-capped ridges close enough to throw a football at. "Even if we did just pass a cow crossing sign. Which begs the question, why did the cow cross the road?"

"To get to the udder side."

"Wait, you mean it's a real joke?"

"Welcome to the country."

Rafa laughs deep and rich. "Well, now I've even done line dancing. So I guess it's official."

"Glad I converted you." Chicory bobs along the side of the road. "Do you know what the purple flowers are?"

Rafa shakes his head.

A logging truck roars by, sending a torrent of air through my hair. "Chicory. Mom told me it can be used as a coffee substitute."

"Let me file that in my random trivia folder." He squeezes my hand. I squeeze back.

I feel good. And Rafa's smiling too as the wind flutters around his open hand dangling out the window.

We descend a hill and the world opens up to soybean fields turning yellow and a sea of corn. The ridges fade in the distance. As we cross into Sparta city limits, Rafa says, "You can drop me at my place. I get the van tonight. Oh, and if your dad ever needs a hand with that fan belt, I help my dad with cars all the time."

My heart flutters. "Cool. His best shot of a car partner in crime is Sage, and she's too young."

Rafa directs me to his house, a small white duplex on the edge of town. Two little pink bikes lay at the base of a maple tree; the one with training wheels must be Flor's. I imagine the room he shares with Omar is a blend of Diego Rivera prints and swim-suit model posters.

When we get a new place, would I still be sharing a room with Hollis? There would definitely be worse fates in life.

"So, can I give you a ride home tonight?" Rafa asks as he squeezes my hand.

"All the way to Cataract?"

"Figured your parents would probably appreciate saving a few bucks on gas. And . . . I could spend more time with you."

I tuck my hands around the back of his head into his short, coarse hair, then pull him in for a kiss. His lips are soft and warm against mine. Rafa's sharp breath tickles my upper lip, mixing with mine. His fingers lace through my hair and cradle the nape of my neck as his tongue gently parts my lips. And his kiss is nice and sweet and innocent. Like Rafa. He's quivering. So am I.

As we part for air, our noses still touch. His eyes are warm pools that I sink into as they drink me in like I'm the only thing that breathes.

He brushes my limp bangs away. "So does this mean we've transcended the f-zone?"

"Um, yeah . . . I mean, I hope so."

He kisses both my cheeks and my forehead. "I'll see you in a few minutes, *mi Rosa bella*. My beautiful Rose."

Millions of butterflies flutter inside me. "Sorry, the German equivalent just isn't as pretty."

"Well, now I'm dying to know." He pokes me in the ribs.

Crap, all I can come up with is, *"du hast wunderschöne Augen."*

"Yeah, well, that's . . . interesting. Thanks for sharing more spit with me."

I tickle him in the side.

"What does it mean?"

"You have beautiful eyes."

"They're just brown."

"With copper in the sun."

Rafa kisses my cheek. *"Tus ojos* are the color of Lake Michigan on a still, summer day."

"Really?"

"No sarcasm." Now he kisses me long and deep, and it feels like I'm touching his soul. It's the most right thing in the universe, and when our lips part I'm starving for more. Rafa's thumb traces down my jawline, sending chills down my spine.

"Crap. I'm distracting you. Go get your siblings." He climbs out. "See you soon."

I blow out a hot breath as I drive toward Lawrence Lawson. And relish that I can have room in my life now for more than just Mom.

Chapter 19

I pick up the kids, fill the gas tank, and take them to West Side Park until Dad's done working. Gretchen drops off Sage and four M&M McFlurries. I love her.

As I watch Sage the Knight fight Hollis the Dragon to rescue Princess Vi from my castle, I can't stop a grin. They're getting better, I think.

At four-thirty, we pick Dad up at the back of Northern's parking lot. He climbs in carrying the Power Rangers lunch bag Grammy packed him. Apparently the red one was his favorite in sixth grade. Dad drops me off at Walmart, then heads off to find Mom.

I hope she passed her drug test.

I cut across the Walmart parking lot. Sunlight beats off the rows of cars, sending white floaters dancing through my field of vision.

As I clock in, someone calls, "Rose, that you?"

It's Tim's voice. I hope I'm not in trouble for calling in yesterday. My fingers find my medal. I slink into his office.

Tim leans back in his office chair. "Tell your mom and dad I know a guy trying to rent an apartment over on Main Street. Three bedroom for six fifty a month. Bet I can get him to drop down the security deposit."

My shoulders relax. "Thanks, Tim."

Rafa waits for me near Layaway, head bowed, framed by an explosion of colorful fake flowers. It reminds me of Rivera's *The Flower Carrier*. When his gaze meets mine, his face breaks into that grin that just melts me.

I'm not sure what official protocol is for PDA while working. Trina's always hanging on Justin, but I'm not going to use her as a role model, so I just weave my fingers through Rafa's.

Rafa's cheek brushes mine as he leans in to whisper, "Just to warn you, my mom sent us a bunch of food. Like more than you and I could eat in three days."

"Good, cuz I love your mom's food." I squeeze his hand.

"You have no idea how much I want to kiss you right now." Rafa's breath tickles my ear, leaving me starving for more.

My face warms.

"That's not helping."

I throw up some jazz hands. My medal falls from my palm.

Rafa scoops it up. A dimpled smile of pure sunshine beams from Rafa's face. "You kept it, huh?"

"Yeah, and it appears to still be working."

Rafa looks around, then pulls me into a Stationary aisle. He steals a quick peck on my cheek. My heart sprouts wings and soars through the skylight over us. We're both laughing as we reach the front end.

Cindy's grinning at me as we stop at the podium to check our registers. "Never knew you were a dancer, Rose."

"Huh?"

"I seen the video." She flails her Wesco pen at me.

Rafa rests his elbows on the podium. "Warned you."

"I literally didn't do anything. It was all Rafa."

He throws his hands up. "What can I say, I'm a miracle worker."

"Well, you better work some miracles on me, then." Bobby leans on the counter, his gut spilling over. "It's my aunt's wedding this weekend, and I gotta outdo my cousin Terrence. He's been taking dance lessons."

Ashlee squeals in delight, clapping her hands.

"Oh, you're serious." Rafa skims through the break schedule. "I have break at eight thirty."

"I'll bring my dancing shoes."

Rafa still looks flabbergasted as he watches Bobby lumber off. *"No manches."*

"Well, you brought this on yourself, King of Sarcasm." I shoulder check him. "I'm buying popcorn for this."

"You two are so cute!" Darlene croons, clutching her hands to her generous bosom. "Ah, to be young and in love."

My face blazes cadmium red.

"I . . . no, I . . ." Rafa scratches the back of his head. "¡Híjole!"

Then a perfectly timed hoard of customers arrives at the Front End.

"Crap, what register am I even on?" I say.

"You're four. I'm five."

Like always.

Bette Midler croons, "You are the wind beneath my wings," but today it can't touch me.

As I yank my register cord, I can't believe how good it feels to be back at Walmart. Today my smiles at customers are actually real.

———

After work, Rafa drives me up to Grammy's. A bag of leftover tamales sits in my lap. Rafa helped make them. The chirping of crickets from fields on both sides of the highway surrounds us in stereo.

"Now, Mr. Former City Boy, you know to watch for deer, right?" I ask as we leave Sparta's lights behind. "My dad's hit like four of them on this road."

"Deer *and* cows? Who knew driving could be dangerous," Rafa jokes. But he flicks on his brights, then hunches over his steering wheel, eyes glued to the road.

We take turns playing our favorite songs. Daddy Yankee and The Chainsmokers. Shinedown and Three Days Grace.

Through the windshield, the sky is clear enough to see the Milky Way stretch across the sky. The stars are specks of titanium white mixed with tiny bits of oranges, reds, and blues spread against a black backdrop touched with deep purple. Millions. Billions. I'm not even a grain of sand in comparison to that, but I am something.

The van headlights strike the "Cataract Welcomes You" sign with a crossed rifle and fishing pole dividing off a duck, white-tailed deer head, and trout. I start the new Shinedown song, the one I first heard in Gretchen's car the day I first met Rafa. Before Mom's overdose. I check Instagram. Aunt Colleen never messaged me back.

Her latest post is a selfie in front of some temple with beehive towers covered with carvings. She looks so much like Mom, except with dyed blonde hair and her trademark red lipstick.

The caption:

I'm nearing the end of my quest to find pure love. And the monks I met today at Angkor Wat (in Cambodia) filled my heart with love like I've never felt before. This was the single most revolutionary experience of my life. XO Sera.

It's pathetic and so utterly selfish of her, jetting around the world hoping complete strangers will donate love to her, while ignoring loved ones who've been here all along.

Rafa reaches across the center console and takes my hand.

"What's wrong?"

I blow out a breath. "Long story. Tell you tomorrow."

As we close in on Grammy's, one of Unrequited Death's new songs starts. "But like a phoenix, we can rise again." Fitting.

Dad texted me at ten o'clock saying Mom appears to have stayed clean all day.

The punch line of Mr. Smith's shitty joke pops into my brain; what happened to the mugger to make him that way? Mom wasn't born an addict, and if she could travel back in time and stop herself from taking heroin the first time, she would. I know that. Mom doesn't want to be *Saturn Devouring Her Children* or *The Broken Column*.

Rafa turns down Grammy's driveway. His headlights cast light through the pine trees to the house, spotlighting Mom and Dad sitting on chairs framing Grammy's front door.

"Well, that's an intervention if I ever saw one," Rafa says as he pulls to a stop behind Dad's truck.

"Yeah . . ." My mouth goes dry.

Rafa's hand slides around the nape of my neck. He kisses my forehead. I want to stay here in his warm van listening to music all night. Feel the light, gentle caress of his tongue on mine.

But Mom and Dad are watching us through the windshield. I have to face this. I curl my fingers around my medal. As I pull away, his fingers slip through my hair.

"See you tomorrow?"

I nod, then climb out. I draw in a slow breath, filling my lungs with cool night air heavy with the smell of pine needles. My heart slows. The glow left in Rafa's wake lingers.

Rafa's van backs out. Crap. Forgot the tamales. As his headlights fade, Grammy's porch light casts light and shadow across Mom's and Dad's faces.

They stand.

Mom and Dad are both here.

For me.

Just me. No other kids even.

I can't remember the last time that happened.

The corners of my medal dig into my hand. My breath becomes white puffs floating up to the stars. Gravel crunches under my combat boots as I walk up to them.

"Well, that Rafa boy's nice." Dad's eyes linger on the end of the driveway. "Big step up from Justin. Don't even think I'll need to threaten him with my shotgun."

"Daryl!" Mom smacks his arm. Her pupils are large in the darkness, meaning she probably hasn't used recently.

"Please don't even say those names in the same sentence," I say.

"First things first." Dad digs his wallet out of his back pocket. He slides out a stack of twenties and holds it out to me.

I shake my head. "We need a new place. Tim even said he knows a guy with a three bedroom for six fifty a month."

His hand inches down. "Six fifty? That ain't bad."

Mom elbows him.

Dad sighs. "Look, it's our job to worry about all that." He holds up the money again. "Kristy's got me working with Couleecap. They're going to help us with first month's rent and the security deposit."

"But you don't believe in handouts," I say.

"I've got to set my pride aside right now, Rosey. And you're going to need that for Belwyn."

I've lost the glow from Rafa. "Yeah, I don't know about the whole Belwyn thing."

"You know I ain't crazy about you being so far away with all them bears up in the mountains, but I already found bear mace for your birthday."

"Bear mace?" I squint at Dad. "No, I won't just abandon the kiddos. I won't."

"No. It's your dream. Take it, Rosey." Dad's voice quivers as he flaps the money in front of me.

Jaw set, I shake my head.

"Rosey . . ." His breath hitches. Tears shine in his eyes.

Don't cry again, Dad.

"Rose, you're not Aunt Colleen. You know that, right?" Mom's voice is strong and firm and confident, like back when she could wrangle four kids into bed at once.

"What are you even talking about?" I ask.

Dad looks equally perplexed.

"I seen she liked some of your stuff on Instagram. And followed you."

My jaw drops.

"Why are you so surprised?" Mom's voice takes on a teasing tone. Just like old Mom. "You know I follow you. You only have like five followers."

I kick at a crushed, faded cigarette butt tucked into the grass, a stray from Grammy's overflowing earthenware ashtray under the chair. A birthday present I made for her back when I was in Mrs. Kenyon's class. "Well, I mean, you're literally never on it, so . . ."

"What's Instagram?" Dad tugs off his Packers hat and rubs his forehead.

"It's like Myspace or whatever you used back in the day, but more for posting pictures," I mutter.

"There ain't any creepy pedos bothering you, are there?" Dad folds his arms.

"No, Dad. My profile's set to private."

"Rose, the only reason I go on it is to check up on you. And it's only gotten interesting the past few weeks, between Colleen and Rafa."

Mom's been cyberstalking me. While in the hospital. It feels kind of good. "It was just a few messages," I say.

"Rosey, I'm glad you're talking to her." Her hand reaches for my face like she used to after french braiding my hair. Then falls.

But I want to feel Mom's touch.

"I'm not," Dad huffs.

Mom rolls her eyes at Dad. "She's our family, and we ain't got much of that."

The folded triangle curls a little in my palm as I tighten my fingers around it. "Not that she cares."

"Rose has a point, Maureen."

Mom shakes her head. Strands of long dishwater-blonde hair fall across her eye. She tucks it behind an ear. "I think Colleen blames herself for my addiction, and that's too much for her. She's scared. But it's not her fault, just like it's not your fault I overdosed, Rose. And it won't be your fault if I . . . I relapse. It's my fault." Somehow her voice is strong and tremulous at the same time.

"Rose. Going to college in California is not the same as what Colleen did. She cut all ties with us until a week ago. You would never do that. Now, if you want, go to college closer to home, but I won't watch you give up your dream."

Mom takes the money from Dad's hand and holds it out. That stubborn gleam flashes in her eyes, like when she out-negotiated my attempts at evading doing math extra credit.

It's Mom. It's really her. And that terrifies me, because I don't want to lose her again. The chill in the night air leaks through my sweatshirt, and I shiver. I hug my arms to my chest so tight it compresses my ribcage.

Dad squares his shoulders like he's preparing to deflect a tackle. "You need to trust me to be the parent. No matter what happens with Mom, I'm the parent. Not you. You're focusing on college. I'm going to start attending a program for family members of addicted loved ones, so I can do a better job at all this."

He's my rock.

Mom's chin trembles as she thrusts the money closer to my face. "And then there's Grammy."

Maybe if I get into Belwyn, it'll give Mom something to hold on to. I take the money.

Mom swipes her wrist across her moisture-rimmed eyes, then lifts her chin. "I need to learn to live with my pain and guilt. Okay? I'm, I'm trying to get into treatment. I will. Then I can work on fixing the stuff in me that's broken. And my lawyer thinks I'm a slam dunk for drug court. That'll help keep me clean. Because I want to get back to who I'm supposed to be. I want to be your mom."

She loves me more than heroin. No doubt. A tear rolls down my cheek. I cuff it away with my sweatshirt sleeve.

"But you were right, Rose, you shouldn't trust me. And you should be angry. Because . . . because"—she presses her fists to her eyes—"I'm an addict, and if I mess up again, that'll hurt you even more. And you've been hurt enough. I won't make any promises, but I'm fighting this one day, one hour, one second at a time."

I unfurl my arms and hug her frail body. Mom gasps. She's trembling as she wraps her skinny arms around me. She smells like Vanilla Field. No sign of Jeremy's cigarette smoke. Mom strokes the back of my head like when she used to snuggle in my bed with me until I fell asleep.

Mom lets me go and grips my shoulders. Her "best smile"

shines on her face, and it looks almost exactly like the one from the yearbook, probably taken around when I was born.

"I love you, Rosey." Mom chokes on happy tears. "You're the best thing that ever happened to me."

Warmth floods my chest, holds it open. The pressure lifts, and I can fill my whole lungs again.

I feel priceless.

Chapter 20

The next morning, I wake up early. Throw on my Nine Inch Nails shirt with the birds flying free. Layer on my thick eyeliner, careful to get both sides even. My mascara brush pulls at my lashes as I put on several coats. I find a hair dryer under the sink beside Epsom salts and ancient Aqua Net and style my hair. It feels good, like I'm myself again.

COW 97 softly plays on the front speakers as Dad drives us to school. The kiddos sleep in the back seat. A brown paper bag sits on my lap with a lunch Mom prepared. I unfold the top and peek in. A peanut butter and chocolate chip sandwich; I know because I saw a bag of chocolate chips sitting on the counter after my shower. She also threw in an applesauce pouch, some chips, and a huge bag of her cookies—enough for Rafa and me. Attached to it is a pink Post-it note with a quick sketch of a rosebud with a few thorns and a drop of dew. Perpendicular to the rose, Mom wrote, "Today's your day to blossom."

I peel off the note and hug it to my chest. I don't know what tomorrow holds, and I won't hold my breath that she'll stay clean, but I can enjoy today.

I pull out my phone and check Instagram. No message from Aunt Colleen. I send her one.

RoseMarie: We're here when you're ready.

"Well, that's a pretty sunrise." Dad slurps the coffee Grammy dumped into her Flying J Travel Center travel mug for him. Today his brow is smooth.

A burst of liquid yellow-orange sunlight fights through black pine trees. The sky—cobalt blue as the base, titanium white, orange, and light yellow around the sun barely peeking over the trees. Dry-brushed rays shoot up behind the purple clouds with peachy golden ripples, reflections, and highlights.

It's a new day. And today my brain is free and clear, and I can focus on what I can control.

Step one: figure out what I need for my Belwyn application.

I open up my email and scroll through the viewbook to the point where Hollis interrupted me all those days ago. The assignment. "Using a medium of your choice, create a response to the following prompt: Hope."

It rushes through me like a tidal wave. Bright, clean colors and images coalesce in my mind. An impressionist dove fights to break free of Goyaesque demon claws and escape into pure-white radiant light. One of the dove's wings is clipped and bleeding, but she's draped in a garland of wildflowers. She has to fight harder now, but she's also learned some hard lessons. The glow spreads through every cell in my entire body.

Hope breaking free.

For the reflection: "My mom's a heroin addict. She's been clean eleven days." I can already feel the brushstrokes in my fingers.

Dad pulls to a stop in front of the school. I check the time. I have twenty minutes until school starts.

I grab my backpack and throw open the heavy door.

"Have a good—"

"Gotta go before I lose it!" I slam the door and run for the entrance.

"Hey, walk!" the custodian calls at my back as I jog toward the art room. When I get there, I head straight for the paints. A thrill rushes up my spine as I mix burnt umber and ultramarine blue with alizarin crimson and titanium white to create a range of colors from black to barely purple white. I can create an infinite spectrum of colors from four tubes. I am alive.

I grab a canvas, a whole world with unlimited possibilities, from the pile by the drying rack and throw it on an easel.

"Rose!" Rafa cuts across the art room. He trips over a stool and nearly face-plants. "Well, that ruined my grand entrance."

I cannot contain my giggle. "If only I'd recorded it, your shiny-new reputation as Lord of the Dance would be ruined."

Rafa clutches his chest with a dramatic gasp. "You wouldn't dare, Queen of Bluntness."

"I might, King of Sarcasm." I waggle my brush at him. "Don't get on my bad side."

"Never, *mi bella Rosa*." Standing behind me, Rafa hugs my waist and pulls me against his chest. I feel his slow heartbeat through my shirt. It beats in time with mine as we study my blank canvas. His lips tickle the spot under my ear like butterfly wings.

My brush slices into white.

Acknowledgments

I'd like to start by thanking my amazing editor Kathy Haake. She's so thorough, she corrected me on how to spell places in my high school home town. I'd also like to thank everyone at Turner Publishing Company, especially Kathleen Timberlake, Heather Howell, and Stephanie Beard for all your hard work bringing *Everything's Not Fine* to life, as well as my agent Claire Anderson-Wheeler.

Everything's Not Fine evolved tremendously over the five years I worked on it, and many people helped along the way, including social workers, sensitivity readers, an authenticity reader, and a police officer. First and foremost, I'd like to thank my friend Anabella Atach for helping me bring create Rafa, and Jan De La Rosa and Nicole Real for supporting around Rafa and his family as well. I'd also like to thank the social workers who answered my millions of questions about Child Protective Services and Taylor Barton for helping me find the right story for me to tell.

And *Everything's Not Fine* never would have been finished without the support of my amazing critique partners, including Rose Deniz, Katya Dove, Dina Von Lowenkraft, and Melissa Bergum as well as the Singapore Writers Group.

And of course, my husband and my family.

Discussion Guide for
Everything's Not Fine

I've loved writing stories since I first picked up a pencil, but I'm also a school psychologist. The biggest thing I see kids and teens facing is stuff beyond their control that rips their lives apart. Oftentimes, these injuries to the psyche are invisible, which can leave kids and teens feeling like they're stranded on an island surrounded by happy people with happy lives. In reality, research shows 58 percent of teens have experienced at least one Adverse Childhood Experience, which includes things such as poverty, neglect, abuse, witnessing domestic violence, and household substance abuse.[1] When it comes to addiction, according to the National Institute on Drug Abuse, more than twenty million people over the age of twelve in the United States are fighting substance abuse addiction.[2] This, in turn, impacts millions of American children.

DISCUSSION QUESTIONS

1. The impact of trauma varies greatly person-to-person, based on things such as age, previous experiences, mitigating factors, and their overall capacity to cope. How does the impact of trauma manifest itself differently in Rose and her family members?

2. Trauma can tear a family apart, but can also bring a family together. How did Mom's overdose affect Rose's family system and the relationships between family members? Compare and contrast the responses of Aunt Colleen and Grammy. What do you think will happen with Aunt Colleen,

AKA Seraphina?

3. What impact did the trauma experienced by Aunt Colleen and Mom at the hands of their stepfather have on them? How did it spread to the next generation?

4. Both Rose and Rafa choose to isolate themselves from others at school. Compare and contrast their reasons, and how and why this changes for each character as the book progresses.

5. Rose and Rafa are both the oldest of four children. Both have also had to make sacrifices as they put their families first. Compare and contrast how that looks for each character and how their families shape their identities.

6. On page 38, Rose's psychology teacher tells a joke about a psychologist's reaction to stumbling across a mugging victim, worrying about what happened to the mugger to make him this way. Discuss how Rose connects this to Mom's addiction and your thoughts on this idea. Are there connections you can make to your own experiences?

7. How does Rose's understanding of her mother and her addiction evolve over time? How did yours?

8. In *Everything's Not Fine*, there's a lot of talk of ignoring the elephant in the room. This is a common analogy for what it can be like living with an addict. After Mom overdoses, it becomes impossible for Rose's family to ignore the elephant, but Aunt Colleen worked so hard to ignore she cut herself off from the family. How does Rose's understanding of the elephant and what to do about it evolve as the story progresses?

9. According to National Institute on Drug Abuse, risk of opioid relapse is higher than for any other drug, with one study showing as many as 91% of those in recovery will relapse.[3] Recovery often takes several tries and can take many years because of the drug's impact on the brain. Discuss the implications of this statistic for Mom and her family.

10. According to the American College of Neuropsychopharmacology, people in need of treatment for opioid addiction may wait months or even years for access to care as the opioid crisis has continued to escalate.[4] Mom almost died of an overdose and wants treatment, yet is on a waiting list and faces issues around insurance and copays. Discuss the barriers Mom faces to accessing care for her addiction and how that impacts Rose and her family.

11. Rose and her family endure a traumatic event, and the ripples of that trauma spread beyond what Rose and her dad can control. One of the most important things as you're facing things beyond your control is to have coping strategies. What are Rose's? What are yours?

12. One lesson Rose learns is the healing power of admitting to those she can trust that everything really isn't fine. Who are Rose's people? Who would yours be?

13. Just like Rose, Mom once used art to cope with her traumas. In the end, Rose draws inspiration from Mom's old painting of a dove trying to escape the blackness. How else does Rose draw strength from Mom?

14. On page 274, the social worker says to Rose, "if you continue holding your breath waiting for her to relapse, you'll suffocate.

Your life must go on." Discuss what this means for Rose, and what it might take for Rose to push forward with her life.

15. What role did Rose's family play in helping Rose discover her resilience? How do Rose's connections to family members evolve across the book?

16. Flowers are frequently mentioned in the book. How does the author symbolically use flowers, particularly "ditch flowers," throughout the book?

17. The author chose to set *Everything's Not Fine* in a small Wisconsin town. How might the story and characters have been different if it had been set in a big city?

SOURCES

1. Child Trends. (2019). *Adverse experiences*. Retrieved January 20, 2020 from https://www.childtrends.org/?indicators=adverse-experiences
2. National Institute on Drug Abuse. (2015). *Drugs of Abuse: Opioids*. Bethesda, MD: National Institute on Drug Abuse. Retrieved January 20, 2020 from http://www.drugabuse.gov/drugs-abuse/opioids.
3. American Addiction Centers Editorial Staff. (2019, September 5). *Opiate Relapse*. Retrieved January 20, 2020 from https://drugabuse.com/opiates/relapse/.
4. American College of Neuropsychopharmacology. "New hope for waitlisted patients addicted to opioids." ScienceDaily, 6 December 2017. Retrieved on January 20, 2020 from https://www.sciencedaily.com/releases/2017/12/171206090621.htm.

CPSIA information can be obtained
at www.ICGtesting.com
Printed in the USA
BVHW031157210520
580065BV00001BA/1